THE VANISHING EYES

Emily Slate Mystery Thriller
Book 11

ALEX SIGMORE

Dark Woods Press, LLC

THE VANISHING EYES: EMILY SLATE MYSTERY THRILLER
BOOK 11

Copyright © 2023 by Alex Sigmore

1st Edition

ebook ISBN 978-1-957536-36-1

Print ISBN 978-1-957536-37-8

Prologue

MAYBE IT'S NOT LEGAL, *but it's right,* Cameron Bright thinks as she locks the side door and double-checks to make sure her guest makes it back out to his car without incident. There aren't any cameras on this side of the building because Louis doesn't want any record of what they're doing, which suits her just fine. It prevents uncomfortable questions later.

She takes a deep breath, reassuring herself that everything will be okay and heads back to her station. She's got the night watch, and other than herself the only other non-patient in the building is Ricardo, and he's down the opposite hall cleaning the floors. She's pretty sure he's never seen her and the others, and even if he did, it would look like business as usual. That's the whole point; it's not like she's *trying* to draw attention to herself. Nothing can look out of the ordinary.

As soon as she's back in her seat, Cameron checks to make sure none of the other patient's night monitors have gone off, but they're all dark. They give everyone a pretty heavy dose of Melatonin every night to encourage sleep and it usually does the job. Even for the ones in chronic pain, like Mrs. Berger. Though she can't help but glance at the trash where Mrs. Berger's meds now lie. She'll have to make sure to dispose of that before she leaves in the morning. No need to leave anything incriminating behind.

As Cameron goes about her duties, she can't help but take a surreptitious glance at the postcard attached to her monitor with a small piece of tape. At the beginning of every shift she takes it out and tapes it back up. It's something she learned from Kyra, who has recently been getting more and more into the power of manifestation. At first it sounded like nothing but a bunch of bull hockey to Cameron: getting what you want by just believing it can happen? The real world didn't work that way, and she should know. How much money had she spent on a degree only to learn that the best she could do was nurse practitioner unless she was willing to drop another hundred grand to become a "real" doctor? She already had all the responsibilities of a doctor, but without the massive paycheck that came with it. Even Dr. Whiteside had been surprised when she'd told him just how much it cost to get an advanced degree these days. He'd been born in a better time, back when everything only cost a quarter of the current prices and people were paid better.

But she'd fixed all that. It hadn't taken Cameron very long to realize that her life prospects were limited if she didn't do something drastic. Even if it was illegal.

And yet, as she stared at the postcard of Hawaii taped to her monitor, she knew she had made the right decision. In only a few days she'd be heading to the islands—on a first-class ticket no less—and all because she'd taken life by the reins and made something happen for her. Kyra would say she manifested it into reality and maybe that was true on some level—in that she had been open to additional opportunities and possibilities that she hadn't considered before.

But it had taken a lot of work and a fair amount of luck to get this far. What had seemed simple in the beginning had turned out to be a lot more complex as she tried to figure out just how she was going to make it work. Thankfully she'd discovered Dr. Whiteside and had realized they both had similar interests and goals. And what had been something of a crazy idea had gelled itself in her mind as actually possible.

That had been six months ago. She'd been terrified they'd be caught at first, until she realized just how little people paid attention in a place like this. Nursing homes were often places for the forgotten, so why would it be a surprise that the company owners and administrators wouldn't be any different?

Cameron glanced at the postcard again and smiled. She'd made the right decision. That much was for sure.

After about twenty minutes Ricardo made his way down the hall, the low hum of the floor buffer the only sound as it passed. He gave Cameron a small nod and went back to his work. She returned the gesture and continued to fill out her evening reports and prepare everything for the morning shift. At least she had the quietest shift. No one wanted third because there wasn't anyone else in the building and the closest on-call nurse was almost ten minutes away. So if there was an emergency Cameron would be on her own until help arrived. But in all the time she'd worked here there had only been two incidents, and neither of them had been any more serious than a patient that needed some help to the bathroom or couldn't get to sleep because their meds had been off. It was the perfect job for her. She didn't need to really talk to anyone, and she was free to operate her little "side business".

After she'd finished all of her duties and made sure the rosters were all set for first shift, Cameron leaned back in her chair and pulled out her phone. She hadn't checked it since Dr. Whiteside had left and she was surprised to see a text from Kyra, asking how her latest date had gone.

Cameron frowned at the memory, but texted back anyway.
Up late?
Doing some reiki work. Couldn't sleep. No more stalling.

Cameron smiled. *Fine. He got freaked out about my $ situation and bailed.*

Another one? Jeez, what is it with guys and money?

No clue. But I figure it's better to find out up front.

She'd been hesitant at first to tell her dates how much she made, because all the so-called advice out there said guys didn't like to hear about money. But then she'd realized what terrible advice that had been and started telling them anyway. She wasn't about to get into a relationship then find out six months down the road it wasn't going to work because the guy was too controlling about money. So lately, she'd been getting real.

Don't sweat it, I'm sure you'll find some hot Hawaiian guy who sweeps you off your feet.

Lol, if I'm lucky.

Actually, she had heard about the phenomenon surrounding people taking vacations to Hawaii. Apparently—and there was data to back this up—people who vacationed to Hawaii had a much higher chance of never returning home than from any other vacation spot on the planet. Maybe that would happen to her, hot Hawaiian guy or not. Maybe she was manifesting it right now. Sure, she'd have to give up this extra income as she wasn't sure she could pull it off over there, but that might not be so bad.

A bad day in Hawaii was still better than a good day anywhere else.

Cameron checked the time and slid her phone in her pocket. She still had to do morning rounds before the first morning shift nurses began to arrive. The day shifts were much busier than her meager shift, requiring at least four nurses per department at all times. Ricardo had probably already finished the floors and had headed home without Cameron even realizing it.

Her board was still green, so she got up and began her individual door checks, making sure to leave every one of them cracked to allow enough light in that the residents knew someone would be checking on them soon. As she made it back to her desk the first kitchen staff were just starting to arrive, and she buzzed them in the front door. Though it was still pitch-black outside. She bet it never stayed this dark in Hawaii.

Soon the place was buzzing with activity as more and more staff began to show up, one by one. Cameron greeted all of them, removing her picture of Hawaii from the monitor and slipping it back in "her" drawer, before locking it.

"Any problems?" Tricia asked as she set her purse on the same desk Cameron used overnight.

"Nope, all quiet," Cameron replied, pulling out her own purse and rummaging through it, looking for her car keys. She was anxious to get home to keep packing—something she'd been working on for a week already. Even though her trip was still a few weeks away it was never too soon to pack. Plus, the earlier she left, the better.

Cameron made sure she clocked out before grabbing her stuff and hauling it over her shoulder. She passed another nurse on the way in, Lottie, she thought her name was, but wasn't a hundred percent sure. They'd brought in some extra help from New Orleans a week or two ago and Cameron hadn't taken the time to learn everyone's name because she really didn't work with them. She always had the night shift and that's why she liked it. She took a deep breath in as she headed out into the morning darkness. Light was just barely beginning to warm the edges of the horizon, but it would still be a good thirty minutes before the sun was actually up. By then, with any luck, she'd be at home and in bed before getting up and doing it all over again tonight.

"*Only a few more days. Only a few more days,*" she whispered as she made her way to her car, parked on the far side of the lot. Part of the reason she did that was parking in that spot helped obscure the one camera that happened to cover the side of the building she used when Dr. Whiteside would make a delivery. The only downside was it became a haul to get out to her car.

But as she walked she thought she could sense a presence behind her. Cameron turned suddenly, looking back at the lights shining from the clinic, but there was no one there. While her job wasn't in the worst part of town, it was in a sparsely populated area. There weren't many other businesses around and really the main road that led back to Bellefleur proper was unlit by any kind of streetlight. It could make for some good stargazing, but right now all Cameron wanted to do was get to her car and get back home. It was probably silly being this nervous, but then again, she'd had a stressful evening. Not necessarily bad, but every time Dr. Whiteside was scheduled to arrive, she couldn't help but get nervous.

Key in hand, Cameron resumed the walk to her car, picking up the pace. But just as she was close enough to reach out and touch her taillight, that feeling of a looming presence returned. When she turned to see what could be causing it, she found a hand clasped over her mouth and another arm wrapped around her midsection, pulling her back. She screamed anyway, but it didn't do any good, as the hand covering her mouth was gloved and muffled all the sound.

She panicked and thrashed back and forth, in an attempt to escape her attacker. But as she did, she felt a sharp pinch at her neck before everything quickly grew dark.

The last image that flashed through Cameron Bright's head as all the synapses in her brain fired at once was the blue and green of her Hawaii postcard, before it all went dark.

Chapter One

"I HAVE A VISUAL," Zara says, the radio in my ear crackling as she speaks.

"Are you sure?" I ask. "We don't want to jump the gun."

"Dead sure. It's him."

I take a deep breath and step out of the car, staring at the building before me. It's an older building that's been repurposed a few times, though not recently. The sign out at the street is probably half as old as the building itself and barely lit every time I drive by at night. But in the daytime it proclaims itself as Washington D.C.'s best Italian since 1959. I've never been to *Osteria del Cuore* myself as it's always seemed more like the type of place the mob would meet rather than an actual, functioning restaurant. It makes me think of one of Washington's local mobsters, Santino Toscani. I wouldn't be surprised to walk in there to see him sitting in a booth surrounded by his goons. But I'm not going inside. Not just yet.

Why Dr. Archer picked this place as our meeting spot I have no idea. But seeing as he's already blown me off three times, I'm not about to let this opportunity slip out of my grasp. For some reason the only person on earth who can tell me more about my mother likes to set appointments and then break them. He contacted me for the first time over three weeks ago, told me it was imperative that we meet and has broken every engagement since. Each time he calls back he has the same excuse: he thinks he's being followed and can't risk it.

But this time, we're ready. I'm done waiting for answers. In my pocket are three separate letters by a woman *claiming* to be my mother, and Dr. Archer knows something about it. I say claiming because my mother is dead—I watched as they lowered her casket into the ground. So whoever is sending me these letters is obviously hoping to provoke a response, and they're going to get one. I've already had to deal with the loss of my husband, an international assassin with a target on my back, my entire family of in-laws being part of some clandestine organization hell-bent on destroying society, and an infiltration of the FBI at the highest levels. I think I can handle a prankster.

But I need to find them first. And seeing as my mother revealed parts of her history to Dr. Archer and no one else when she was alive, he's the only one who might be able to help me track this person down. Whoever is sending me these letters, they knew my mother, and strangely, they seem to know me. So far, Dr. Archer's behavior isn't winning him any points, and makes me suspect that even *he* could be the one responsible.

"He's heading away from the back exit, looking over his shoulder," Zara says again. "And not doing a very good job of it. East along the alley. Looks like he's turning…south."

"Got it," I reply, not bothering to tap the speaker in my ear. I want to keep the line of communication open between us in case Archer somehow spots Zara. We both saw him enter the restaurant before she took up a position around back as we expected him to ditch again. I can't understand why he insists on playing this cat and mouse game. He'll show up to a location, then leave only minutes later, missing our meeting entirely. I would arrive at the locations before him, except he only gives me about twenty minutes notice each time. I guess he doesn't think I'm brave enough to use all the resources at my disposal to track him down.

So far Zara has managed to pull images of him, so we at least know what he looks like. I can't discount Archer's suspicious behavior. Part of me hopes that it *is* him, because at least this will all be over soon if that's really the case.

"You're gonna miss him," Zara chides. She's been a little more on edge ever since her ordeal at the hands of the terrorist known as Simon Magus. Even though we were able to stop the man and prevent him from hijacking the entire economic system, Zara suffered a lot of trauma. We took a short vacation after Archer blew me off the first time, just enough to get away and recharge. I really hoped it would give her the mental reset she needed, but she's been more despondent since we came back. I know she needs time, but I've been so distracted by this Archer nonsense I haven't been able to be there for her like I should. Another reason why I want this all to be over.

"Cool your jets, I've got him right where I want him," I whisper as I hurry up to a tall hedge that comes right up to the sidewalk. I've made my way around *Osteria del Cuore* and come up on the south side, making my way to intercept Archer. My plan is to confront, interrogate and arrest him if necessary. If for no other reason that he's been wasting my time. But he is moving quicker than I expected. He pops out from behind the hedge, his head down as he makes his way down the sidewalk to the parking lot another half block away. His hands are shoved in his coat pockets and he's doing his best to look like a man who does not want to be bothered.

"Archer!" I call out, causing him to look up in surprise. I'm virtually running at him in a sprint now, determined to get my hands on him. His eyes go wide, and he takes off a second later, headed in the direction of the lot.

"Told you!" Zara says in my ear as I also catch the sound of a car door opening.

"Dr. Archer, stop!" I yell, but it does no good. The problem is, Archer isn't a young man. According to the information we found online he's in his mid-sixties, and he's attempting to sprint down a sidewalk in the middle of winter. He doesn't see the ice patch before it's too late.

"Shit," I say as I see him slip on the ice and I rush to catch up to him and grab him before he falls, breaking a hip or worse on the hard concrete.

I get to him just in time, grabbing him from under the shoulders and hoisting him back up. Zara appears from off to my right and out of breath.

"Look, just let me go, I don't want any trouble," Archer says, attempting to wiggle out of my grasp.

"I don't think so," I say. "You've been jerking me along for three weeks now. I'm done playing games. You and I are going to sit down and have a conversation."

He turns to me. "Wait, you're Emily? Emily Slate?" His glasses are thick and shield dark brown eyes. While his hair is thinning, it's still darker than I would have expected for a man of his age. He also seems thin and frail, though I'm not letting go of him until I'm sure he won't try to run again.

"That's right," I say, giving his arm a little pull as it to emphasize how much he's put me through. "We're doing this, right now."

He looks furtively behind us. "But——"

"No," I say. "I'm done playing around. Talk to me, tell me about my mother."

He glances around a few more times. "Not here," he says. "They could be out there, watching."

"Who?" Zara asks.

Archer reaches into his pocket and produces an envelope, shoving it in my hand. "*Them.*"

I turn the envelope over and a shudder runs down my back. It's exactly the same style as the envelopes I've been receiving. Inside is a letter, which I remove and unfold. There's only a single line of typed text:

STOP TALKING TO HER.

"I RECEIVED THAT THE DAY AFTER WE SPOKE ON THE PHONE," he says, grabbing the letter and putting it back in his pocket. "I have two more just like it at home. I get one every day after we make an arrangement. Someone is watching us." He's jittery, like someone is dealing him several electric shocks per minute.

I have to admit I'm gobsmacked. Here I was thinking Archer might be the perpetrator behind this whole thing, only to find out he's receiving his own letters? Who could be doing this, and how do they know we've been in communication? Bad memories of Camille sneak into my subconscious and I push them away before they can take hold. She's dead and the Organization is dismantled. No, this is something else. It feels more...*personal*. Almost like the past is reaching forward, taking hold of me and attempting to drag me back.

"C'mon," I tell him. "Let's take this inside."

Chapter Two

Unsurprisingly, the inside of the restaurant was just what I'd pictured. The walls are all covered in dark red and browns, and the tables and booths look like they've been here for at least two decades. Everything is clad in heavy woods, and there is dark mood lighting which keeps the place dim, even though it's bright outside. What few windows adorn the rooms are covered in heavy curtains, each with its own layer of dust. And the tile floor looks like it hasn't had a good cleaning since the last presidential election.

A bored-looking server takes us to a small table where Zara and I take one side while Archer takes another, scanning the restaurant for any other patrons. "There was an older man and woman here when I was here earlier. Where did they go?"

"Jeez," Zara says. "Calm down. They were leaving as I was running up to catch you."

Archer nods a few times, more to himself before he hunkers down, looking at us over the rim of his glasses.

"Let me see that letter again," I say, holding out my hand. Archer fishes it out of his pocket again and puts it on the table between us. I reach into my coat and pull out the three letters

I've received. As I suspected, the envelopes are all the same brand and type. "It seems we have a common problem."

"I wish I'd never contacted you," Archer says, shaking his head. "I should have left well enough alone."

"Left what alone?" I ask.

"This business with Margaret," he replies. "She told me her secrets in confidence, under the assumption I would never reveal them. But then you came looking, I thought you had a right to know. She warned me and I should have listened. I now realize it may not have been her privacy she was concerned about, but rather my safety. And yours as well."

"I don't understand," I say, frustrated. "Please, just tell me what you know."

The waiter who seated us returns with waters for each of us, though he doesn't look at anyone as he sets them down. Only arrives and departs without another word.

"Great service here," Zara quips.

"You are going to get all of us killed," Archer whispers. "You, your friend here and especially me. Just tear the letters up. Throw them away, burn them. And get on with your life."

Zara scoffs. "You obviously don't know Em very well."

"Nor do I want to after this," he replies. "It was a mistake ever calling you to begin with. *I* should have left it alone. Now I'm giving you the same advice." He moves to get up and leave.

"Mr. Archer," I say in a stern and loud enough voice that he hunkers back down into his seat looking behind him again.

"Shh," he says. "Don't use my real name."

"I don't think you realize who you're dealing with here." I point to the letters. "These suggest a threat of some sort. Yours more than any of them. But it wouldn't be too much of a stretch for me to bring a case against you, seeing as you are the only other person in possession of a letter. I could even argue you created a fake letter in order to shift the blame away from yourself."

"You wouldn't," he says. "It would never hold up."

No, I wouldn't. But right now, I'm so frustrated I'm not willing to give him an inch. "You can take that chance, or you can tell me what you know," I reply. "I don't take kindly to someone attempting to extort me, whether that's financially or, in this case, emotionally. I'm going to find this person. And you're going to help me." He pinches his features as he studies us again. It's not hard to tell he's scared half to death, of what, I have no idea. But whatever it is has him on edge.

He looks down at the letters between us. His breathing has slowed some and he seems less jumpy, though I'd still be willing to bet if someone dropped a glass in the kitchen he'd take off for the door.

Archer carefully picks the first one up, reading it silently. Then the next two. "Your mother...she had a lot of... demons," he says.

"What?"

"In our discussions," he says. "She would always talk about how she didn't know how things got so out of hand, that it felt like someone else was living her life, right up until the moment she left. Until she decided to put it all behind and start over."

"Is that what this *pain* refers to in these last two letters?" I ask. I re-read the messages again.

Precious Emily,

You don't know the pain I've carried around all these years. Pain that could have been prevented. If only they had listened.

And then from the third letter:

Exquisite Emily,

I had to leave everyone behind because of what I'd done. No one would have understood. The pain was too great.

IT'S ALL VERY CRYPTIC, ALMOST TO THE POINT WHERE THEY could be referring to anything. But Archer seems to know something. He exhales, like he's letting go of a weight. "She's talking about the incident with her family...something she described to me as...illegal."

I pause, taking it in. "Which was what?"

"We...we never got that far in our sessions," he replies. "I tried to get her to open up about it on more than one occasion, but she insisted that if anyone ever found out, she'd be arrested. She was afraid of spending the rest of her life in jail. Of losing you. And before I could get anything more, she stopped coming to our meetings. I tried calling a few times, but the very nature of our meetings required that I not attempt too hard. It was always understood that Margaret could leave at any time and never return."

"What the hell kind of therapy is that?" Zara asks. "You just let her quit?"

"The nature of our discussions was very painful for her, almost physically so," he replied. "And I knew it would take a long time before she was finally comfortable telling her truth. So we worked on it slowly. But she always had the option to leave if things got too difficult. I trusted Margaret to come back when she was ready. I just...I didn't realize she'd died."

"When was your last session?" I ask.

"About two weeks before her death," he says. "I knew she'd been having some health trouble, but she always covered it well. I didn't know just how sick she was."

I remember those days. Everything seemed to happen so fast. One day she was fine, she was...Mom, and it seemed like the next she was this frail person who could barely stand. "She had a glioblastoma. By the time they found it and tried to begin treatment…" I trail off.

"I'm very sorry," he says.

I glance over to Zara and wipe my eyes. I didn't mean for this meeting to get emotional. That's not why we're here. But to know she was afraid of some legal repercussions for something she did when she was younger doesn't sit well with me. In my experience, anytime someone creates a brand-new identity in a new town, leaving her entire family behind, it's usually because they did something *really* bad. Mom was obviously running from her past, but it's only now that I realize she was also running from the consequences of her actions.

I reset myself and turn back to Archer. "She never hinted at what it could be?"

"All I know was it happened when she was still young. A teenager, I believe."

I can't help but wonder if Mom was using Dr. Archer as a kind of deathbed confessional. How long did she know the cancer was terminal? And was she trying to unburden herself before she died? I'm still not even sure how long before she knew. She complained of headaches a lot, but I don't think she realized until it was already close. At least, that's what I choose to believe, and hope is true. The last thing I'd want to think is she'd been carrying the knowledge around that she would die young for a long time.

"Was there anything else?"

"Just that she could never go back. Getting away from her family was the only way she could ever live a normal life. The last thing she ever wanted was them tracking her down."

"I don't understand," I say. "She always told me her family was dead. That's why I never had any grandparents to go see or any cousins on my mom's side."

He hunches and looks around again. "She believed they were still alive. But, I don't know for sure."

I look down at the letters. "Do you think they're the ones responsible?"

"I don't know how, but then again nothing about any of this makes sense."

I sit back in the booth, still trying to absorb the shock. "I can't believe she lied to us. Did my dad know?"

"No one knew," he replies. "She didn't want them to. Especially not you. But I've been carrying this weight around for fifteen years. I thought it might finally be time to tell someone. Obviously, I didn't realize things could still be dangerous or I never would have…" He pulls back and bites his lip. Light gray hairs dance on his chin, like he's been trying to grow a beard and hasn't been successful. "None of that matters now."

"Archer," I say. "I need to know what's coming. I need to know what I'm up against."

"I wish I could tell you," he replies. "But that's something Margaret took to her grave."

"Then I'll just have to go to the source," I say, standing.

"Where's the source?" Zara asks, getting up at the same time.

"A small town named Millridge. It's in Ohio." I turn to Archer. "I assume she at least wasn't lying about that part. About where she was born."

He winces. "Whatever this is, whatever you're doing, your mother wanted you to have no part in it. She did what she did to protect you and your father. Of that much I'm absolutely sure."

"Maybe if I'd never received one of these I wouldn't care," I say, gathering up my letters and putting them back in my pocket. "But if my mother was involved in some illegal activity, something so severe she had to cut off all communication with her family, then I have to know what it is. And obviously someone out there wants me to know it too. The only problem is they don't know who they're dealing with. I've dealt with a stalker before, and I'm not about to live with it one day longer than I have to. I'm going to find them, and put an end to this farce." I leave him at the table as Zara trots closely behind.

"Hey, hey wait a second," Archer says, following us. "That's it?"

"You didn't want to talk to us in the first place," I tell him.

"I just don't want this to come back on me," he says, pulling out his letter again. "I've already received one of these damn things. You're going to put a stop to it, yes?"

I nod. "I'm a woman of my word." I pull a card out of my coat and hand it to him. "Here. If anything else comes to mind, or you see anything strange, call me."

He looks at the address printed on it once before shoving it in his pocket and pushing past us to the door. He's out into the midday sunlight before I can utter another syllable. "Great guy," I tell Zara.

"Oh, the best," she says. "I just wish he'd had more for you."

"Yeah," I say. "So do I."

Chapter Three

"So. When are we going to talk about it?" I ask as we ride the elevator up to our floor inside the J. Edgar Hoover building. Zara has been uncharacteristically quiet the entire ride and it's beginning to worry me. After the events up in New York, and after Dr. Archer blew me off the first time, we finally took a short vacation, just to get away from it all. But the entire time she seemed far away, like she wasn't really present. I didn't try to force her to talk about her time with Magus, and I know how close both of us came to losing our lives, but still. I don't like this new, subdued Zara. It's like something isn't quite right in the universe.

"What?" Zara asks as the elevator doors open.

"Your valentine," I say.

"Pssh, it's not that big of a deal," she replies.

"You think *he* sent it, don't you?"

She rolls her eyes at me and leads me into our department, which is bustling for a Monday afternoon. Even in the dead of winter, crooks don't slow down. There are at least a dozen cases on my desk that need my attention and I can't help but feel a twinge of guilt at spending extra time trying to track down my own answers.

"That's not a no," I say, following her over to her desk. A little over a week ago, on Valentine's Day, Zara texted me the picture of a postcard she'd received in the mail. It didn't contain a message, only a postmark from Manchester, England and it was the image of a small coastal town named Whitby. I looked it up; apparently the setting partially served as the inspiration for Bram Stoker's *Dracula*. A fact both of us were very interested to hear.

"You know, for someone who has been receiving random letters in the mail, I'd think you'd be more sensitive to this." She slumps down in her chair, removing her sidearm and placing it in the drawer beside her desk.

"C'mon," I say, feeling more playful than I have in a while. "You know it's from Theo, I think he wanted to wish you a happy Valentine's Day. Who else could have sent it?"

"Who else knows my home address, you mean?" she asks. "Even if it was from him, so what? It's not like I'll ever see him again."

"I still want to know how he survived that gunshot wound to the stomach," I say, taking my own seat across from her. She's given me all the details of her time with Magus, including when Theo—seemingly one of Magus's right-hand men decided to defect and help her. But it turned out Theo wasn't part of the cult either. He later told us he'd once been with MI6, though now he's more of an "independent contractor," which I take to mean mercenary. Not to mention Zara saw him shot in the stomach, only for him to appear to help us remove the exploding vest Magus had fitted on Zara in a last, desperate attempt to disrupt the world's economy. I could tell at the time Zara was smitten, and given that she broke up with her then-boyfriend Raoul not more than a day later, I feel like I'm on to something here.

But she hasn't been ready to talk about that, either. Still, I have to wonder if Theo is secretly keeping tabs on Zara because he feels the same way.

As I'm running through the possibilities in my head I realize Zara has engrossed herself back into her work again—something she's been doing a lot of lately. Gone is the happy, boisterous and sometimes irreverent woman I once knew, and instead I see someone who needs help. She's been through a lot and needs a place to vent. As much as I can't believe I'm about to suggest it, I think maybe some time with Dr. Frost might be in order.

Just as I'm about to grab her attention, my desk phone rings. "Slate," I say, picking it up.

"I need to see you a minute," my boss, Fletcher Wallace, says on the other end. I look up, giving Zara one of my trademark "what now" looks that she always catches, but she's involved in whatever she's working on.

"Hey," I say after I hang up and am already standing to head into Wallace's office. "Thanks for your help today. He probably would have gotten away if you hadn't been there."

"Sure," she replies. "No problem." And it seems like that's all I'm going to get out of her. I'm going to need to do something drastic to get her out of this funk, which more than likely means we'll need to hit up a karaoke bar. I bet if I—the perpetual introvert—got up on stage it would shake her from this thing.

I leave her at our desks, worry still coursing through my veins. I've never seen her like this before and I'm not quite sure what to do about it. While I like the idea of Dr. Frost, she probably won't want to see him because she's heard me complaining about him so much. But I'd be willing to bet Frost can give me a referral to someone else.

"Slate, good. Come in," Wallace says, motioning to me as soon as he sees me at his door. Like every other day his suit is well-pressed and immaculate, though today he's removed his jacket which is hanging on a hangar hooked over a knob on a filing cabinet behind him. Underneath he's got on a pinstripe shirt complete with overalls. Combined with the horn-rim glasses it makes my boss look like he stepped out of the 1940s.

"What's up?" I ask. While we've had our differences in the past, including the time where he had to almost tranquilize me, I've decided I'm not going to let Fletcher Wallace get under my skin anymore. I have bigger things to worry about than his strict adherence to the rules and regulations. And honestly, it's not worth the energy.

"Got a new case for you." He picks up a folder and hands it across the desk to me. I don't bother sitting down; these meetings rarely take more than a few minutes.

"I've already got a backlog from my time off," I say.

"I know. But this is of some urgency and requires your… unique talents."

I stare at him over the edge of the folder as I open it. "What's that supposed to mean?"

"Read the file."

I give it a cursory look. It involves the murder of a young woman down in Louisiana. "Her body was found by the side of the road…" My brow furrows as I read the rest.

"Go on," Wallace says.

"…drained of all its blood?" I look up again. "What is this?"

He nods. "Keep going." I read over the rest of the report. The coroner states no cause of death can be found, other than two small puncture wounds at the base of the neck." I shut the folder and throw it back down on his desk, doing everything I can not to bite my lip in frustration. "What is this, a joke?"

He holds up one hand in a "who knows" gesture. "Doesn't really matter. The locals have requested federal help; they don't know what to do with it down there."

"So send someone from the New Orleans office," I say.

"No dice. I'm sending you."

"Why?" I don't need this right now. I've already got a ton of work here, not to mention I need to follow up on this

Archer angle. If he's telling the truth, I need to get to Ohio and start investigating my mother's supposed activities, not head down to Louisiana to deal with someone's idea of a bad practical joke. Now I'm sorry I even mentioned anything about Dracula to Zara.

"Because of your record," he says. "You're good at this kind of stuff, and weird cases like this tend to require someone with the skills to think outside the box."

"But—"

"Unless you have a more pressing matter," he says, the snark unmistakable in his voice. Does he know I've been pursuing this situation with my mother on company time? This is where Wallace and I butt heads. Where I could have confided in Janice about this latest development in my personal life, it's not something I'm willing to share with him. Wallace already knows more about me than I'm comfortable with, and I really don't need him knowing my personal business. Not to mention the last time I got the Bureau involved it almost cost me my life and my job. I'm not making that mistake again.

"No," I finally say. "Can I at least take a flight this time?"

He glares at me over the top of his glasses. "You get one flight. No second chances, no screw ups. You miss the plane and you're driving. And *I'll* make your travel arrangements. The Bureau is still paying off that private plane fiasco, which they should be garnishing your wages for. And don't think I didn't suggest it to them, but Deputy Director Simmons overrode me."

I try not to smile but I know it partially reaches my lips anyway. Wallace only narrows his gaze. "Get started. You'll leave first thing in the morning. I want you down there while everything is still fresh."

I nod. "I'll let Zara know."

"Slate," Wallace says, stopping me before I get to the door.

"You'll be handling this one on your own. Agent Foley won't be joining you."

I thought maybe with a new assignment it would give Zara a chance to think about something else, rather than being stuck in this office. Her field assignments have been particularly light lately; this would give her a good chance to get out and away from it all for a while. She's like me, she does better when she has a goal in front of her, rather than just a "vacation" where we do nothing but sit around all day soaking up the sun. Not to mention it's still somewhat warm in Louisiana at this time of year. "But—"

"Apparently she hasn't informed you yet," Wallace says. "But Agent Foley has requested reassignment. She's retiring from fieldwork."

Chapter Four

"HEY, OW," Zara says as I pull her by the arm until we reach the south stairwell. I push through the security door and wait until it closes behind us. The sound echoes down the concrete stairwell. I pause a moment, listening for anyone above or below us, but it's quiet. No one ever uses these stairs unless there's an emergency, because doing so locks us out of the entire building and we have to go all the way down to the main floor to get back in.

"Why didn't you tell me?" I hiss at Zara, so mad I can practically feel steam billowing from my ears.

"Because I knew you'd react like this. I'm not like you, Em. I can't keep doing this job. It's too hard."

"Too hard? You took to fieldwork faster than anyone I've ever known! That operation you pulled off with Magus? A ten-year veteran would have struggled, but you managed to breeze right through it. And I'm not just blowing smoke up your ass. If I didn't think you were suited for it, I'd tell you."

She shakes her head vehemently. "That's the problem. I can't do something like that again. I got cocky, thought I could do what you did and go undercover. You know, really take one of the big ones down."

"You did!"

"Yeah, and it almost killed us both. If Theo hadn't showed up—" She turns away and I see the glint of tears swimming in her eyes. "I just...can't. I need you to accept that."

I take her hands in mine. "Of course I accept that. I just wish you could have told me. I never meant to put extra pressure on you."

"I know," she says, turning back to me and the tears are already running down her cheeks. "But I didn't want to disappoint you."

I pull her into a hug. Given I have a couple inches on her, I'm able to really pull her close and there's not much she can do about it. I hate that I've been so wrapped up in my own shit that I didn't even see what was happening to her right in front of me. Zara really was a prodigy—even Janice thought so back when she was still in charge of our department. But I don't want to try and force her to do anything she's not ready for. The whole experience with Magus has really shaken her confidence; I don't blame her for wanting to sit somewhere it's safe for a while.

I pull away and look straight into her eyes. "Promise me something."

"What?" She sniffs and runs her palm under her nose.

"You won't dismiss the idea of coming back someday. Maybe even someday far in the future. You're just...you're too damn talented to sit behind a desk all day."

She smiles a little and I see a bit of that Zara I've been missing lately. "Yeah, okay. I can do that."

"Did Wallace tell you about the case?"

"I think he was going to, before I told him I wanted the transfer." She pulls away from me and sits on the nearest step. "I hope you're going somewhere warm."

I take a seat beside her. "Warmer than here, at least. It's a town called Bellefleur, about an hour outside New Orleans.

Apparently they had a…weird death down there and aren't sure how to handle it."

She looks up, interest flaring in her eyes. "How weird?"

"As in the victim is missing her bodily fluids and the only potential cause look like two evenly-spaced holes at the base of her neck."

Her eyebrows raise so high I think they're going to jump off her brow and fly away on their own. "You're kidding."

"I wish I was. Obviously, someone is trying to make the death look supernatural. Wallace wants me down there to figure out what's going on."

"What are you going to do about Ohio?" she asks, pulling her legs up and hugging them.

"I don't know," I say. "I wish I could be in two places at once. For some reason I feel like this thing with Archer is urgent. Like if I don't act soon, I might lose the opportunity for something forever."

"Probably because someone has eyes on him," she replies. "And you too."

"And me too," I say. "I seem to be everyone's favorite subject these days. Remember back when things were simple? I'd just get a case, work it—you'd help on the other end of the phone, and then we'd go out and have a pizza after we caught the guy?"

"Sure seemed simpler back then," she replies.

"Yeah, it did." I look to the side, thinking I heard someone a few stories down enter the stairwell, but when I listen more carefully, there's nothing. "Will you—can you watch Timber for me while I'm gone? I'm going to see if Liam can't find his way up to Ohio, maybe sniff out some contacts, or some basic information." When this case is over, I need to get up there. But in the meantime, I'm sure I can convince my boyfriend FBI agent to take a short trip for me. It doesn't have to be anything big; I'm just looking for evidence that Archer isn't yanking my chain. Something that would show my mother's family *is* still alive, and maybe something about this, *incident* that caused her to leave everything behind. Maybe even figure out if they're the ones behind these letters or not.

"Of course," she says. "I'd love to take him. It's been a while since Timber and I have had a chance to hang out together."

"Not too many snacks," I chide. "Last time you watched him he came home two pounds heavier."

"Growing boys need their nutrients," she says, sounding more and more like the Zara I'm used to. Maybe this is what she really needs: a reset of sorts. I'm sure telling me about her decision has been weighing on her, and while I'll miss her being by my side in Louisiana, I'm not about to suggest she put herself in the crosshairs if she isn't ready. Our job isn't the kind you can just power through, despite that being part of the old creed. Now we know what kind of psychological and emotional damage that kind of pressure can do to agents; and no one wants an agent in the field who can't handle it. That's how people get killed. Zara is making the right choice. The brave choice.

I help her up and hug her again. "You know you can tell me anything, right?"

"Yeah, I know," she replies. "It's just…sometimes you're like super agent, you know?"

I bark out a laugh, letting her go. "Super agent? Do I have to remind you I practically got my face smashed in because I wasn't quick enough?" Even though it's been a good month, my face is still sore in places from my confrontation with Brodie Tyler. At least I don't have to wear the nose brace anymore.

"You know what I mean," she says, laughing. "There isn't any case you can't handle."

I yank on the door before remembering that it's locked from the outside. We'll have to walk all the way down and come back through security to get back into the office. I start the long trudge down the stairs. "Maybe that's why Wallace is sending me. Maybe no one else wants to touch this case."

"I know I sure wouldn't," Zara says.

"Why's that?" I ask.

"Because. Catching a vampire is nearly impossible."

I turn around to smack her in the arm, but she deftly dodges it and instead her laugh echoes all the way down the stairs.

Chapter Five

I CATCH the sound of the door opening and closing just as I throw the last of my things into my suitcase. I'm not the kind of person who can wait until the last minute to pack. And given Wallace's warning about not missing my flight, I'm not taking any chances. In fact, I might sleep in my clothes tonight.

Timber jumps off the bed at the sound of Liam coming in and runs to the door. He always gets a little depressed when I have to go away, so he ends up sitting on my bed, giving me the biggest puppy dog eyes he can while I try to pack and not feel like a horrible mama. But hopefully he'll have fun staying with Zara. Despite my warnings, I have no doubt she'll spoil the crap out of him.

"Hey, you here?" Liam asks from the hallway as I hear the jingle of Timber's collar as he's probably assaulting Liam.

"Back here," I call out, closing my suitcase to make sure everything fits.

"Hey," he says, rounding the corner. "Missed you today." He plants a longing kiss on my lips.

"I missed you too," I admit.

"You weren't in the weekly briefing this morning." He

tosses his jacket on one of the chairs in the bedroom. Liam has been staying over so much I've officially designated that his chair, where he can pile whatever he wants on it.

"No, Zara and I had a...thing. I finally talked to Archer."

His eyes grow wide. "You're kidding. He showed up for once?"

I lead him through the entire operation, including both me and Zara staking out the place and finding a way to corner the man before he finally coughed up what he knew. But to be honest, I'm not sure I believe it. It's going to take a lot more than the word of a man who was my mother's supposed therapist before I believe his accusations.

"So what are you going to do?" Liam asks, looking at my suitcase. "Headed up there to find out?"

"I wish. Wallace assigned me to a new case. I'm flying out first thing in the morning."

He grins. My folly with the airline is public knowledge around the office, but Liam was one of the first to know. "I can't believe he actually caved."

"I'm sure I'll be in fourth class or whatever the worst seat on the plane is, my knees up to my chest."

"At least you're not driving. That's what...a fifteen-hour trip?"

"I have no idea," I say, turning back to my suitcase and squishing it closed before pulling the zipper all the way around. I'll have to stuff a few more toiletries in there first thing in the morning, but otherwise, I'm ready. I pull the suitcase off the bed and wheel it down the hallway, setting it right up next to the front door. Timber whines.

I get down on my knees and rub his head, which turns into a full-body rub, causing him to wiggle that little butt of his. "I'm not leaving yet, baby. One more night," I tell him. The more I do this the worse I feel. Back when Matt—

No, I'm not doing that anymore. Dr. Frost says I've been too eager to compare my current situation to my previous one, especially when it seemed like that previous one was superior. He says all I'm doing is reminiscing on a life that can never be and instead I need to be focused on the here and now instead.

"You're gonna be staying with Auntie Zara, won't that be fun?" I say and he whines again this time, but it's the excited kind and he looks so happy he might actually pee on the floor. "Okay, c'mon, let's take you out." I grab his leash and have him out on the yellowing grass patch before he loses it.

Liam watches from the door, a small smile on his face.

"What are you grinning about?" I ask, unable to keep myself from smiling at his earnestness.

"Just appreciating the moment," he replies, crossing his arms.

"What? Watching my dog pee on the same spot he's peed on a hundred times before?"

He shrugs. "What can I say? I'm a simple man."

I scoff, doing my best to hide my emotions. Sometimes I don't know how I got so lucky as to find someone like him. "Hey, feel free to tell me no to what I'm about to ask." Timber has finished his duties and we trot back up the few steps to the porch and door. Liam steps aside to allow us to pass.

"Let me guess, it has something to do with going to Ohio for you?" he says, closing the door behind us.

I let Timber off his leash and he immediately goes for the water bowl, refilling the well. I turn back to Liam. "I see you learned about anticipating your opponent's moves in Quantico after all."

"Sometimes I'm not as dumb as I look." I love it when he does this self-deprecating thing. It's so damn charming. Liam is actually quite intelligent, becoming an agent in such a short amount of time. Like Zara, he's managed to impress his superiors, which in this case happen to include Wallace.

"If Wallace hadn't just dropped this in my lap—"

"Em, it's no problem," he says. "I've got a couple of days after working overtime while you and Zara were taking a break. I can spend a day or two up in Ohio, snooping around."

"Just the bare minimum, though," I tell him. "I'm just looking for confirmation that Archer isn't jerking me around. If we can at least figure out if Mom's family *is* still alive, maybe I can figure out what she did that was so terrible."

"You showed him the letters?" Liam asks.

I nod. "And he showed me one of his own. Whoever is doing this is close." A year ago that might have given me pause. But I've seen this movie before. And I'm not about to let anyone else get the jump on me. Which is why I'm so determined to cut this thing off at the source, so I can finally get on with my life, once and for all.

"Shouldn't be a problem. After all, I already sound like I come from the hill country. There's not much difference between a Virginia accent and an Ohio one, is there?"

I laugh. "I have no idea. But it's not like I'm asking you to go full hillbilly. Just ask around, don't stick out, and for the love of god don't let them know you're with the FBI."

He quirks one edge of his mouth. "You act like I've never done this before. I *was* a cop for a couple of years. I know how to blend in."

"Okay. Thank you. Seriously. I'd do it myself, but something tells me we don't have a lot of time left. And who knows if more letters are already on the way." So far they have been coming at pretty regular intervals. But at the same time they feel like they are building to something. What, I have no idea.

"I assume this is why Timber is staying with Zara," Liam jokes.

I make a face that causes him to laugh, though I was a little serious because I wasn't sure if he'd be mad I already sort of committed him to it. But his good mood tells me I'm in the clear, so I take the opportunity to change the subject. "Did you hear? About her request?"

He nods. "She came and told me after you left. That

means she won't be working in the same office anymore, doesn't it?"

"Probably," I reply. I'd gotten so used to Zara being there I almost forgot what it was like before she became a field agent. "More than likely she'll go back to working remotely from home, or from the Intelligence division whenever her work requires a top secure clearance."

"What does that mean for you two?"

"We'll still see each other," I say. Though it won't be the same. Zara and I have always been close, ever since we both started working at the Bureau. She was the one who found me, though. And ever since she's moved into our division, we've grown a lot closer, especially since we worked a lot of cases together. Now, I'll probably only see her in person if we make plans outside of work. It doesn't leave a good feeling in my stomach.

Liam seems to sense my discomfort and instead heads into the kitchen. "Can I at least feed you one more time before you have to go? Or is it an early flight?"

I check my phone to find Wallace has sent over the flight info. My face falls when I see the time. My guess is the earlier the flight, the cheaper it is. "You might as well fix eggs and bacon."

Tomorrow is going to be a long day.

Chapter Six

My flight gets into Louis Armstrong International Airport before eight and I'm in a rental car and on the road by nine. Wallace wasn't kidding when he said *no frills*. He'd had me in the very back of the plane, on an airline I've never flown before but have heard about how…economical it typically is. And they weren't kidding; I didn't even get a bag of nuts on the trip.

Still, I manage to grab a quick breakfast from one of the airport kiosks before I head out and get on the road. I'm anxious to miss all the morning traffic, but I'm only half successful. It's a little cooler than I anticipated, but at least it isn't sticky season yet. While I'm glad to get away from the frigid temps in Washington, I'm grateful I'm not here in "sweat through your shirt" weather.

I take the 310 south until I hit Highway 90 where everything just flattens out as the road runs through the small towns of southern Louisiana. The towns themselves are quaint, usually with a couple of gas stations, fast-food restaurants and not much else. In between are long swaths of nothing but swampland on both sides of the road, as if I need any reminder that things here aren't particularly great for these communities. Many of them seem stuck, unable to improve or grow and just feel as though a lot of the people have given up. Often the road will elevate on long, low bridges with pylons that disappear into the muck. The bridges also have high fences to keep people from accidentally falling off. I can't imagine what kind of logistical nightmare it is to try and find a body that's been swallowed up by the bayou.

After about an hour of driving I make it to the city of Bellefleur, population around fifteen thousand. Though "city" is a generous term. From all accounts, it looks no bigger than a small town, though I'm used to the sprawling suburbs of D.C. It sits right on the Bayou Laforche with a downtown that looks like a smaller version of New Orleans. The buildings are two to three stories, and most are French-inspired, seeing as this city has been here since around the time of the Louisiana Purchase. It's a cute place, but it's not difficult to tell the city has seen better days. My guess is damage from all the recent hurricanes has started to become too much for these people, and the city doesn't have the same visibility or support of somewhere like New Orleans.

Still, I'm not looking for a place to settle down when I'm old. I'm here because I need to find out just what the hell is going on with this body that's been found. With any luck, I can determine the killer, find them, and wrap this up quick. But because the local LEOs have requested our assistance, this has now become a federal case. I can't leave until the case is closed or we've exhausted all potential avenues.

I pass through the rest of downtown on my way to the police station, which happens to be a multi-story brick building set off the side of the road with a large parking area. I follow the signs directing me to guest parking and step out into the morning sun. It's barely cool enough for a jacket, but I'm sure it will be freezing inside, so I keep my suit coat on. There's the thick scent of something organic in the air, but I can't quite place it. But it smells of earthy moss, like a forest right after a heavy rain. I also catch the whiff of something industrial somewhere, but don't see any smokestacks.

Heading into the building, I find myself directed to the left before I'm even greeted by someone. A large partition sections off an area of the building, from the floor to about chest height and what looks to me like bullet-proof glass the rest of the way up. It reminds me of a bank teller's counter, except with much higher security.

An older man in uniform, probably in his sixties or seventies sits on the other side of the glass reading a newspaper, his name tag telling me his last name is Cropper.

"Excuse me," I say, holding up my badge to the glass so he can clearly see it. "I'm looking for Captain Decker."

The man looks at the badge a minute and puts his paper down. "You're here about the Bright case." I nod. He smacks his gums once, though I'm not sure if he's actually got anything in there or not. "Sorry, Decker is out of town. Had to leave this mornin'. Detective Lowe took over the case."

"Where can I find Detective Lowe?" I ask.

He points me to a door that's close by. "I'll buzz you in. Just look for the desk. He's here somewhere."

An ear-splitting buzz comes out of nowhere and I wince, heading for the door. As soon as I open it, the noise thankfully stops and I find myself in a small corridor that leads to the other side of the partition where Sergeant Cropper sits. "Back thataway." He motions, then goes back to his newspaper.

I miss having Zara here to exchange a snide glance with, but I press on, passing different offices and desks, none of which belong to the man I'm looking for. Finally, I have to stop a helpful-looking officer who shows me that Lowe's desk is near the back, almost in the far corner of the building. Normally people like corner desks, but Lowe's is set in the middle of what looks like a storage area. Large, white evidence boxes surround his desk along with some old furniture that seems to be falling apart. A middle-aged man sits at the desk, staring intently at his computer. His skin is a couple shades darker than mine, and his hair has begun to recede, though his face is clean-shaven. Still, his cheeks are wide enough that he almost looks like he has jowls, and a frameless pair of lenses sit on his considerable nose.

"Detective Lowe?" I ask, walking up.

He glances up, surprise on his face, like he doesn't get many visitors. "Yes?"

"I'm Special Agent Emily Slate. With the FBI." I show him my badge.

"Oh," he says, standing. "Thanks for coming down so quickly. I'm Bill, though most everyone here just calls me Lowe."

I give his hand a quick shake. "I've read the file and what evidence you've found so far. I'd be interested to hear your theories about what's going on here."

"Isn't it obvious?" he asks, a look of concern crossing his brow. "We have a vampire on the loose."

I wait for the punchline, but it doesn't come. My features fall as I realize that Detective Lowe is serious. "A vampire."

"I don't know what else to call it," he says, turning his monitor around so that I can see. "I've been going over the reports from the coroner for the past day. There is no other indication to how she died." On the screen is a close-up image of two puncture marks, evenly-spaced, in skin that has almost become translucent. The wounds are gaping, having not healed, which means the victim was either dead at the time they were made, or they were the direct cause. But a long enough sharp object, driven straight through that part of the body could easily cause death just as easily.

It's the lack of body fluids that bothers me.

"But you don't seriously believe that someone is going around...biting people and draining them of their blood." I can't believe I'm having this conversation. If Zara were here she'd be cracking up by now.

He regards me with something I'd have to call suspicion, but it's fleeting. "Have you ever been to Bellefleur, Agent Slate?"

I straighten. "No, why?"

"Lot of superstitious people around here. We have a long history that goes way back. Things around here…they linger."

The way he says it makes me think the man believes he's hosting Tales from the Crypt. "I'm sorry. Linger?"

"Spirits. Supernatural beings. Whatever you want to call them. If they really *do* exist, they exist here."

I pause. "I don't mean to be rude. But you can't be serious."

"Oh, he's serious, all right." I turn to see another sergeant with a coffee cup in hand walking up. He's tall, with a chiseled jaw and a smirk on his face. "Brett Jackson," he says holding out his hand, which I shake as well. Jackson has a much stronger grip than Lowe. "Lowe here likes to think himself the *expert* on all things unexplained that go on in Bellefleur. But most of the time he's just makin' shit up out of thin air."

While I can appreciate Jackson's stance, his cockiness and condescending tone tell me a lot more about the man. "So what do you believe happened?"

"Someone got creative with an ice pick," he says, shrugging. "Doesn't really matter. No prints on the body means we don't have a suspect. Just a poor girl who deserves more than someone making up crazy theories about what could have happened to her. Her family deserves better than that." He shoots Lowe another look before addressing me again. "There's really no need to waste the Bureau's time on something like this. Lowe convinced Captain Decker we needed your help, but I think we have things well under control."

"If it was an ice pick, how do you explain the lack of any residual internal damage?" Lowe asks. "There's nothing below the surface to indicate whatever made the puncture was more than a couple of inches long."

Jackson glares at Lowe. "Whatever it is, it *wasn't* a vampire you crazy bastard. How you haven't been fired yet is a mystery to me."

"Maybe I'll add it to my list of unexplained occurrences around here," Lowe fires back.

Jackson just scoffs before turning back to me. "Captain Decker will be back in a few days. You may want to hold off your investigation until then, at least until we can get all of this figured out."

Nobody tells me when to start or end an investigation. While I might agree with Jackson, I don't like his attitude. "Part of the reason I'm here now is because I want to get a look at the body before too much time passes."

"What are you, a medical doctor or something?" Jackson asks, his tone now turning condescending toward me.

"Not at all. But I do have a lot of experience in this area. More than you might expect."

He shoots me and Lowe another look before shaking his head and returning from the direction from which he came.

"Sorry about him," Lowe says. "Most people around here have a healthy respect for the unexplained. Jackson isn't one of them. He's just an asshole."

I turn back to him. "I'm sorry to admit that I don't believe you either."

He shrugs. "That's okay. At least you're nice about it. Maybe you're right, and something else is going on here. I just haven't found the evidence for it. But hopefully, with your help, we can figure out what's going on."

"Sounds good to me," I say. "Can I see the body?"

"Sure." He half-scrambles around his desk and squeezes past me to lead me down a different corridor which heads to the back of the building. I have to admit I kind of want Lowe to be right just to see the look on Jackson's face, but I know it isn't possible. Lowe might just be a little more eccentric than most officers on the job. Still, he comes across to me as having his heart in the right place, even if his theory is too wild to be true.

"It's right down here," he says. "I'm sure you've been in a ton of morgues before, but ours is on the main level because the ground is too soft down here to have any buildings with basements. It's an unfortunate side effect of living so close to sea-level."

"How large is your force here?" I ask, just as a way to keep the conversation moving.

"About sixty officers total," he says. "But we also work closely with the Lafourche Parish Sheriff's office to include the surrounding areas."

"Any tension between you?" I ask, remembering my debacle in Mardel.

"Not really. More often than not you'll find both of us on a scene. In fact, it was a State Trooper who found poor Ms. Bright. Just lying there, on the side of the road like a piece of discarded trash." He pushes through some double doors, though he holds one for me.

"I assume you have a CSI team at the location where the body was found?"

He nods. "We did, but there was a lot of rain that night so there wasn't much left." A sign points us to the morgue and Lowe leads me down to another door, though this one is metal. He scans his badge across the electronic keypad which turns green. "She'll be just down here. Ready?"

I hold out my hands. "It's what I came for."

He nods. "Okay. Hold on to your butt."

Chapter Seven

As SOON AS we head through the metal door, I feel like we've entered a different building entirely. The lighting in this corridor is much brighter, and the walls are painted cinder block. Lowe leads me around a corner where the space opens up to reveal several offices, with the morgue through an open frame way near the back. I follow him into the morgue itself, where a wall of refrigeration units sits on the far side. A door opposite the units leads to what I assume is a loading dock outside. At the end of the room are a number of unused gurneys and a few small desks, each with their own computers. A woman sits at one with her back to us, typing.

"Dr. Hansen?" Lowe asks.

The woman turns. She's got long, blonde hair that's been pulled up into a messy bun, with strands sticking out everywhere. She's also wearing a lab coat covered by a black smock and I notice a couple of rubber gloves on the table beside her. Like Lowe, she wears a pair of glasses which she removes as soon as she sees us.

"Oh, Bill, you startled me," she says, standing. "I was just working on our mystery patient here."

"Rani, this is Special Agent Emily Slate with the FBI," he

says, introducing me. "Agent Slate, this is Dr. Rani Hansen, our resident coroner, and honestly the only one in about fifty miles."

I take her hand and give is a quick shake. "You're working on Cameron Bright?"

She nods. "Just finished up and put her back into storage. But if you'd like I can pull her out again."

"If you don't mind," I say, pulling a pair of nitrile gloves out of my pocket and slipping them on.

"I guess this one was weird enough to involve the FBI, huh?" she asks, going over to one of the square refrigerator doors and opening it. I catch the top of the girl's head, her dark hair the only thing visible until Hansen pulls the shelf out.

"That was my call," Lowe says. "Thankfully Decker agreed."

I'm not really listening though, instead I'm staring at the deceased form of Cameron Bright. I've seen my fair share of dead bodies, but still her appearance is immediately startling. She's completely nude and every inch of her skin has taken on a waxy sheen, while her skin color is almost an alabaster. It is like someone has come along and spray-painted her.

"Strange, isn't it?" Hansen asks. "I'd never seen anything like it before, either. But that's what happens when you drain a body of all its blood."

"How is that possible?" I ask.

"Well, generally, if a person is still alive, all it would take is a large enough cut on a big artery and the person would bleed out in only a few minutes. Though there would still be some residual fluids as the heart slowed down and stopped. But we're not seeing that here, and there were no other injuries on the victim other than the two puncture wounds right here, at the base of the neck."

I stare at the giant Y-section that's been cut into Cameron Bright, allowing Dr. Hansen to access the inner body cavity, though she's been sewn back up. "And the autopsy didn't reveal anything else?"

"Not so far. But I want to take another look. Still, examining a body like this is difficult. We're not seeing the regular kinds of bruising that would be typical in a dead body. Due of course, to the lack of fluids."

She almost doesn't look real. I hadn't realized just how much a splash of purple on the lips or the sallowness around the eyes made a corpse seem more…lifelike, for lack of a better word. I carefully reach down and pull back one of her eyelids. The eye underneath is cloudy, though I can still see where the woman once had dark brown eyes. It's times like this when I wish I had a medical degree.

"So, I say, walking around the body to look at the puncture wounds on the neck. "What do you think happened?"

"Hard to say," Hansen says. "But whoever did this has some medical knowledge."

I look over to Lowe. "One of the other officers suggested someone might have taken some kind of ice pick to her neck."

"If that's the case it was an extremely thin ice pick, and it didn't penetrate very deep. But whatever punctured the skin *did* hit the carotid. And there is no indication of the killer breaking the skin more than once."

I furrow my brow. Generally, in an attack, things are tense, the victim would be thrashing about. So to hit the intended target on the first and second tries without missing is a minor miracle in itself. "Any indication of sedatives in her system anywhere?"

"Nothing residual. But without the blood to test, it's much more difficult to tell," Hansen says.

I take a step back. "So the attacker stabbed her, with something small and thin, twice…and she bled out?"

Hansen pinches her features together. "That's all we have to go on right now."

I turn to her. "But in your professional opinion, that's what you're saying?"

She shoots a glance to Lowe, then back to me. "I...really don't have enough information to make an informed judgement," she says.

"Okay then," I say, not liking where this is heading. "*Off the record.* What happened?"

"I can't exactly explain it, not in traditional medical terms," she says. "But I believe someone drained the blood from her and the evidence seems to indicate she could have been a willing participant."

I can't believe this. What is it with people down here? She might as well have just come out and said she believes the exact same thing as Lowe. The only problem is, vampires aren't real, and whatever killed this girl most certainly was. I find myself agreeing more and more with Sergeant Jackson, as much as I hate to admit it.

I take a few steps back, pulling my gloves off and tossing them in the trash.

"Perhaps we'd be more comfortable in my office," Hansen says. "I can show you some literature on the subject."

"Literature? Are you saying you have documentation of previous attacks like this?" There was nothing in the file to indicate this was part of any pattern. But intrigued, I follow Dr. Hansen out of the morgue after she's closed Cameron's body back into the drawer.

She leads us down the other direction until we come to her office, which is a small room lined with shelves. Most of the shelves are full of books, and a few have begun overflowing with errant papers. Though I notice a few other items as well. A large quartz crystal sits on one of the shelves, next to a feather and what looks like a rattle of some sort. As Dr. Hansen rounds her desk, I notice her slip a deck of cards in one of the drawers. I didn't get a good look, but they looked larger than normal playing cards. And underneath her calendar on her desk, I notice the edge of some kind of design peeking out. There are also a number of wooden circles, all on different shelves and all with different runes carved on them.

"Collector of antiquities?" I ask, looking around.

Hansen follows my gaze. "What? Oh, I guess you could say that. When you do this job long enough you start to get a little superstitious about things I suppose. Plus, I've always enjoyed little trinkets and baubles." She reaches up on one of the shelves and pulls a few older books down. They certainly don't look like medical journals. Instead, they look like something one might find in the fantasy section at the local bookstore.

As she flips through the first book, I turn my attention to Lowe. He doesn't seem surprised by anything in the office, which tells me he's been in here before. I might have just stumbled into two *believers* who happen to be working for the local government. Not the best people I want on a case like this. Their biases are most certainly affecting their judgement.

"Here we go," Hansen says, turning the book and handing it to me. "There was record of an incident in 1927 of a young woman being found in a similar manner. And another incident in 1944." I read through the transcripts in the book, which seem like little more than memoirs, though there are some accompanying drawings, which depict a young woman lying on the ground, with some kind of tube hooked up to her neck. But the drawing is so old I can barely make out any of the details.

I take a deep breath. "You're saying that we should take these accounts on their face value?"

Hansen shrugs. "Unless you have a better idea. I remember reading about these when I was young. Woman dying around the times of the first and second world wars, drained of all their blood. A few young men too."

I close the book and look at the cover. *Incidents of Para-*

normal or *Parasituational Activity, Collected Works Volume 2* by E.G. Blundht. "This is unsubstantiated nonsense," I say, handing the book back to her. "Probably someone's attempt at swindling people at the beginning of the century. I've seen far better cons."

"But," Lowe says, stepping forward. "What if they are connected? What if whatever is out there doing this was dormant for all this time."

"Sergeant, I think you've let your imagination run away with you," I tell him. "There are no such things as immortal beings who drain the blood of the living to maintain their immortality and youth. I may not be a scientist, but I know for sure it isn't possible."

"Possible or not, *someone* killed that woman," he replies.

"I agree. Though I believe it's much more likely we're dealing with someone *real*, someone who wants to play games with us. A sick and twisted person with way too much time on their hands." I turn back to Dr. Hansen. "I appreciate your theories, but I'd like to bring my own medical examiner in on this."

Her face turns downward. "Why?"

I sigh. While I don't enjoy this, it's necessary. "To be honest, I don't think you're up for the job. You're too willing to believe in some supernatural element and I don't have time to try and hold your hand through this. We have a killer out there that needs to be found. Speculating about some fictional monster isn't doing anyone any good."

She places the book back on the shelf. "Careful, Agent. These monsters may not be as fictional as you think. Bellefleur has a special...energy about it. It attracts all sorts of strange creatures."

Smile and nod, Emily. I do as my subconscious suggests. "Thank you, anyway, for your theories. But I'll be contacting the New Orleans field office. Expect another coroner here by tomorrow." I make my way past Detective Lowe and head for the door.

"Don't discount the possibility, Agent," Hansen calls after me. "You never know *what* is out there."

Sure I do. A bunch of kooks dressed up to look like cops, that's what.

Chapter Eight

WHILE LOWE OFFERED to accompany me to the nursing home where Cameron Bright worked, I politely declined, telling him I tended to work better alone. My hope is he doesn't think I'm just blowing him off, though he could suspect it. He doesn't strike me as a stupid person, but I don't think I can listen to any more theories about how there could be a real-life vampire walking the streets of Bellefleur and draining victims of their blood.

At most this is a case of extreme exsanguination, probably caused by someone with an irrational fetish of some sort. I could be looking for someone who is obsessed with the occult or even *believes* themselves to be a vampire of some sort, but I won't buy into the myth. This crime was perpetrated by a very sick, but also very *human* individual. I just need to dig a little deeper than it seems Lowe wants to go.

While I'm not thrilled with the idea, part of me wants to speak to Sergeant Jackson again, to find out if anyone else has determined what could have happened. But seeing as their coroner seems to be just as eccentric as Lowe, I'm not sure they've made any progress. I really wish I could speak with Captain Decker, for no other reason than to find out *why* he assigned Lowe to the job knowing the man's predications for the supernatural.

By the time I get to Loving Hearts Senior Living, I've managed to calm down a hair. I don't know what it is about people who just refuse to accept evidence right in front of them, but it really bothers me. It's like they are being willfully blind to reality. My goal is to determine the cause of this poor young woman's death as soon as possible, find the killer and put all of this to rest before anyone else can even suggest the word *vampire* to me one more time.

As I pull into the parking lot, I notice a car off to the side that is surrounded by police tape. Cameron Bright's car, no doubt. They still haven't moved it. I wonder if the CSI team has even had a chance to give it a once-over. I park near the front and as the midday sun hits me, I decide to leave my overcoat in the car. It's just warm enough that I don't think I'll need it for another few hours.

Inside the lobby is decorated in what I can only describe as nineties contemporary. The rugs on the floor are worn, but clean, and the neutral colors give the entire place a very bland feel. I imagine that's probably on purpose, but at the same time, it doesn't seem like a place I'd like to wake up every day.

Says the girl who has trouble even mounting a new photograph on the wall every six months. I still have boxes from my move that I haven't unpacked, and it's been well over a year. I'm not one who should be questioning anyone's décor choices.

There seems to be no check-in desk, so I make my way down one of the hallways until I find a door marked "office." It's open so I knock on the side as a woman working at the closest window looks up. "Can I help you?" she asks, eyeing my appearance.

"I'm Agent Emily Slate, with the FBI. I'm investigating the death of Cameron Bright."

Her face falls as she stands. "Oh, yes. I'm Tricia. We all

loved Cameron. She brought such a young energy to this place. I told Mr. Gallagher he needed to take her off the night shift but he refused to do it. This place was always so…well, bright with her here."

I pull out my phone and check my notes about the case. "Wait, Tricia Caldwell? You were the last person to see or speak with Cameron, weren't you?"

She nods. "The first shift has about five nurses on it, but we all get here at different times. Cameron usually waits until we're all here before she heads out."

"Is that what happened on the day she disappeared?" I ask.

"Oh, no, she seemed like she was in more of a hurry to leave than usual. I was the third nurse in, and I remember her checking to make sure we were good before heading out." She dabs one corner of her eye with a nearby tissue. "I sure am going to miss that girl."

I sense a presence to my right and turn to see a heavyset man in his forties approaching from an adjacent office. "Did I hear you're here about Cameron?" he asks.

I nod, showing him my badge. "Are you Louis Gallagher?"

"In the flesh." He gives my hand a hearty shake. "I'm surprised to see someone from the FBI. Not that I'm not glad you're here. Whoever did this to Cameron has a lot to answer for. We're glad you're taking it seriously."

I arch an eyebrow. "Are there deaths in this town that *aren't* taken seriously?" I ask, tugging on the thread I'm not even sure he knows he left dangling.

"Well, no. I mean, the police do a fine job, I suppose. But most of the time it's someone who has died of a drug overdose, or it's a domestic situation. But for someone to be taken and then left on the side of the road…it's just…unnatural."

Ah, shit. Not another one. I decide to ignore it. "Did you know Ms. Bright well?"

"I should hope so," he says, shoving his thumbs into his

waistband. "I'm the one who interviewed and hired her. We only accept the best here at Loving Hearts and Cameron passed our interviews with flying colors. I know this was probably only a stepping stone in her career, but we were happy to have her."

I check over my notes again. "Can you tell me anything about her last night here? Did anything out of the ordinary happen?"

Gallagher shoots a glance at Tricia, who returns to her computer. "Nothing that isn't normal for a place like this," she says.

"What does that mean?"

"It means we lost a resident that night," Gallagher replies. "Mrs. Berger. She was ninety-two. And to be completely honest with you, we had all been hoping for it."

"Really," I say.

His mouth turns into a frown. "Agent Slate, you have to understand, for some people death is a gift. We see it first-hand here. Many of our older residents who have been with us long-term have complex health issues, or they're fighting terminal diseases. It breaks our hearts to see them in so much pain day in and day out. No one wishes for it. But sometimes the body hangs on, despite the person wanting to go."

"Sometimes people need permission from their loved ones," Tricia says. "And sometimes they just won't go."

"Isn't that what Hospice is for?" I ask.

"Hospice is only for when we already know death is close. As a way to prepare our residents and their families for the days and weeks ahead. But there are some cases, such as Mrs. Berger, where there is no clear indicator that she's ready. We just see the constant pain every day. I think we were all relieved when Tricia found her that morning."

I perk up. "Wait, she died overnight, but Cameron wasn't the one who took care of her?"

"She probably didn't know," Tricia says. "Usually we only

have one nurse on night shift, which means there is one nurse to check seventy-two residents."

I turn back to Gallagher. "Isn't that a little light for a place of this size?"

"Not at all. Very little happens at night; we only keep a nurse here for emergencies. But we've only had that happen, what, twice? In the past five years?"

"Something like that," Tricia says.

"I think I'd like to see Mrs. Berger's room, if that's all right," I say. I'm not sure what I'm looking for, but my curiosity is beginning to get the better of me.

"Of course," Gallagher says. "I'll be happy to escort you." He holds out one hand, indicating we should head back out into the hallway. "I will warn you, though, we've already cleaned the room, so I'm not sure what you're expecting to find. We have an excellent team who comes in and delivers the remains to our local morgue. It's very bad to keep them around for more than a few hours."

"I can imagine," I say, thinking of how even after only a few hours bodies begin to smell and putrefy.

Gallagher leads us to an adjacent hallway and I get to peek into rooms with their doors open. Each is decorated mostly the same, but contains furniture and knick-knacks from each of the residents' personal lives. Some are inside, staring out the windows or watching TV, and I can't help but feel a profound sense of sadness. I know if either of my parents were still alive, I never would have let them end up in a place like this. I understand the need, especially for people without families, but I'd be willing to bet more people here than not have families that could take them in.

But instead, they're here. And I can almost feel the loneliness radiating off them. Who knows, maybe I'll end up in a place like this. It isn't like I have any kids of my own, and no other family to take me in. I may be staring at my own future as I pass each of these rooms.

Gallagher finally stops at an open door, but the room is empty. I take a few steps inside and am overcome with the smell of bleach and cleaning products. Everything has been removed so it is little more than a box with a window and a bathroom. "Is this room already claimed for a new resident?"

"Yes, we have a substantial waiting list," he replies. "They should be bringing in some of the furniture today. The new resident is due to move in on Thursday."

I'm not sure what I was expecting to see here, because there literally is nothing. Strange to think this is where a person died—where they drew their last breath before leaving this world. At least, I hope, it was peaceful. A far better end than Cameron Bright was given.

I sigh and turn, only for something across the hall to catch my eye. "That's an emergency exit door, isn't it?"

Gallagher follows my gaze. "Yes, why?"

I point to the metal bar that allows the door to open and close. It's loose in its housing. "I think it's broken." As soon as I give the door a light push, it opens immediately to the bright sun outside.

"Yes, it broke a few months ago. We just haven't had it repaired yet."

There's something else about this place. I look down the hallway, following the ceiling. "You don't have any security cameras."

Gallagher winces. "We tried them, about five years ago. But the residents didn't like feeling like they were being watched all the time. Some even refused to come out of their rooms until we removed them. We tried to explain they were only for security, but you know how some people can be. Set in their ways."

What he's really saying is older people don't like adopting to new technology. Not that I can blame them. When I found a hidden camera in my apartment, I was livid, not to mention feeling violated. I suppose this place operates less like a commercial building and more like a makeshift residential one. And the people who inhabit it aren't used to cameras being part of their everyday lives. But I'd be willing to be in another sixty years, people won't blink twice at being recorded all day long.

"What about outside cameras?" I ask, pushing through the door and heading outside.

"We have them on the back loading dock, and at the front entrance," Gallagher says.

"But the front camera didn't pick up Cameron Bright leaving, did it?" I look up to the top of the building, then down along the small alleyway on this side of the building. It's bordered by tall brush and bushes on the other side.

"No, I don't believe it did."

"Then it's conceivable she left out of this door."

He sighs. "A lot of the nurses do it. It's easier to get to their cars and they don't have to engage with the residents that sit out front, as awful as that sounds. But imagine you care for people for eight or ten hours a day. You'd just want to go home and rest too." He pauses. "I've asked them not to use this door, though."

I'm only half listening, instead I'm focusing more on the accessibility of this alleyway. This side of the door has no handle, and no other way to access it. It's just a flat metal door on this side, which means no one could come in this way. But they could leave, especially if it's no longer linked to the emergency alarm system. I crouch down and take a good look at the pavement. There's a dark, oily spot on the ground, indicating a car was here recently.

"Does anyone normally park here?" I ask.

"No, it would block the alleyway," he replies.

"And you don't get any deliveries in this side of the building."

He shakes his head. "That's what the loading dock is for."

I nod, pulling out my phone and calling Lowe. "Detective Lowe speaking."

"It's Slate. I need a CSI team to head back down to Loving Hearts."

"Why?" he asks.

"Because I may have found evidence of the car that took Cameron Bright."

Chapter Nine

AFTER SPENDING a good hour with the Bellefleur police team at Loving Hearts, I decide to find out if there could be anyone who had a grudge against her, or any reason to hurt her. I'd spent some additional time interviewing some of the other staff, but no one seemed to know Cameron as well as Tricia and Mr. Gallagher. It seemed she was something of a loner. Though I did learn she had specifically *requested* the third shift, which I find interesting. Why would a bright, young woman in the prime of her life request the one assignment that kept her apart from all her coworkers, and meant she needed to be up all night long? I get that some people are heavy introverts, but from what I've learned, Cameron wasn't like that at all. She enjoyed interacting with people and all the residents loved her.

So why sequester herself voluntarily?

I don't want to waste too much time chasing something that may not lead anywhere. After all, some people just have their preferences for certain environments. Zara is much the same way. She's great whether she's alone or in a big crowd; one of those people who can shift seamlessly between an introverted and extroverted state. She likes both. I, however, am not that way.

Still, I'm hoping to speak to a few of Cameron's non-work friends as well. As soon as I find some.

While Lowe manages things at the nursing home, I head to the south side of the city to the address of Cameron's next-of-kin, her mother. The houses around here are all older, one-story and not very big. And there are a lot of trailer homes mixed in, instead of being in their own "parks" like they are back in D.C. I get the feeling people around here don't have much, but what little they do have, they stretch to make ends meet.

I pull up to a small, white house that sits in a secluded community, but I wouldn't go as far to call it a subdivision. It's just a collection of houses and streets that branches off the main road. A few plots of flowers dot the landscape in front of the house and though the siding looks worn, at least it's clean.

I approach and rap on the screen door, hoping anyone inside can hear me. I also get the feeling this is the kind of place where every neighbor is watching me from their windows. It isn't like there's a lot else happening around here.

A moment later the inner door opens to reveal a small woman, maybe five-one or five-two, her graying hair pulled back into a bun. Her eyes are sunken in and have the telltale redness of someone who has been crying nonstop. But when she sees me her face contorts into something of a rage.

"What th'hell do you want?"

I hold up my badge. "I'm Agent Slate with the FBI, here about your daughter? I'm very sorry for your loss, Mrs. Bright."

"She wasn't your daughter, what do you care?" the woman spits.

I've seen this before. The misplaced anger, the fury with nowhere to go. She would probably act this way to the mailman if he came by, so I do my best not to take it personally. "I'd like to ask you some questions, if you don't mind."

"I do," she replies. "You people won't even let me see her.

All I want to do is bury my daughter in peace. Why can't you just leave me alone?"

"Mrs. Bright, I'm sure the Bellefleur police are only trying to protect—"

"I don't need protectin'," she says. "Do I look like a shy violet to you? I was an E.R. nurse for fifteen years and I've seen the gamut of the terrible things out there. So don't tell me they're doin' it for my own good 'cause I don't buy it."

I see this will take a different approach. "I'll be honest, Mrs. Bright. I've been in the FBI for almost five years, and I've seen my fair share of bodies. Still, I have to admit how... unprepared I was to see your daughter."

She glares at me a moment, then turns away from the door, leaving it open. "Don't matter anyhow." I'm going to take that as an invitation. I open the screen door and step inside. The house is sparse, but clean and well-kept. A small couch sits to one side of the first room, facing a TV that backs up to a picture window with the curtains drawn. The room behind the living room is the kitchen, but they're so close I can practically peer into it even from my vantage point at the door. Mrs. Bright is rummaging around in there, and I hear the clinking of what sound like mugs or cups before she returns to the living room with a mug in hand. As she passes I catch a whiff of gin.

Mrs. Bright sits on the couch and indicates a chair that's pushed up into the corner. "Well? Get on with it if you're gettin'. Ask your questions."

I take a seat across from her, resting my elbows on my knees. "I'm not trying to tell you what to do, but when I lost my husband, I found it helped to talk about him a little, even to people who didn't know him. At first I thought it was the worst idea in the world, because I wanted to keep all of those memories to myself. But I realized later that by sharing who he was with other people, it helped heal the wound that had been left by his absence." Of course, I don't mention that he managed to lie to me the entire time we were married and that I didn't really know him at all. But I need Mrs. Bright to trust me, and she's not going to do that if I can't be a little vulnerable for her.

"Sorry to hear that," she says, softening a little. "But I don't need to be talking about Cammie."

"I spoke to her coworkers...and her boss. Everyone really seemed to love her."

Mrs. Bright makes a sad sort of face, then takes a sip from her mug.

"Can you tell me if there was anyone you were worried about? Anyone Cammie said might have been bothering her?"

"Not that she ever told me. Then again, we ain't talked much lately."

I look up. "Was there a particular reason?"

Mrs. Bright stares at me a minute, then runs her tongue over the top of her teeth before taking a long, thoughtful sip from her mug. "Your husband. That the worst thing that ever happened to you?"

I'm thrown by the question, not sure where she's going with this. "No," I answer honestly. Maybe at one time it was. But no longer. Instead, my mind goes to a hundred other situations. I only now realize just how unimportant it has become to me. But mainly I'm thinking about holding on to Zara, that bomb strapped between us, and not knowing if either of us would be walking out of that building alive.

Mrs. Bright nods again. "You swear to me you'll find the man who did this?"

"On my life," I say with the same honesty. No matter what, I don't let anything get in the way of giving a victim's family some kind of closure, though I know that's not always possible. But I will do everything in my power to make it so.

She lets out a long breath. "I think Cammie was lyin' to me."

"About what?"

"I think she was into somethin'…dangerous."

I try not to show my surprise. This is the first I'm hearing of anything other than Cameron was a strait-laced, perfect employee and friend. Everyone has skeletons in their closet, I don't care who they are. "Do you have an idea what?"

"Jus' that it has somethin' to do with extra money. I told you, I worked for the E.R. for fifteen years. I know how much a nurse makes. And it sure as hell ain't enough to fly off to Hawaii for a week."

"She was going to Hawaii?" I ask.

"In a week or so. Was really excited about it too."

"By herself?" I ask. The woman nods.

"And you don't think it's possible she saved up for—"

"Cameron was drownin' in student debt," the woman says, her words slurring ever so slightly. "Look around, it ain't like I could have afforded to pay for her school. She took on loan after loan to get her degree, only to find out she'd need somethin' more advanced to make any real money. But then, about six months ago, she stopped complainin' about her bills. Never said a word about it, but I realized somethin' was different. She took me out to dinner, always had nice clothes. Now unless she won the lottery and didn't tell no one, I'd like to know where all that extra money was coming from."

"Okay," I say. "I'll look into it. Thank you." An undisclosed money source could provide a motive to the murder, seeing as right now we have nothing. I'll need to pull her bank records to find out for sure. And I want to get a look at her apartment. Maybe there's some explanation there of the extra income. "Just one more question. Did Cameron have a boyfriend? Or anyone she saw regularly, even if they weren't 'official'?"

Mrs. Bright rolls her eyes and finishes off the mug. "Wouldn't know. She never talked to me about that stuff."

"All right," I say. "Well, thank you for your time." I pull out one of my cards and leave it on the coffee table between us. "If you think of anything else that might be useful, feel free to give me a call. That's my personal number on there."

I get up and head for the door.

"Agent Slate?" I turn back to the woman, whose eyes are swimming. I'm not sure if it's the alcohol or if she's just finally started to open herself up. "Don't let me down."

"No ma'am," I reply. "I give you my word."

Chapter Ten

IT'S GROWING LATE by the time I get to Cameron's condo, because the first address I went to was her old apartment, the one listed on her driver's license. But a quick call with Detective Lowe informed me that she just moved into this place only a few weeks ago. And given the apartment complex I just left; the condo is a significant upgrade. At least from the outside. The property has a gate that requires a code, despite being in a nicer part of town. There may be some truth to Mrs. Bright's assumptions after all.

As soon as I pull up to the condo, Lowe is already there, standing outside his car and looking up at the unit. Cameron's unit was on level two, and the property has large windows that would allow anyone to see inside from the parking lot, assuming the curtains weren't drawn like they are now. Someone could have been stalking her for a while, keeping a watch from out here. I take a cursory look at the parking lot as soon as I get out of the car, trying to figure out the best hiding spot if someone was keeping tabs.

"What are you doing?" Lowe asks, coming over.

"Just testing out a theory," I say, checking the surrounding bushes for any footprints or other evidence that could have been left behind. But everything looks clean. "Just a thought. Do you have the key?"

He nods. "From her personal effects."

"And what of the oil stain?" I ask. "Did you test it yet?"

"Results should be back in the morning," he replies. I doubt an oil stain is going to give us very much in the way of identifying whoever had parked there. I'm not even sure it's related to Cameron's disappearance, but the evidence is light on this one so I'll take what I can get. "You look tired."

"I had an early flight this morning," I say, climbing the stairs until we reach the second floor. "I spoke with Mrs. Bright. She believes Cameron had a secondary means of income. We'll need to pull her bank records."

"I'll get right on it," Lowe says. "You think someone killed her for money?"

"It's a good a reason as any," I say, stepping into the room after he's opened the door. There's a small keypad beside the door with a red light. Lowe pulls a piece of paper out of his pocket and enters the code. "Who knows, someone could have kidnapped her in an attempt to extort her and things might have gone bad."

"Bad enough that they drained her of all her blood?" he asks as I flip on the lights. We're met with a clean, modern condo, full of what looks like new furniture.

"That's the part I haven't figured out yet." An extortion would more than likely be attempted by someone who wanted or needed the money, rather than someone looking to send a message. And even if that were the case, who were they sending a message to? It isn't like Bellefleur has an organized crime base. At least, I don't *think* they do.

"Have you already been here once before?" I ask.

He nods. "First time I had to call the security company to come turn off the system. They gave me the access code."

"CSI come through here?"

"Didn't see the need. Nothing was disturbed. And we

know she wasn't abducted from here. Her car is still at the nursing home."

All of which is true, but that doesn't mean there isn't something valuable that can be learned here. I stroll through the apartment, keeping a sharp eye for anything that might be suspicious. Her kitchen is nice and updated, and features a home cappuccino machine, along with a few other high-end appliances. I pull a pair of gloves out before I start going through the drawers and cabinets, but I don't find anything other than well-organized dishes and glasses.

The condo is a two-bedroom. The first is smaller, and contains only a yoga mat, a humidifier, and a couple of soft lights, along with a Bluetooth speaker. It's not hard to figure out what this room was used for. Again, I'm struck that Cameron would prefer to do yoga in her own home rather than go out and join a class or group. That tells me a lot, actually, and I'm starting to believe this persona that everyone saw in the times she did have to interact with people might have been nothing more than a carefully crafted mask.

The second bedroom is decorated like much of the rest of the condo. Modern and upscale. When I open her closet, I'm surprised to see more than one name-brand bag, along with some very expensive shoes and clothes. All of it screams luxury.

"This didn't strike you as odd when you came through the first time?" I ask Lowe, who has meandered into the room, looking around.

"What?"

"All these expensive designer clothes?"

He squints, looking at the closet. "Oh, I guess I don't really pay much attention to that kind of thing. It's not really my field of expertise."

Right. This isn't New York, or LA. He's a small-town detective, probably used to filling out traffic reports and responding to domestic abuse calls. I guess I can't blame the guy.

After counting at least ten thousand dollars' worth of clothes and accessories in her closet, I turn to the rest of the bedroom. As far as I can tell, Cameron Bright didn't own a safe. And after a thorough search of her drawers, bathroom and virtually every hiding spot I can think of, I have to conclude she wasn't keeping any kind of cash hoard in her place. Which means it has to all be in the bank. Good, there's a better chance of us tracing it that way. But now I'm beginning to lend more credence to Mrs. Bright's suspicions. Even if Cameron had a well-paying job, this is still a lot for someone in their twenties.

"When can you pull the bank records?" I ask Lowe as we're doing one last sweep of the place.

"This evening if you want. I'd be happy to stay late unless you want to do it."

"I would, but I'm beat," I say, snapping off my gloves. Whatever Cameron Bright had gotten herself into, there isn't any evidence of it here. And I have to admit, the expensive items aren't damming enough on their own. There's always the chance that Cameron has maxed out several credit cards to afford this kind of lifestyle.

Again, it's odd. None of her coworkers said anything about any of this. One would think if she had these expensive things, she'd have some of them with her when she got to work, but maybe she didn't want anyone to know.

"And see if you can't pull the flight records to Hawaii from New Orleans over the next couple of weeks. Her mother said she was planning a trip."

"Must be nice," Lowe says. "Wish I could afford a trip every now and again."

I think back to my time at the beach with Zara. What should have been a relaxing girl's trip was fraught with more anxiety than I was willing to admit. I may try to call her tonight, with the excuse that I'm just checking up on Timber.

"I need the name of a good motel in town," I tell Lowe as we're locking up Cameron Bright's apartment. "Something on the…economical side." I just hope it doesn't have cockroaches.

"Best bet is probably the Gator Motel. It's right off Talbot Ave, behind the gas station."

I turn to him. "Be straight with me. How bad is it?"

He makes something of a pained face. "I wouldn't say it's *bad*, necessarily. I mean, if you want something nicer you can always stay at the Chenêville House. It's this big historical home that's right off the canal. I think they added it to the National Register of Historical Sites. Plantation-style home with all the amenities." He pauses. "'course, people say it's haunted." He shoots me a wink.

Yeah. Paranormal activity notwithstanding, Wallace would kill me if I stayed in a place like that. "Thanks anyway."

Gator Motel it is.

Chapter Eleven

"I'm TELLING YOU; this has to be the weirdest case I've ever seen." I'm lying on my back, staring at the popcorn ceiling of a room at the Gator Motel, which happens to be one of the most "affordable" places I've ever stayed in my entire career with the FBI. The wall behind me is painted a vibrant red, while the wall across from me is a corresponding yellow-ish-green, conjuring up images of the last time I was sick on the bathroom floor after Zara's insistence at a fifth cosmopolitan. But the room is clean enough, though the bathroom sink isn't actually *in* the bathroom. Instead, it's right outside the bathroom, which itself only contains the toilet and shower.

"So what do you –ink really happened?" Liam asks. His phone doesn't have the best reception, because he's driving through West Virginia at the moment on his way to Ohio. It seems like every third word cuts out.

"I don't have any idea, but it's like the people around here *want* it to be something supernatural. Like the existence of a real-life vampire would confirm all their beliefs about the world. Even the coroner. The *coroner,* Liam. She's got all this… I dunno, stuff in her office. I mean, it's innocuous enough at first, but jeez! How does a woman like that maintain any kind of professionalism?"

"Not everyone is ¬ike you. Some of us can se¬arate our work lives from our personal lives."

"Very funny," I say, but he's right, of course. It's not like I have much of a personal life beyond work. But if I did, I wouldn't suddenly buy a cauldron and attempt black magic.

"It just doesn't make sense," I tell him. "This girl, she had some sort of side hustle going on. Something involving a lot of money. I think *that's* what got her killed. Not some random attack in the night."

"Any leads?" he asks.

"Not really. But I'm waiting on the bank records. And I spoke to the New Orleans office. They're sending down a medical examiner tomorrow. Someone who can look at the body with a clear mind."

"Probably not ¬oing too ¬well with the ¬cal coroner."

"What was that?" I ask. "You broke up."

"I said, it's probably not helping your working relationship with the local coroner."

I roll over, staring at the brown door to the motel. "At this point I don't really care."

"You'll figure it out," he says in that maddeningly reassuring tone. "¬ou always do."

"Easy for you to say, you're a thousand miles away," I say.

"Careful," he chides. "I'll turn this car around right now, missy."

I laugh, partially from exhaustion before a silence stretches out between us.

"You miss her, don't you?"

I groan. "Is it that obvious? I'm a grown woman; I should be able to deal with a case on my own! I used to do this all the time, why am I having such a problem with it now?"

"Because you got used to h¬ving Zara around," he says. "It's hard to get unused to that. Especially when the two of you support each other so well. I'd bet she's probably missing you just as bad."

"Maybe," I say. "But I don't want to call and put any pressure on her. I'm sure she's dealing with enough right now. At least she has Timber to keep her company."

"Any—ing I can do?" he asks.

"Yeah, figure out how someone drained a body of all its blood without any other signs of force or struggle."

"They —ave her something," he says. "To knock her out."

"But there is no trace of it in her body, and with the blood effectively missing, we can't prove that."

He's quiet a moment and I'm afraid that he might have cut off. "Have you thought about someone adjacent to the medical field?"

"Adjacent?" I ask. "Like who?"

"Taxidermist? Or even someone —ith movie production experience?"

I sit up. "What does a movie have to do with anything?"

"You're looking —or someone who likes drama. And some movie productions have dedicated staff to make wounds look real. Maybe even someone who has a medical background."

Huh. I hadn't considered that. Though I'm not sure there are any movie productions down here in Bellefleur. But New Orleans is often the setting for movies and TV shows. I suppose someone could have migrated down from an in-progress production.

"Okay, I'll check it. Thanks."

"I —now it's a long shot, but it sounds like you need —ome leads."

"I do, thanks," I say. Though I'm growing frustrated not being able to hear him properly. "Listen, I'm going to go. Call me tomorrow once you're set up. And be safe driving."

"Good luck," he says. "And Emily. I love you." *That* comes through clear as a bell.

"I love you too," I say. "Goodnight." I lay on the bed a few minutes longer pondering whether Liam's suggestions could have any merit. The taxidermy angle is interesting, and a good possibility. Though I don't know much about the process, it won't hurt to study up to see if someone with those skills could possibly do this to Cameron. I think the movie thing is too much of a stretch, though he is right about one thing: I'm dealing with someone who likes to be dramatic. No one would leave a body in that position if they didn't want a reaction. Still, a quick search for any movie or TV productions in the area would be prudent.

However, right now, I need sleep. Usually Zara is the one reminding me I need to slow down and without her here I feel like I've been running at full steam all day. I take a few minutes to wash my face and slip into sweats before I head back to the bed. I'm not entirely sure this place doesn't have cockroaches, so I'm cautious about where I step and what I touch. I think tomorrow I'll grab some disinfectant for the room, just in case.

I spend a couple of minutes catching up on some reports and doing some light research on taxidermy before my eyelids refuse to stay open any longer. There's no denying it, I have to relent and get at least a few hours if I want to be of any use tomorrow. I hope to meet the medical examiner as soon as she comes in and hopefully we can get a solid understanding of what could have happened here.

Finally, I give up and turn out the light, and I don't even feel my head hit the pillow.

$\sim$

I WAKE UP WITH A JOLT, FUMBLING FOR THE LIGHT AND MY GUN in the same motion. As soon as my hand is on my weapon I find the light with my other and flip it on. The room is empty, just as I left it when I went to sleep. But my heart is pounding.

The time on the clock next to the bed says three-twenty-three. I pause, listening for any errant sound, but there's nothing other than the rumbling of a truck rolling by in the distance. Still, I know what I felt. I'm not a heavy sleeper by any means, and somewhere in that space between sleep and awake I *felt* someone in this room with me.

Keeping the gun in one hand, I slowly pull back the covers and get out of bed. Underneath the bed is nothing, it's not large enough for someone to squeeze under there, but I check anyway. I run my hand over my suitcase which is still propped open, half my clothes spilling out from where I was too tired to put them away. And given the state of this place, I feel like they're better served in my suitcase anyway. Still, it feels like something is...*off*. I can still feel it in this room, though I don't know how to describe it. It's just a...sensation that someone else is here.

I tiptoe to the bathroom, the door is partially propped open, but the light inside is off. There is no sound I can hear, but I keep my own breathing to a minimum, trying to determine if I can hear anyone else. Adrenaline is pumping through my veins and my gaze is laser-focused on the dark room ahead of me. They *have* to be in there. There's nowhere else to go and the chain is still on the front door. How they got in here to begin with I have no idea, but I'm not going to worry about that right now.

In one swift move I push the door all the way to the wall as to crush anyone who might be hiding behind it between the door and the wall, but there's no one. I have the light on in half a second but all I'm looking at is an empty bathroom. No one in the tub, behind the curtain or anywhere else. I also don't see any footprints anywhere to indicate someone *was* here.

Relaxing a hair, I drop my guard and begin a thorough inspection of my room again. As far as I can tell, nothing is out of place, nothing has been moved or tampered with. My laptop is right where I left it, and you'd think that's the first thing a thief would go for.

I don't like this; something isn't right. Despite everything I've been through, I've had enough training that I don't just wake up in the middle of the night for no reason. Someone was here, I'm sure of it. The room has a small window opposite the door. It's barely large enough for a small enough person to get through, but I check it anyway. The hinges are loose and with a little force it opens, but I don't see how that would be possible from the outside, at least not without some kind of specialized tool. The motel backs up to a grassy patch and then heavy woods. I peer out into the night, but don't see anything out there. But it *feels* like something is watching me and the hair on the back of my neck raises. My adrenaline is pumping again, and I shut the window, locking it tight, and draw the curtains.

Why am I so *jumpy*? I am not this person. Normally I'm in control, but I can't seem to get my heart out of my throat. I take a few deep breaths and climb back into bed. As much as I hate to do it, I keep the light on, and my firearm at my side, with the safety on. After about thirty minutes I find myself beginning to drift off again, but I still can't get that creepy feeling out of my bones. Eventually though, sleep overtakes me. Though somewhere deep in my subconscious, I fear I may not wake up again.

Chapter Twelve

"GOOD MORNING." Detective Lowe's bright face darkens as soon as he gets a good look at me. I know he's spotted the bags under my eyes and is wondering just what I got up to last night.

"Hmm," I say, heading for the station's coffee machine. It might be slightly burned and smelling of old leather but at this point I really don't care. I didn't manage a lot of sleep last night and when it did come, it was broken and not enough to reach the deep REM I really needed to rejuvenate me. The coffee tastes like ass but at least it wakes me up a little.

"Hotel not good?" Lowe asks.

I take a seat in one of the other chairs in the small break area. Fortunately we're the only two people in here at the moment. "Have you had reports of break-ins recently? Anyone complaining of people coming into their homes during the night?"

His face contorts to one of concern. "No, why? What happened?"

I shake my head. "Nothing. Don't worry about it. Let's just press on. The medical examiner from the field office in New

Orleans should be here by ten. I want to have as much information as possible before she gets here."

"Rani's not going to like that," he says, shuffling some papers in front of him.

"I don't really care," I say. "If she didn't want someone checking her work, maybe she shouldn't have suggested to me that we might be dealing with an otherworldly being here."

He chuckles, revealing a side of him I hadn't seen before. At least he knows how preposterous it sounds, even if he does believe it. "You did ask her off the record. But I guess I can't complain. After all, I'm the one who invited you down here."

I take another sip of the coffee and it almost turns my stomach. But it's enough to keep me awake. I'm not sure I trust Lowe to point me in the direction of a reputable coffee shop, but at least it will give me a chance to bug Zara about something. "Where are we on the bank records?"

"I was just going over those," Lowe says. "I've pulled everything for the past year." He hands me the stack of papers he'd been reviewing when I came in. I didn't actually expect him to print them out, and it takes me more than a few minutes to flip through them.

"Looks like she was making regular cash deposits," I say, going over all the documents. "Somewhat irregularly. I don't see a pattern, do you?"

"No, she'll make one, then another a few weeks later, then maybe another right after that. Whatever she was doing, it wasn't consistent."

"But it paid well," I say. Over the last six months, Cameron Bright has deposited almost sixty thousand dollars into her account. Now more than ever I'm inclined to believe this is what she died for. Whatever she was involved in, something must have gone bad. "Check with the nursing home. See if they have any record of missing drugs over the past six months."

"Right," Lowe says, picking up the phone. As I'm waiting for an answer, my cell phone rings.

"Slate."

"Agent Slate, this is Special Agent Lori Phillips, in from New Orleans. I've arrived at the station, where should I meet you?"

She's early, I think. *Finally, someone with some professionalism.* "Just head through to the back. I'll meet you and direct you to the morgue." I indicate to Lowe to keep on Loving Hearts until he gets an answer, and he nods in agreement. Despite the lack of sleep, I'm feeling better about things this morning. No more running around chasing ghosts.

I meet Special Agent Phillips halfway as she's making her way in, carrying a large case full of what I can only assume is medical equipment. She's tall, with broad shoulders and long dark hair that's pinned at the base of her neck. "Agent Slate?"

I give her hand a shake. "Pleasure to meet you. Thanks for coming down so quickly."

"When my SAC informed me of your request I could hardly refuse," she replies. "I'm surprised our office didn't pick this up. They said they flew you in from D.C.?"

I do everything I can to keep my cheeks from flushing. "My own boss and I have something of a...let's call it a healthy rivalry. I think he thought it would be funny, despite his insistence that I'm an 'expert' on things like this."

She arches an eyebrow. "You often deal with bodies drained of their fluids?"

I laugh. Special Agent Phillips has something of a similar taste in humor, which puts me even more at ease. "No, just death in general. It seems every other case I'm dealing with a new kind of killer."

"Well, I'm just happy to get a look at this one. Is the morgue here in the building?" It's not hard to tell she's anxious to get a look at Ms. Bright, and I can't blame her. I imagine any medical professional would be interested in seeing what we have here.

"Right this way." I direct her through the back of the building, until we reach the metal door I first came to with Lowe. Since I don't have a keycard, I have to knock and look up at the camera before someone buzzes us through. When we reach the morgue itself, I'm surprised to find Dr. Hansen inside again, working at one of the stations. I figured she'd be in her office.

"Oh," she says, looking up. "Good morning."

"Dr. Hansen, this is Special Agent Phillips from New Orleans," I say, making the introductions. "She's here to take a look at Cameron Bright."

Hansen stands and offers a stiff hand to Phillips. What warmth I felt from Phillips immediately cools between the two women. I'm sure Hansen sees Phillips as a challenge to her authority, because that's exactly how it's meant. I don't want to come right out and say it, but I'm not about to let someone with a belief in the supernatural lead this investigation around like a dog on a leash.

"I understand you have something of a mystery here," Phillips says, attempting to keep the awkwardness to a minimum.

"Yes," Hansen says, shooting me a look. "It's been difficult to explain with…conventional methods."

"Mind if I take a look?" Phillips asks.

"Not at all," she replies, heading over to the coolers. "She's in here. Take all the time you need." Hansen returns to her computer, shuts it off and heads out of the morgue, presumably back to her office.

Phillips exchanges a look with me. "I hope your reception was better."

"Right up until the point when she suggested this might be the work of the type of being afraid of garlic and mirrors," I say, not bothering to hide the sarcasm in my voice.

Phillips chuckles and opens up the cooler, having set her bag off to the side. We're hit with a blast of cool air as I gaze upon what's left of Cameron Bright for the second time in two days. "Well," Phillips said. "You weren't kidding."

"Let me guess, you've never seen anything like it," I say.

"Not exactly, no. But I have seen bodies where individuals have attempted to remove most of the fluid for crude mummification purposes, though it wasn't successful," she replies. "Though I've only ever seen a body drained from the bottom, where the blood tends to pool after death. Coincidentally that's how it's done for embalming as well. It's just easier to remove the body's fluids that way. But this…" She trails off as she examines the body, which has begun to take on a shriveled and waxy appearance. Phillips takes a few moments to inspect the holes around her neck, even taking a few tools out of her case to measure them.

I stand back and let her work, my arms crossed, confident she'll come up with something. After about twenty minutes of inspection, she stands back. "Agent Slate, I'm afraid to inform you Bellefleur has a vampire on its hands."

For a second I'm in shock, and it must show on my face because she bursts out laughing. "I'm sorry, I couldn't resist."

As soon as I realize she's not serious I can't help but grin. That's something Zara would have pulled on me too, and she probably would have gotten away with it. How many times has she told me I need to stop taking things so seriously? "I guess I can't blame you," I say, chuckling. "I left myself wide open for that one."

"Seriously though, I'd like to get a look at the autopsy report, to see what Dr. Hansen found."

"Do you at least have an idea of what it could be?" I ask.

"Maybe. But I don't want to speculate just yet. Not until I'm sure. I'd also like to suggest we move the body back to the New Orleans office. I have more sophisticated equipment there that can help me determine what killed this young woman."

Finally, some progress. "I'm sure we can get Dr. Hansen to send you a copy of the report."

"Great," she says. "In the meantime, I'm going to do a more thorough investigation, it will take me a day or so to arrange transport for her body back up to my office."

"I'll talk with Dr. Hansen, she'll probably be more amenable if the request comes just from me."

Phillips makes a small pointing motion with her hand. "That's a good thought. I'll be in here if you need me."

I nod, thanking her, then head out and over to Dr. Hansen's office. The door is closed, so I give it a quick knock.

"Yes?"

"Excuse me," I say, opening the door and stepping in. "Can you email me a copy of your autopsy report from yesterday?"

Dr. Hansen looks up, and there's a visible cloud over her face that wasn't present earlier. Strangely, the entire office seems darker, even though the lights are on and I can't identify anything that's changed. But all her baubles and trinkets are still in place, and it takes considerable willpower for me not to stare at them.

"Does she really need it?" Hansen asks. "If she's doing her own investigation?"

"She'd like to know what you found," I say. "And she wants to arrange to have the body transported back to New Orleans where she can do a thorough examination."

Hansen pinches her features and opens her mouth to say something before thinking better of it. Instead, she turns to her computer and types out what I assume is a frustrated email. "Anything else?"

"No, but thank you," I say. Part of me feels bad; she's obviously upset about the situation, but it's also a situation of her own making. If she truly believes Cameron Bright was killed by some supernatural force, I'm not sure she belongs in her position. That kind of thinking can be incredibly harmful to the families of victims, causing them to endure more trauma than they already have. I can't imagine going up to Cameron Bright's mother and telling her with a straight face that the coroner believes *Nosferatu* murdered her daughter. I almost can't imagine anything more disrespectful.

My phone buzzes letting me know an email has come through and I give Dr. Hansen a final nod, before heading out to rejoin Phillips. But before I can, my phone buzzes again, this time indicating a call.

"Slate."

"It's Lowe. We might have something."

Chapter Thirteen

As soon as I get back to Lowe's desk, he's already gathering his stuff. "I just got a call from the mechanic that sits across the street from Loving Hearts. They have cameras all over their property and one of them might have caught something that night."

"Great," I say, feeling a rush of adrenaline that allows me to leave the coffee on the edge of his desk. I'm not sure I can touch that stuff again. We head out to the parking lot and I give him a quick rundown of what little Phillips has found so far, though I leave out the obvious animosity from Dr. Hansen. I'm reasonably sure we can all get through this like adults; I just hope Hansen stays out of Special Agent Phillips's way until after we've transferred the body.

I drive us over to the nursing home again, except this time I pull into the business across the street, which sits cattycorner to Lovely Hearts. It's a four-stall mechanic garage belonging to Daryl, if the sign is to be believed. "*Daryl's Custom Car Care*," I read aloud as we pull in. Sure enough, there's a camera above every stall and on every corner of the building. Currently all the stall doors are down and without windows, we can't see inside. But there is a small office area to the left, so I pull in right next to it.

"Is this our only viable angle?" I ask as we get out of the car.

"I checked with all of the other surrounding businesses; this was the only one with a camera that shot over the fence and into that alleyway," Lowe says. "But if we can get a good look at the car, maybe we can pull some of the surrounding cameras, see if we can spot it on the street anywhere."

"That's good thinking," I say as we head into the garage. Despite his beliefs, Lowe is actually doing some solid police work here, which is more than I can say for Hansen.

As we enter the garage, a man comes into the office portion from a side door, wiping his hands with a rag. He's built like a linebacker, and his arms are covered in detailed tattoos. "Help ya'll?"

I pull out my badge. "I'm Agent Emily Slate, with the FBI, I believe you spoke with Detective Lowe on the phone?"

"Oh, right," the guy says, tossing the rag behind him into a small bucket. "About the cameras." He holds out his hand for me to shake. "Daryl Oke." His grip is strong and even though I don't think he's trying to; I feel like if I don't get my hand back quick he might accidentally break it. Lowe makes his handshake just as brief.

"I assume you're the owner?" I ask, indicating the sign on the door.

"That's me. Been open for about five years now. Doin' okay, as much as I could expect in a place like this. People still gotta drive, right?"

"Do you mind if we take a look at your camera footage?" I ask, growing impatient. "It's of some urgency."

"Sure, sure," he says. "Come on 'round here, I route everything into this one system." We both circle the main partition and find there are three different monitors on the other side, two of which show nothing but camera feeds. The third has a spreadsheet on it, populated with financial information.

"This is all eight cameras," Oke says. "I got four here in the front, two on the sides and two 'round back."

I check all the feeds and sure enough, one of them shoots directly on the alleyway where we found the oil stain, though it's far away. "Can you rewind this one, back early Sunday morning?"

"What time?"

"Let's start at nine p.m. the night before and go from there." Oke taps a few buttons and the image changes to a night picture. In the bottom corner shows the time as nine p.m. "Now speed it up until you see something."

"But isn't that the start of Bright's shift?" Lowe asks.

"I just want to cover my bases," I say, watching the camera. Sure enough, what looks like a cargo van pulls into the parking lot around one-thirty a.m. "Whoa, slow it down." We watch as we see someone get out of the van, but as they circle we lose sight of them. And with the van in the way we can't see the door from this angle. We've also got no good shot of the license plate.

I realize I might have a good opportunity here. While I don't have a clue what the make and model of that vehicle are, there's someone in this room that's an expert on vehicles. "Do you recognize that van?" I ask.

"I do," Daryl says. "That's a twenty-nineteen Chevy Express."

"Have you seen this van before?" Although I try not to, I can't help but get my hopes up.

"Not that exact van, I don't think." He heads over to the third monitor with the financial info and pulls up another program, doing a search. "Nah, I've got a green Express in here, but not a white one. Guess they use a different mechanic." He smiles at us.

I turn back to the screen and watch. Whoever was driving

they sure are spending a long time in the nursing home. As soon as I'm getting impatient enough to tell Daryl to speed it up again, the figure returns, though this time I can clearly see they are carrying something in one hand. Some sort of bag or satchel. I turn to Lowe. "Did you figure out if they were missing any narcotics?"

"They're checking their records," he says. "Gallagher said he'd get back to us."

Moments later, the form drives away, leaving the alleyway empty. The whole interaction took maybe thirty minutes.

I let Daryl fast-forward through the rest of the footage, but there's nothing else there. No one else in or out of the alleyway. And whoever was driving the van didn't take Cameron, at least not then because her coworkers remember seeing her until she checked out at five a.m. Unfortunately, Daryl's does *not* have a camera that captures their parking lot well.

"Damn," I say, banging my fist on the counter. They may not have been our kidnapper, but I'm convinced whatever we just witnessed has to do with Cameron's death somehow. I just don't know how yet. "How far back does your footage go?"

"Only about two weeks, then it's wiped to make room for new footage," Daryl replies.

"Would you do me a favor and go back though the footage, see if you see that van appear at any other times?"

He gives me sort of a pained look. "Lady, I don't mind helpin' but I got a business to run. I have an Impala out there that's going to need some serious work and I really don't want to be here all night."

"I'll do it," Lowe says, surprising me. "You take care of whatever you need to do. I can grab a ride from another officer back to the station."

"You sure?" I ask, impressed with his initiative. I don't know if he's doing it *to* impress me, or if Lowe always has this kind of work ethic, but I definitely appreciate it.

"Yeah, I'll let you know if I find anything."

I give him a nod. "All right. Thanks." I turn to Mr. Oke. "Appreciate your help. You're in good hands with Lowe here."

He gives me a two-fingered salute before heading back into the garage area. And I head back out to the car, both of us leaving Lowe to his work.

∼

AFTER CALLING IN AN APB ON A WHITE CHEVY EXPRESS, I head back over to the station to assist Phillips in any way I can. I'd sent her the autopsy, but she remains tight-lipped about her theories until she can confirm them. Part of me can respect that, not wanting to add to the spread of gossip, especially in this case; but I also find it maddening. If she thinks she has an answer to what really happened to Cameron, I'm virtually chomping at the bit to hear it. But Agent Phillips strikes me as the kind of person who doesn't speculate. Whatever she's doing, she's not going to reveal her findings until she's ready. Finally accepting I'm not going to get anything out of her by just standing around waiting, I head back out, hoping to clear my head. I check back with Lowe who says he's fine and not to worry, he'll be finished soon. It seems like no one needs me at the moment, which doesn't leave me with the best feeling. I'm sure Dr. Frost would love to unpack that little nugget. Thankfully, he's not here right now. But I do find myself growing antsy. I need something to burn off some of this excess energy. Strange, I should still be exhausted from last night, but I'm completely wired. Getting back into the rental car, I pull out my phone.

"Hello?"

"Hey," I say, putting the car into drive and pulling out of the station. "I need help."

"What's wrong?" Zara asks, her voice on high alert.

"I need the name of a good coffee place, like right now.

The swill they have down here isn't fit for human consumption."

She laughs, then lets out a breath. "You scared me there for a second."

"Sorry," I say, not realizing that might have been triggering for her. "I wasn't thinking."

"It's okay," she says, and I can hear her typing in the background. "How's it going down there?"

"I know you don't want to hear this, but I could really use your help. Liam didn't really seem to believe me when I told him, but the people down here are a little nuts."

"Only a little?" she asks. "I only get involved if people are a lot nuts."

I smirk and pull on the main road, headed for nowhere in particular. I just need to drive. "Okay, then they're a lot nuts. At least two people down here believe we're dealing with an honest-to-god Dracula."

"Yeah, I can see that," she says.

"*What?* You cannot," I say.

"No, I mean I can see *why* they believe that, not that I agree with them," she says. "Looks like the best coffee place is going to be a joint called *Tudo's*. Do you know it?"

"I don't think so," I say. "Where is it?"

"Tiger street? I didn't know they had tigers in Louisiana."

"I think it's a sports thing," I say.

"Ohhhh, gotcha."

"Okay, so *why* do you think they believe it?"

"'cause you're down in the spookiest place in the country. Haven't you ever seen *True Blood?* Vampires and werewolves and all kinds of stuff."

I have to keep from making a face. "Z. That's fiction."

"I know. But think about what that kind of reputation does to a community. Especially if it's built on the back of actual local legends and stories that have been passed down from generation to generation. It's ingrained in the culture. I'm surprised you're not running into more of it."

I guess she's right. People take pride in the places they live, especially if it can help drive tourism dollars. But still, to make those kind of assumptions about an official investigation? I'm not sure that's something I can get past. "Yeah, I suppose." I peer down the main road that runs through Bellefleur, looking for anything that says *Tudo's* or Tiger Street.

I can feel that uncomfortable awkwardness beginning again; the same thing that was there the entire time we were on our short vacation. I know she needs time to recover, but I want her to know that I will be here for her in any way she needs me to be. But I also have to remember we both process our trauma in different ways. Where I have to keep barreling in on a case and keep myself busy, Zara is more introspective and needs time, more than anything.

"How's my boy holding up?" I ask, keeping it in safe territory.

"Just bein' an angel like always," she says. "But I'm keeping him this time."

"The hell you are," I say.

"Yeah," she jests. "Wanna fight about it? I bet he'd come to me first if I called him."

"He would not!" I know she's just messing with me, and I'm glad to have a little bit of the old Zara back.

"He is being a little clingy, though," she says, more serious this time. "I really think he needs a buddy."

I've been toying with that idea ever since the whole fiasco with my in-laws. Timber had stayed with them for a bit, and I know he had loved being around their two dogs. "Yeah, you gonna keep two of them when I'm gone?"

"Are you kidding? If they're all as sweet as him, I'll keep every dog in the world."

I chuckle. "Well, maybe. I need to think about it." Liam and I still haven't decided exactly where our relationship is going. I think back to his question to me about moving in together. The more I've been thinking about it, the more it makes sense. And it would be a lot easier to get a second dog if we were both living under the same roof. It's not like we don't already spend ninety percent of our free time at either my place or his. And he hasn't been pushy or even pressuring at all. He's letting me get there on my own time. Something I'm not sure he realizes just how much I appreciate.

"Is everything okay?" Zara asks. "You went a little quiet there."

"Yeah, just—" I finally spot a small sandwich stand on the side of the road with the word *Tudo's* written on it and an arrow. "There it is."

"What?" she asks.

"The coffee place. Not big on advertising down here."

"Well, I hope it's as good as the yelp reviews," she says.

"I'll be sure to let you know." I pause a moment as I pull into the small parking lot. Tudo's is barely a shack much less an actual coffee house. "Are you okay? Do you need anything?"

"No, I'm good," Zara replies. "Just keeping myself busy with a few cases here. Wallace has me watching two different operations involving the Toscanis."

"You're kidding," I say. Both Zara and I have had our fair share of run-ins with the Toscanis, especially their little toad of a crime boss, Santino. "What are they into now?"

"I'll have to tell you when you get back," she says. "Probably not best to discuss on an open line."

"Good call," I say, though I'm a little disappointed. Wallace must know about my history with the Toscanis, and yet he's shuffled me down here to deal with this. I really don't understand my boss sometimes. I find myself gripping the steering wheel hard enough that my knuckles are white. I just can't seem to calm my nerves.

"Em?" Zara asks. That's the third time I've gone quiet.

"I need to tell you something," I say. "Because I can't seem to get it out of my mind. But I swear someone was in my motel room last night."

"Someone like…"

"An intruder," I say. "But nothing was missing and the only way they could have come in was through a small window barely big enough to fit through."

"Was the window locked?" she asks.

"Yes, but it was easy enough to jimmy open if you knew what you were doing. I asked the locals about it and even the motel proprietor, but they say they haven't encountered any break-ins lately. But I know what I felt, Z. Someone was in there, I'm sure of it."

"Can you move rooms?" she asks.

"Probably. But who would want to come into my room and why? Just to stare at me?"

"Who knows, but at least we're sure about one thing," she says, her voice deadly serious.

"What's that?"

"It definitely wasn't a vampire. You have to invite them in, remember?"

Before I can even get a word out I can hear her cracking up on the other end. "Just for that I'm gonna—"

"Em, I love you, but you are too serious sometimes," she says, still laughing. "Just change rooms and get one with a better lock. Or change hotels. It was probably just some crackhead looking for a quick score."

"I dunno," I say. "It felt like someone was just…watching. I want to find out who it was."

"If you do, make sure you have backup," she says. "And don't go off trying to do it on your own like you always do."

I roll my eyes. "Yes, Mom."

"I'm serious, Em. If you think it really is a threat, then don't try to do this on your own. Get the locals on a stakeout of the motel."

"But you could be right, it might have been nothing more than a transient. And they just got out before I saw them." I finally release the wheel. I don't think I realized just how much of this I'd been holding in all morning. I've had enough bad experiences with unwanted people coming into my personal space that I should have realized it was taking more of a toll than I thought. Maybe coffee isn't the thing I need right now.

"To be honest, I don't know if I trust them. They'll probably try to convince me it was the ghost of some long-dead confederate general or something." I try to imagine asking Lowe to be my backup on something like this. Then again, I could always speak to that other sergeant, Jackson. He seemed to have a more level head on his shoulders.

"Just make sure they have your back," she says, dead serious this time. "I can't go through that again. Not like with Magus."

I nod, even though she can't see me. "I know. I'll be careful, I promise."

"Okay," she says. "The closest place that serves some nice, hot tea is a seafood restaurant just around the corner from you."

I smile. Zara always seems to know what I need, even when I don't ask. "You're the best. Take care of my boy and I'll see you in a few days."

"I will. And, Em, be careful."

Chapter Fourteen

THE REST of the afternoon passes with relative quiet. I'm able to sit down and calm my nerves with some nice, black tea, and I even enjoy some of the local food while I'm waiting on either an update from Phillips or Lowe. I consider texting or calling again, but deep down I know it won't do any good and I'll just end up looking needy. Wow, Frost is going to have a field day with me when I get back. Apparently, I'm still dealing with some stuff that hasn't come up in our sessions yet. At least now I know the man has my back. He's proved that much, at least.

Part of me thinks Zara is right, and it may not be worth spending time chasing someone who may or may not have been in my room. That's not what I'm here for. By the time it's growing dark out, I start heading back to the motel, with the full intention of switching to a different room with a more secure window. It isn't like the Gator Motel is packed with travelers. I think I only saw one or two other cars in the lot last night.

As soon as I pull into the space in front of my unit, my phone buzzes. I look to see it's Lowe calling.

Jesus, took you long enough. "Slate. Did you find anything else on the van?"

"No, that's not why I'm calling," he says. "We have a situation. I need you to head over to one-four-seven Rochenoire Drive. It's on the west end of town."

"Why, what's going on?" I ask.

"We've got another body."

I SEE THE LIGHTS LONG BEFORE I PULL UP. THIS PART OF TOWN doesn't have any streetlights to illuminate the neighborhoods, so the flashing red, blue and yellows are easily visible from a distance. When I arrive a fire truck is blocking most of the house while an ambulance sits in the driveway and the home is surrounded by three other Bellefleur police vehicles. There's even a Lafourche Parish Sherriff's office vehicle on site.

I'm out and badge myself past the officer standing watch, keeping the growing crowd of neighbors and pedestrians away from the scene. Lowe meets me halfway down the drive, his face ashen, like he hasn't seen the sun in a month.

"Sorry to call like this, but it's a real mess in there," he says, wiping his brow. The heat of the day hasn't exactly dissipated with the setting of the sun.

"Who's the victim?" I ask, heading straight for the house. He walks in step with me.

"Dr. Sonny Whiteside. He's well-known in town for making house calls when people can't get to the hospital."

"He's a medical doctor?" I ask. Lowe nods. "What happened?"

"Wife found him after coming home from her weekly gin rummy game. She said when she left he wasn't home yet, but that wasn't strange as he worked odd hours sometimes." He stops just short of the door, and I can see there's something else.

"What?"

"It's just…I knew Dr. Whiteside. Most of us here did. One of the only doctors in town that would still come to you. Most of 'em these days are tied up with insurance companies or hospitals, but he was all about his patients. He was a kind man, great bedside manner. He watched over my mother when she got sick. I just don't…I guess I don't understand how people can be so savage sometimes."

I approach him, trying to remain empathetic. I may not agree with Lowe's assessment of our case, but that doesn't mean he doesn't deserve sympathy. "I'm sorry," I say. "Are we looking at the same M.O.?"

Lowe looks up at me and I can tell something is very wrong. "Not exactly." He heads past me into the house, leading me down the hallway. Officers fill the home with activity. An older woman is sitting in the living room, her head in her hands, sobbing, as an officer stands close with her hand on the woman's back. The entire scene is chaos. There are people everywhere, in every part of the house, looking through things. It's almost like a raid.

"What is—" I can't get the words out before Lowe leads me to the back room, where another officer stands guard next to an open door. He steps out of the way so I can see inside.

"Holy *fuck*."

It's as if the entire room has been splattered with red paint. Except it's not paint. It's blood. In the middle is a bed, which has been effectively *broken in half*. And in the middle of the bed lies a figure, covered in dark crimson from head to toe. His clothes have been shredded and his face is almost unrecognizable, but I can see a few hints of what probably used to be a white moustache and trim beard.

I can't even step into the room without leaving a footprint in the blood that is seeping into the carpet, the walls, the curtains…*everything.* "What in the hell? Has anyone been in here?"

Lowe shakes his head. "I've called in the closest CSI team, but they were out on a job in Thibodaux. They won't be here for another forty-five minutes."

This doesn't even look like a murder scene. It looks like an animal attack of some kind. The crimson curtains flutter as a small breeze blows in through the open window. It's been broken out of its frame and there is glass and wood everywhere. I point to the window. "Entry point?"

"And exit," Lowe says.

I have to cover my mouth as I survey the scene again. In all my years as an agent, I've never seen anything as...*savage* as this. The man has literally been shredded. "I want to see the outside."

Lowe nods and leads me through the kitchen in the back, which has a side door already standing open. The mood in the house is apprehensive, and each officer I pass is either trying to keep themselves busy or speaking between themselves in low tones. Possibly spreading gossip about what they've witnessed.

Another officer stands close to the door and steps out of the way as we exit. "I've called in almost everyone for this one, and Lafourche is providing the backup," he says. I spot Sergeant Jackson out of the corner of my eye, he's over with some of the other officers helping to set up a perimeter around the back of the home. He no longer seems combative like before and even gives Lowe a respectful nod as we pass. There's a detached garage that sits a few feet away, with a footpath leading to it, but we step off and head to the right instead.

Lowe leads me around through the backyard where the team is setting up large spotlights, like the kind they use on construction sites at night. Obviously I'm not the only one anxious to get a look at the outside of the home.

"Right here," Lowe says, pointing to the outside of the same window. As one of the bright spotlights comes on, illuminating the area, I look for any other sign of an animal entry into the home. But there are no claw marks around the shattered window frame.

"What kind of local animal could have done this?" I ask.

"Pretty much just a bobcat or a bear," he says. "We don't have a lot of mammals large enough to cause that kind of damage. 'course there's also an alligator, but—"

"—doesn't match the marks on the body," I say. The wounds on Dr. Whiteside were long and deep, like they were from something with big claws. "We need to get a Zoologist down here. See if they can identify what made those marks."

"Hansen can probably do it," Lowe says. "We've had to deal with animal attacks before."

I turn to him. "Like this?"

"Well, no," he admits. "Never seen anything like this before."

I nod, trying to figure out what could have broken through this window, attacked Dr. Whiteside enough to leave a scene like that, and then just vanish in the night. "Maybe Agent Phillips can assist. If the two of them work together they might actually come up with something plausible." I scan the ground for any footprints or markings, but there is nothing. "Are we sure this was the only entry and exit point?"

"The wife said she had to open the bedroom door when she came home. A splatter pattern on the back of the door seems to indicate it was closed when the attack happened, and there are no traces of blood anywhere else in the house. At least, no one has found any yet."

If that's the case, the animal wouldn't have closed the door behind them once they were in the bedroom, unless it was just an unlucky accident. "At any rate, I want to do a full sweep of the entire property. Let's make sure we're not missing something." What kind of animal doesn't leave tracks to follow? Especially something that can do this kind of damage. If it was a bear, there should be prints leading away from the house, the ground isn't exactly dry and solid. And now that I look, there are no tufts of hair or anything that would indicate a big predator made it out this window.

"Have you checked the entire house? All the closets and storage areas?"

Lowe nods. "Why?"

The possibility of the animal hiding somewhere in the house had crossed my mind, but that's preposterous. An animal big enough to do this, even scared, wouldn't just hunker down and wait for people to leave. It would be fighting back with everything it had. "No reason. Never mind."

I head back around to the front of the house and call Phillips, informing her of the situation and asking her to come down as soon as possible. I want her taking point on this as I trust her assessment. At least she'll look at this with a clear eye. But my first priority is to secure the scene. I order Lowe to get everyone out of the house, including the wife. While most of the officers had gloves on, we don't need to contaminate the scene any more than it already is. The officer I saw with Mrs. Whiteside earlier leads her over to the ambulance where she's given a blanket. No longer crying, she's just staring at the house, her short, silver hair tussled from all the excitement.

"Mrs. Whiteside?" I ask, approaching gingerly. "I'm Special Agent Slate with the FBI." She doesn't seem to acknowledge me in any way, only grips the blanket and stares at the house, where the lights from the emergency vehicles light up the outside walls.

"Do you mind if I ask you a few questions about your husband?"

"No." Her voice is quiet and stoic. I'm not even sure she's blinked.

"Can you tell me what time you left for your game?"

"Six," she says. "Always at six. Every third Wednesday of the month." She's obviously in shock, her answers are coming clipped and emotionless.

"And what time did you arrive home?"

"Eight-thirty-two."

I wince, knowing the memories of the night will be seared in her subconscious forever. She has a long road ahead of her, one I do not envy. I can't imagine finding Liam like that. In fact, I probably wouldn't be doing as good as Mrs. Whiteside here. "Do you know where your husband was before he came home?"

"No."

"Do you keep anything…exotic in your home? Anything that might have attracted a wild animal?" I know I'm reaching, but from the way the body has been shredded and the state of the bed, I don't know how we *can't* assume this was an animal attack. Still, I've seen animal attacks in the past. And they've never been like this.

"No," she says again.

"Do you know if your husband was having any problems with anyone around town?" I ask. My thought goes back to Zara's comment about tigers. It's possible someone could be keeping exotic pets, even training them to attack people on command. But if that's true, it has to be a short list.

"Everyone loved Sonny," Mrs. Whiteside says, having kept her gaze on the home. "Why would anyone want to hurt him?"

I can't answer that until I have more information. While I'd like to press her on the question, I'm not about to put her through any more trauma, not tonight. I may need to wait a few days before I can speak with her again. Sometimes people are better a few days later and sometimes they're much, much worse. And it's difficult to tell which is which until you're there with the person.

Mrs. Whiteside strikes me as someone who can hold it together for a short time, but very soon she's going to have a breakdown of immense proportions. I'll need to make sure to tell Lowe to keep an eye on her and arrange for some counseling. I leave the woman be and find Lowe again, informing him we'll need a list of everyone in the county who is registered to own an exotic animal of any size. Though if someone did sic a tiger or something else on Mr. Whiteside, I'm guessing they're probably not registered. Still, we have to start somewhere. People like that tend to run in circles. Someone will have heard something.

I check my watch and realize it's not even nine-thirty yet. And as I stare at the gaggle of onlookers from the street, I realize maybe I should have gotten that coffee after all.

It's going to be a long night.

Chapter Fifteen

"GIVE ME GOOD NEWS," I say, walking into the morgue where Agent Phillips is already set up with what remains of Dr. Whiteside. She arrived at the scene and helped the CSI team down from New Orleans collect him so they could transport him here. And while the team stayed on site, Phillips came back here to get started on the body as soon as possible. She's already managed to cut his clothes off him and fully expose the deep gashes that run all the way from his upper left shoulder down across his chest and midsection to his pelvis.

I thought I had been prepared to see the carnage, but it even turns my stomach and I need a moment to gather myself upon seeing the man's remains. Usually I deal with bodies that have had time to decompose, but Dr. Whiteside is still fresh and the smell is even more pungent than it was back in his home. I'm assuming that's because his intestines have been punctured, allowing all his bodily gases to escape.

When I turn back, it's almost like I'm looking at a victim of a terrible car accident, instead of someone who was killed in his own home. I just hope I never get used to something like this. I never want to reach that point in my career where it doesn't faze me.

"You okay?" Phillips asks, her mouth hidden behind a mask. She's also wearing goggles and rubber gloves that have been stained with Dr. Whiteside's blood.

"Fine, go ahead," I say.

"I hate to say this, Agent Slate, but I'm at a loss. At least, until I make a more thorough investigation. But at first glance, I couldn't tell you *what* kind of animal did this." She points to the slash marks that begin at his upper shoulder. "These claw marks are too far apart to be from a bear, though they do follow a similar shredding pattern. I'd say we're looking for an animal with five, maybe six-inch-long claws."

"How big do bear claws get?" I ask.

"Black bears average from two to three inches. Even a grizzly bear, which can have claws longer than four inches, *could* have done this, but last time I checked there were no grizzlies in the bayou." She points to the chest area. "The larger problem is the spacing. The 'paw' is much too massive to belong to any bear, or any other animal I've ever encountered. It's virtually as wide as the chest itself."

"Can you tell how many times he was struck?"

Her eyes widen like she can't quite believe what she's about to say. "Just one. One long, deep swipe created all this damage," she says. "Probably killed him in an instant as I haven't found any evidence of defensive wounds. But, interestingly, I also believe his back is broken, possibly an impact trauma. Which could possibly explain the bed. I'll have a better idea once I get some x-rays."

I pinch the bridge of my nose as I try to work out what she's telling me. "So something broke in through Dr. Whiteside's house, picked him up and threw him, hard enough to break his back *and* the bed, took one swipe at him which painted the room in the man's blood, and then left the same way?"

Agent Phillips pulls off one of her gloves, then pulls her

mask down with her free hand and sets the glasses up on the top of her head. "It doesn't make any sense."

"No, it doesn't," I say.

"Hey!" I turn to see Dr. Hansen appear in the doorway; her hair tussled like she's been sleeping on it. "What's going on here?"

I pinch my features. "Agent Phillips is attempting to do an autopsy. I thought Detective Lowe told you what was going on."

"I haven't had cell service, I had to take my daughter to work. Her car broke down." She stops short when she looks around me and gets a good look at Dr. Whiteside. "Oh. My. God." The bag and coat she had under her arm fall to the ground as she approaches slowly, not taking her eyes off what remains of the body. "What happened?"

"That's what we're trying to figure out," I say. "Agent Phillips says whatever animal did this must have had very long claws. But that's about as far as we've made it." Lowe promised he'd get on a list of exotic animal owners in the county, but something like that will take time.

"Do you mind if I take a look?" Hansen asks. I notice the dark circles under her eyes now that she's closer. She definitely seems more frazzled than yesterday, though I don't know why.

"No, please," Phillips says, stepping back. "If you can offer a theory I'm sure we'd be happy to hear it."

Hansen takes a moment to put on a smock and gloves of her own, though she foregoes the mask and goggles. Instead, she pulls out a few measuring instruments from a nearby examination cabinet and begins paying close attention to the wounds on Dr. Whiteside.

"You wouldn't know of anyone in the area who might be keeping a grizzly bear captive, would you?" I ask. Though I don't have the first clue how someone could have even attempted to train such an animal. As far as I know, they can't be domesticated. Which means the probability of someone having done this on purpose is slim to none.

"I don't think this was a grizzly," she says, examining the wounds closely. "Agent Phillips is only partially right. A grizzly's paw can be this size, but the wounds don't line up. Look here, the middle slash begins at the highest point on the shoulder, while the next two digits on the left and right start much lower. A grizzly—or any bear for that matter—has very regular claws. If this had been done by a bear, you'd see four or five similar slashes, all starting and ending along the same line. But what you see here is a different pattern, matching that of an animal with a more dexterous hand."

She's beginning to lose me. Also I didn't realize Hansen was such an expert in animal injuries, though Lowe did say they'd had some experience with them in the past. "Okay, so if it wasn't a grizzly, then what? A lion?"

Hansen continues to measure the distance between the slashes with her instrument. Finally, she looks up, her face serious. "There's only one kind of creature that could have made wounds like this." I incline my head, indicating I'm waiting with bated breath. She lets out a long sigh. "What we're looking at here is the work of a werewolf."

Chapter Sixteen

"I CAN'T TAKE these people seriously," I say, fuming. "What are they going to say next? That space aliens have invaded people's brains? That someone saw a person carried off by a centaur? It's ludicrous!"

"Have you spoken to Wallace about it?" Liam asks, trying to hide the smile in his voice and not doing a very good job at it.

I grimace. "You know what, I think this is exactly why Wallace sent me down here. I think he knew how 'off-the-wall' this case was and he assigned me to it just so no one else would have to deal with this bullshit." I had really hoped Wallace and I had move past our differences, but it seems that's just not the case. I don't know if he knew just how deep the rabbit hole went on this one, but I can imagine him in his office, chuckling at the thought of me trying to navigate a superstitious town and its obviously inept police force.

No sooner had Hansen said "werewolf" than I somehow started hearing it all over the station, even after dismissing it out of hand and doing my very best not to berate the woman in public. Thankfully I had Phillips there by my side to back me up, but some of the skepticism I'd felt when I'd first arrived to deal with the "vampire" case had all but disappeared as soon as the rumors started getting around. Maybe because so many people got a good look at the body. Apparently, people around here no longer think Lowe is as crazy as he first sounded. But I couldn't stay in that environment any longer and had to get out, which meant it was either drive around in the dead of night or go back to the motel. Because it was already so late I decided to deal with the room change tomorrow.

"I just don't get it," I say, flopping back on the bed again. "I don't see how people—smart, capable people can get so wrapped up in something like this. Detective Lowe is a good officer, he knows how to perform an investigation. And yet I'd be willing to bet he was the first one to believe Hansen's allegations about whatever killed Dr. Whiteside."

"So what do you think it is?" Liam asks.

"My bet is someone let their pet grizzly out of its cage, and there was something that attracted it to Dr. Whiteside's house," I say. "Because anything else sounds ludicrous. But I'm going to have to call in *another* expert who can give me some real information on animal attacks. Agent Phillips isn't as well-versed as I'd like her to be, and I don't trust a word that comes out of Hansen's mouth. Despite the fact *she* believes everything she's saying." I know I'm rambling, but I'm just frustrated. I keep running into these roadblocks and it's all completely unavoidable.

"Do you at least know what killed your first victim?"

I let out a long breath. "No. I was too worked up to remember to ask Phillips before I left. This whole thing has me on edge, Liam. I feel like I'm going crazy down here." I haven't told him about the presence I felt in my room last night. I can tell Zara because I know she can handle it; but Liam will honest-to-god take the next flight down if he thinks I'm in any real danger. And I need him where he is right now. But I'm glad he can't see my face, because I'm just now realizing I've spent this entire call unloading my problems and frustrations.

"I'm sorry," I say. "I don't mean to call you just to complain."

"Hey, that's what I'm here for, isn't it?" he asks. "If you can't complain to me, then what good am I?"

Okay, I deserve a little ribbing. Especially considering he's gone all the way up to Ohio for *me*. Yet again. "Tell me about your day. And I don't even care if it has anything to do with my family or not. Just…how are you?"

"I feel like I'm really getting the hang of trucker talk," he says. "I switched the CB over to the local channels as I was driving, doing my best Ernest impersonation. I think I pulled it off pretty well." Before I can comment, he switches into a heavy southern accent. *"Breaker, breaker one-nine come on back y'hear? This is Big Bobby haulin' the redwood express."*

I laugh. "Why on earth would you do that?"

"Partially from boredom. There isn't a lot to look at on the way. And I'm still practicing my blending skills. Gotta be able to fit in up here, especially if I'm going to be digging for dirt."

I roll over, a smile on my face. "Please tell me you've already bought your first pair of overalls."

"I don't think we need to go *that* crazy," he says, laughing. "But if the occasion calls for it…"

I take a deep breath. "You're too good, you know that?"

"Nah, you just wait until the World Cup comes around next year. I turn into an absolute monster. In fact, you could say I even wolf out."

"That's not funny!" I yell. How is it both he *and* Zara know exactly which of my buttons to push?

"Sorry, Em. You're too easy of a target," he says.

"Do you and Zara get on calls and conspire without me?" I ask.

"Only occasionally. I assume that means you've spoken to her. How is she?"

I get up and walk over to the window that looks out on the back of the property, making sure the lock is down and in place. "She's doing okay. I think she just needs time to heal."

"You *both* do," he says. "A week off from work wasn't long enough. And honestly, given what the two of you did, Wallace should have given you a month off."

I turn back to the room, pacing. "You know I don't do well when I don't have something to keep me occupied. And I could only get Zara on so many excursions. She just wanted to sit around and not go out, which was very un-Zara-like of her. Meanwhile, I was going nuts sitting in one place. If we'd had to stay another week I think I might have had an aneurysm."

"She'll be okay," he reassures me. "She helped track down Archer, didn't she?"

"Under protest," I remind him. "I guess I'm too impatient. I just want my friend back."

"She'll be there for you, when you really need her," he says. "Trust me."

We talk a while longer about non-work-related stuff but it's too late for me to bring up the moving in together thing again. Liam has to be the one to remind me just how late it is and that I need to get some sleep if I'm going to navigate this menagerie tomorrow. Though seeing as it's already past midnight, I guess really I'll be dealing with it later this morning.

After we've said our goodbyes and I've gotten ready for bed, I take one more look at the window, just to make sure it's as locked. I double-check the door too but it's solid. Or, at least as solid as an old motel room door can get. Still, I'm anxious. And I don't know how much sleep I'll be getting tonight. Part of me thinks I should just move anyway, go to another motel somewhere else in town but the other part insists I'm being silly and that it's not a big deal. At this point I'm not even sure someone *was* in my room. Maybe all this talk of cryptids is getting in my head.

Regardless, I stuff my gun under my pillow as soon as I climb into bed. I've never had to do that before, not even when Camille was stalking me. But something about this feels different. I hate to say it, but I almost feel like if someone *was* here, they weren't friendly.

Stop it, Emily. Stop it right now. You are not this person. I refuse to let fear drive me on this. I am a grown woman who is proficient in martial arts, has extensive weapons training and more experience taking down perpetrators than most ten-year veterans. Not to mention vampires, werewolves and ghosts are *not real.* I've let this town get in my head and I'm not going to do it anymore.

I turn off the light and do my best to let my unconscious mind take over.

I FIND MYSELF SITTING ON DR. FROST'S COUCH. IN FRONT OF me are the three letters I've received, all laid out in order. Each one seems like a piece of a larger puzzle, but the more I try to look at them and decipher their words, the more the words scramble themselves on the page.

I look up to see Dr. Frost sitting across from me, one leg crossed over the other and he's saying something, but I can't quite make it out. He's not looking at me as he's talking; instead he's focused on the letters, pointing to each of them in turn. It's like he's trying to get me to understand something about them, but when I try to tell him I can't hear what he's saying, my words come out in a mumble.

His face contorts, like he's getting upset. I'm trying to explain that I don't know what he's saying when he finally stands, and insists I look at each of the letters, his finger pointing to the one in the middle over and over again. I don't understand what he's trying to tell me, but I can feel him growing angrier by the second. It's like he's mad at *me*, but I don't know why.

Suddenly, he flips the table between us out of the way, scattering the letters and begins bearing down on me. I can practically *feel* his breath on me as I try to pull back into the couch. My hand slides underneath one of the pillows beside me, there's supposed to be something there…but it's not.

My eyes snap open as I realize my gun is missing from under my pillow. And in a split second I *feel* the other person in the room with me. I immediately roll to the side as a blade slices through the air and drives into the mattress where I was laying only seconds before. It's pitch-black in the room; the light I had on earlier has gone out. Which means I'm at a disadvantage. I feel a foot drive itself into my midsection as I'm trying to find my bearings and get up, and all the air leaves my lungs. I stop myself from flopping over and making myself a target and instead scramble to my feet as I see the glint of the knife swinging in my direction.

My body feels sluggish, like it won't do what I need it to. Panic sets in, I can't seem to defend myself. I scramble over to the small table in the room and throw it in the direction of my attacker, who is *fast*. I'm going for the door, but feel the slice of the knife as it comes down and opens up my left arm, causing me to cry out and flop back against the wall in pain. Steeling myself, I try to take a defensive stance, but the fact I've already been hit means whoever is in here is faster, *stronger*. I can't beat them. What is happening to me?

I feel a knee drive itself into my midsection again, and the power of it takes me to my knees. But a hand grabs the back of my hair, pulling me back up. I swing forward with my elbow and connect with some part of them, causing the attacker to let go of my hair. I go for the door again, but this time I feel the steel of the knife at my neck. They have me pinned against the wall, where I'm almost sitting at the small dresser that is pushed up against it. The blade is already cutting into my skin and a thousand thoughts flash through my mind. But foremost is the one telling me this is how I'm going to die. In a shitty motel in the middle of nowhere at the hands of a killer I don't even know. I couldn't even protect myself. How was I ever supposed to protect anyone else?

I can't go down without a fight. Even if I'm going to die, it needs to be kicking and screaming. As the knife tugs at the skin of my neck, causing warm blood to run down onto the sweatshirt I always sleep in, I grab the attacker's hand, doing everything I can to twist the knife in the other direction. I can't see this person, nor have they said anything, but I think it's a woman—a strong one at that. Maybe in my dying moments I can at least use the knife against them as well. Leave a trail for someone to follow.

The door to the room swings open, bathing the entire room in the glow of the parking lot lights. A silhouette stands in the door, and I get a brief look at my attacker, decked out all in black, with a baclava covering her face. But her eyes are a deep crimson—most likely contacts, though they add to her menacing appearance.

"*Freeze!*"

I can't believe my ears. When I saw the silhouette in the door, I automatically assumed it was my attacker's accomplice. But I couldn't have been more wrong.

"Step away slowly or I put a bullet in your skull," Zara says, standing in the door like Rambo, her gun trained on my would-be assassin.

For a second I look into those crimson eyes, and I think she's going to go through with it. But she steps back, removing the blade from my throat. I feel even more blood gush from the wound and hold my palm around my neck to stanch the flow as best I can.

"Put the knife down and place your hands behind your head," Zara orders. I want to ask what she's doing here, but

I'm afraid if I talk it might exacerbate my wound. I need an ambulance.

Just as the assassin looks like she might comply, I see something in her gaze and she takes off in the opposite direction through the room. She's *fast*, whoever she is. Zara squeezes off two shots, but both hit the wall as the woman runs for the window that is *clearly open* and dives through it like a professional gymnast. Zara fires again for good measure, but the woman is already gone.

"Oh my god, Em," she says, rushing up to me. Her voice is ragged, and somewhere deep I feel a deep-seated guilt for putting her in this position, though I still don't know how or why she's here. I try waving her off, telling her to go after the other woman, but she grabs me by the shoulders instead, helping me down so I'm sitting on the ground. "Don't worry, I'm calling an ambulance."

I try to shake my head, but my neck hurts and instead I manage to squeak out. "Go. After. Her."

"This is Special Agent Foley with the FBI; I need an ambulance to the Gator Motel. I have a knife victim who is bleeding profusely. Room thirteen." She hangs up the phone before running into the bathroom and flipping on the light. She comes back with a handful of towels and without missing a beat, begins ripping them into strips, before bandaging my arm. "Keep your hand on your neck, we don't know how deep it is," she orders.

"But the...woman," I manage to say.

"Will get away," Zara says. "Right now you need to let me save your life. Got it?"

Right. Priorities.

Chapter Seventeen

"THERE'S OUR PATIENT," Zara says, coming into my hospital room with two coffees in one hand and a bag in the other. I'm sitting up in the bed, one bandage on my neck and another on my left arm. I look to see if she's brought anyone with her, but apparently she's just using the royal "we".

She hands me one of the coffees before taking a seat across from me in the only chair in the room, like we're both just sitting at our desks and it's another day at work.

The ambulance managed to get to the motel in record time and was able to stop the bleeding enough to get me to the only hospital in town, which looks more like a mall than actual hospital. Thankfully neither wound was severe enough to cause any lasting damage, though I have stitches along both my neck and my arm. The doctors said if the blade on my neck had gone half an inch deeper, I would have bled out in less than two minutes.

But in all the hustle and bustle, I hadn't had a chance to speak with Zara or even ask what she's doing here. I'm just glad she showed up when she did. How that person managed to get the drop on me I don't know, but they're not going to get away with it.

"Z, what are—" I manage to squeak out after a sip of the coffee coats my dry throat.

"Call it intuition." She shrugs. "You did say you needed my help on this one."

I give her a skeptical eyebrow raise.

"Okay, fine. After we talked yesterday—well, the other day, I got to thinking about what you said about field work. Specifically, about how we got to see cases no one else ever could. And when you started telling me about this case about this 'vampire', I just couldn't get it out of my head. So yesterday afternoon I went to Wallace and got him to approve some additional manpower."

"And he did it?" I croak.

"I may have insinuated that the case was bigger than you originally anticipated," she says, with a sly smile. "But this is just a one-time thing. And *only* because you were so rattled. I had to come down and see it for myself. After this, I'm back to intelligence for good." I open my mouth, but before I can say anything she holds up her free hand. "Don't worry, I spoke with Thea yesterday. She's watching Timber for you until we get back."

I breathe a sigh of relief. Though I still can't believe she's actually here. I can feel my eyes begin to well up and I try to push the feeling back down before she notices. But Zara is sharp, and she stands, comes over and sits on the edge of my bed, taking my hand. "I'm just glad you're okay."

"Odd time of the night to show up," I say.

She shrugs. "Not really. I took the last flight out of D.C. Then I had to get a car to drive down here, then I had to talk to the motel manager and convince him I knew you and to give me a key to the room. All in all, I think I made good time."

"I think you did too," I say. I can't believe she's actually here. And she doesn't seem as mopey as she has lately. Maybe she really did just need an intriguing case to bring her out of her funk. "If you think the vampire case is strange, wait until you hear about the second murder."

"There's a *second?*" She sits with rapt attention as I slowly tell her all about Dr. Whiteside and the condition of his body we'd found only hours earlier. When I finally finish, she's gawking at me like I have two heads. "Wow. *What* is going on down here?"

"That's the question I'd like answered," I say, attempting to sit up some more.

"Oh, I brought some clothes from your room," she says, indicating the bag. "Your other ones were completely soaked in your blood."

"Thanks," I tell her. I'm sure the nurses threw everything I had on away before they stitched me up. I lift my arm and try to flex it as much as I can, but a dull ache radiates through the joints as I try to move it. I'm embarrassed more than anything. Embarrassed someone was able to get the drop on me, embarrassed I couldn't get my footing under me to fight back. Maybe Liam was right, and I was more traumatized by the events with Simon Magus than I was willing to admit. I should have been able to take my attacker without a problem. Had it not been for Zara, I'd be in a body bag instead of a recovery bed. "You didn't tell Liam did you?"

"Oh, no. I'm leaving you to deal with that hornet's nest. I'm not getting into it." She gets up and heads back over to her chair, sipping on her coffee. I'm relieved about that much, at least. I'll give him the entire story, but not until I'm up and moving around some more. The last thing I want is him coming down here to find me in *another* hospital bed. I did that to him once already. Never again.

Speaking of which, I need to get out of here. I'm sure they'd like to keep me for observation, but someone tried to kill me last night and I'm not about to sit around and wait for someone else to find out who. Now that Zara is here, I'm feeling reinvigorated, stronger. Together, we can finally attack this thing head-on. I don't know if she knows how much being here means to me, but it's given me a new energy.

"Toss me those clothes," I say. "I need to get changed."

I extricate myself from the bed and remove the IV attached to my hand, rubbing the sore spot where the needle was under the skin. More than likely I needed a good pint of blood after the amount I lost last night. Zara tosses me the bag which I catch with my good hand and then head into the bathroom to change. As I'm putting on the fresh set of clothes I hear voices in the other room. More than likely Zara speaking with one of the nurses. I don't care what they say, they can't keep me here any longer than I want to be here.

But when I leave the bathroom I'm surprised to find Detective Lowe in the room instead.

"Agent Slate," he says. "I came as soon as I got the report from the station. Glad to see you weren't seriously injured."

"Em isn't one to let a few paper cuts slow her down," Zara says, winking at me.

"Detective," I say, pulling my sore arm through my suit jacket. "It seems like your town has a sudden and serious murder problem."

"That's why I'm here. We've had some developments surrounding the attempt on your life. I've had officers canvassing the entire motel. They found a couple of soft footprints outside the window from where your attacker ran off. Looks like they headed into the woods where we lost the trail. But we weren't able to get a solid print due to the softness of the ground."

"Of course not," I say. "It was a woman. That much I'm sure of. And she was wearing crimson contacts."

Lowe furrows his brow. "She had *red* eyes?"

"Yes, but they were *contacts*," I reiterate. "But I didn't get a good look at her face, though her build was similar to mine."

"Okay," Lowe says. "I'll make sure we keep a lookout."

"Are we sure it wasn't the werewolf?" Zara asks. I shoot

her a nasty look. "What? Maybe that black ski mask was covering up fur."

Lowe acts like he hasn't heard her. "I have some additional bad news. We haven't been able to recover your badge or your service weapon. Both are missing from the crime scene, presumably taken by your would-be killer."

This just keeps getting stranger and stranger. "Who would want to kill Em anyway?" Zara asks.

"That's the other bit of bad news I have, I'm afraid," Lowe says, his face falling. "I was on my way here when I got the call from Jackson. Agent Phillips is dead."

Chapter Eighteen

I don't even bother checking out of the hospital. Instead, I gather what few things I brought with me, including my phone and head back out to the parking lot. Zara and I pile into her car while we follow Lowe over to the other crime scene. Neither Zara nor I say a word on the way. Thankfully, she's not trying to baby me, which I appreciate more than she knows. The last thing I need is someone thinking I can't get back to work because I was attacked. This case has turned from what looked like a novelty into something deadly serious. We have three bodies on our hands, and I'm still struggling to understand our first victim, much less the other two. Not to mention someone tried to kill me as well, and I haven't even been on this case more than three days yet. Whoever is doing this, they're moving fast and clean, and they aren't going to make this easy for us.

Lowe pulls into the parking lot of the Ramada Inn, which is almost a mirror image of the Gator Motel, except a little nicer on the outside. I probably would have come here last night if I'd ended up switching rooms. As I get out of the car, I try turning my head a little too fast and feel the tug of the stitches in my neck underneath the bandage. I have to remember to be careful with myself for a few days.

Much like Dr. Whiteside's house last night, the place is a flurry of activity. Four other patrol cars sit in the parking lot and part of the property is taped off with police tape to keep any onlookers out. Zara and I follow Lowe as we head down the line of doors leading to different rooms. The seventh door is already open, and I catch the flash of a picture being taken from somewhere inside.

When we turn the corner and gaze upon the room, I'm struck at just how similar it is to my room at the Gator Motel. The layout is almost identical, except that everything is flipped. Even the sink is outside the bathroom. And there is a small window at the far end of the room, just like at my motel.

A couple of techs are already in the room gathering evidence, while another takes photographs of everything. Lying in the middle of the bed is Special Agent Phillips, her eyes wide open. She looks like she could sit up and begin talking at any moment, were it not for the massive gash across her neck. Deep pools of crimson have formed on either side of the pillow and bedsheets. I also notice she's been stabbed a few times in random areas on her body.

"That could have been me," I say.

"But it wasn't," Zara says quietly.

"No, I mean look. It's the exact same M.O. Whoever came after me was obviously the same person who killed Agent Phillips. This doesn't match the other two deaths at all."

"I don't understand," Lowe says. "So someone wanted to kill both you and Agent Phillips last night?"

"Looks that way," I say, stepping into the room. I had left Agent Phillips back at the morgue to continue examining Dr. Whiteside's body, but I could tell she had been tired. She may have finished up not long after I left.

"Damn," Lowe says. "If it was the same person, then I

doubt we'll get anything usable. We weren't able to pull any good prints off your room."

"That's because she had gloves on," Zara says. "And a ski mask that covered her hair. I'm not sure you'll find any forensic evidence here either."

"Still, it won't hurt to look," I say, stepping into the room. "Has anyone checked for her badge and weapon?"

"They're not here." I turn to see Sergeant Jackson standing in the doorway behind us. Apparently, he's the one in charge of the scene. But I realize he seems to be more upset with me than anything else as he's scowling at me. "What have you brought to our town?"

"Me?" I ask. "What are you talking about?"

"You tell me. You show up to investigate one death, and now we've got two more on our hands. Our department isn't equipped to handle this kind of thing."

I turn all the way to face him. "Are you saying this is my fault? That I brought this here with me? Let me remind you, you had a problem long before I showed up. And someone just tried to murder me in my sleep last night. So I don't think I should be the one on the receiving end of your anger, *sergeant*."

He huffs, then turns around and leaves. I catch a few of the techs go back to what they were doing. "What's his deal? I thought he didn't believe in any of this stuff. And now he thinks I brought it with me?"

"Everyone's been on edge since we found Dr. Whiteside last night," Lowe says. "I know some of the stuff I can put out there is...far-fetched. But look at what we're dealing with here."

I turn my attention back to Agent Phillips. Avoiding the techs, I move in closer to get a good look. I didn't know her long, but she was a capable agent. And she was going to put a stop to all this nonsense. I notice for the first time a ring on her left ring finger. "Dammit," I whisper.

"Sorry," Zara says. "I know this isn't easy."

"It never is." I turn to her. "When you told Wallace what was going on down here, how did he seem?"

"What do you mean?" she asks.

"Did he seem to take you seriously? Like this was a real threat?"

"I guess, but that was before we knew there was a second body. And definitely before an agent was killed. What are you thinking?"

"That someone doesn't want the FBI here," I say. "There *was* someone in my room the other night. They were probably preparing to do *this*, and got scared off when I woke up. But look, there's nothing that even suggests anything supernatural here. Just a plain, old-fashioned murder. Like mine would have been."

"Em—," she begins.

"No, I think we're looking at two different killers," I say.

"I thought you said Dr. Whiteside was killed by an animal," she says.

"I'm not so sure of that anymore," I say. "Maybe—"

"Oh, my, god." Both Zara and I turn at the same time to see Dr. Hansen, standing in the door. Her jacket is wrinkled and her hair is still in the same tangle of strands I saw it in last night. The dark circles under her eyes are even deeper now, like she hasn't gotten any sleep. "I...I heard about it through the station, but I didn't...I mean, who could have...?" She covers her mouth with her hand and turns, heading back outside.

I indicate for Lowe to stay with the techs and make sure they bag everything while Zara and I follow Dr. Hansen out into the parking lot. "Doctor?" I ask. "Are you all right?"

She's still holding her hand over her mouth and nods a few times, before she gets a good look at me and her eyes go to the bandage on my neck. "What happened?" she asks.

I point to the room. "That. Had my partner not shown up

in the nick of time." I turn to Zara. "Dr. Hansen, this is Special Agent Zara Foley."

Zara shakes Dr. Hansen's hand. "Temporarily back on duty."

Hansen returns her attention to me, specifically to my bandage again. "You mean to tell me someone attacked you? Overnight?"

"Yes," I say. "Why, does that mean something to you?"

"No, it just seems odd that someone would go after both of you in the same night," she says. Her eyes have gone a little glassy and her words have softened. She's pondering something, though I can't tell what. But I can't help but notice that Dr. Hansen has a similar build to the woman who attacked me. And I don't see any reason why she couldn't wear crimson contacts.

"I...I'll need to prepare the morgue," Hansen says. "I spent most of the night on Dr. Whiteside after Phillips left. You'll be glad to know I've managed to confirm we're not dealing with a bear or any kind of large cat," she says. "I went back to double-check the patterns and compared them with other animal attacks over the past decade. Nothing lined up."

That means she still believes her original hypothesis, even if she's not willing to say it out loud in front of Zara. She might be a little gun-shy after my last outburst, for which I can't blame her. But at the same time, I'm not sure I should be allowing her to look at the bodies.

"I'd like to take a look at the forensic evidence when we get a chance," Zara says, drawing Dr. Hansen's attention. "I love stuff like this."

"Oh?" Hansen asks, perking up. "Are you a fellow cryptid believer?"

"Tried and true," Zara says, holding up a salute, then leaning in, like she's conspiring with Hansen. "They don't like us to talk about it in the FBI. I've been trying to get Em here to come around for years, but she's too stubborn to realize that the truth has been right in front of her all along."

"Yes, exactly!" Hansen says, not attempting to hide her excitement. "There is so much about our world that we think we know, and yet, it turns out we've only scratched the surface of what's out there."

"I can't wait to read your findings," Zara adds.

"Great," Hansen says. "I'll head back over now to prepare to examine Agent Phillips. Maybe we can at least shed some light on what's happening here." She heads off without another word while I stare at Zara in disbelief.

"What the hell was that?" There's more than a hint of impatience in my voice.

She gives me a little smirk. "What's that saying? You attract more flies with honey than vinegar?"

"Are you saying I'm vinegar?"

"No, but we need to find out what's going on here. And my bet is she's at the center of it."

Chapter Nineteen

LEAVE it to Zara to know just how to get this investigation back on track. While I *really* want to give her the old "told you so" in regard to her skills as an investigator, somehow I manage to bite my tongue as we head back to Bellefleur's police station. Instead, I call Wallace and to give him an update on our situation and hopefully get some additional resources at our disposal.

"Why is it every time I give you an assignment you get in the middle of some conspiracy?" Wallace barks as I finish explaining to him we now have three murders on our hands.

I roll my eyes at Zara seeing as we can both hear him on the speaker. "I don't know what to tell you. Someone in this town is gunning for FBI agents." I neglect to mention they took my badge and weapon, though I can't quite figure out why. It's not as if they can use my badge with any kind of authority. And the rounds in my weapon have already been cataloged. If anyone shoots someone with it, we'll be able to match up the bullet to the gun almost immediately.

I can practically hear his exasperation on the other side. Maybe when he started Wallace could pull off the stoic atti-tude, but I haven't seen that side of him in a while. "At least you are all right, correct? Do you need…anything?" His hesitation makes me think he's uncomfortable asking.

"I have a few cuts, but nothing that won't heal in time," I reply, surprised by his concern and also downplaying my own injuries.

"That's not a glowing reassurance, Slate," he says. "If you want to return to D.C. you'd be perfectly within—"

"*No*," I say, too quickly. "No one takes a swipe at me and gets away with it. I'm not coming back until we have this suspect…or *suspects* in custody."

"Then you believe more than one person is responsible?"

"It's just a hunch for the moment," I add. "But whoever is doing this obviously thinks they can intimidate us. I'd like to request additional resources from the New Orleans office." I don't care what it takes, I'll *fill* this town with FBI agents if I have to.

"If what you say is true and someone really is targeting you, then sending in additional agents may not be the best idea," he says. "That's just giving your unsub more targets to hit."

"What's the alternative?" I argue. "Leave?"

"Of course not," he says. "Has there been a similar response to the local police? Does it seem like anyone is targeting them?"

"No, but that's probably because everyone down here is brainwashed," I say without meaning to.

"I'm sorry?"

I really don't want to get into the culture of superstition that seems to surround this town, not right now. Plus, I'm not even sure Wallace would believe me. "Nothing. But we do need people here who aren't so…*close* to the situation."

Nice save. Zara mouths with a smile on her lips.

"Let me see what I can do," he says. "In the meantime, both you and Agent Foley keep your heads down. I don't like the idea of you working without any backup. And keep me in the loop. I'll contact the New Orleans office and see if I can't smooth things over with the SAC, seeing as it was his agent who was killed."

"I appreciate that," I say. I wasn't looking forward to making that call, especially since I was the one who requested Agent Phillips in the first place.

"And I want regular check-ins. Understand, Slate? I don't hear from you or Foley every twelve hours, I'm sending in the cavalry."

"Yes, sir." He hangs up without another word. "That went better than I expected."

"I keep telling you, Wallace has really mellowed. I think that whole situation with Magus really humbled him," Zara says.

She could be right. I haven't spent much time around the man ever since then, just the occasional meeting here and there. He had been the one who tried to keep me off the case when Zara was missing, only for us to find out the ATF team who had been brought in to counter Magus had been compromised. In the end Wallace had ended up with egg on his face, though we hadn't been there to see it in person. I'd been too busy trying to make sure Zara was okay.

"Here it is," I motion to the building as Zara pulls in. "So, when are you going to tell me your theory about Hansen?"

"Oh, no. This is your operation. I'm just here for you to bounce ideas off of," she says.

"And to save my life."

"Yes, that too. Had I known I couldn't leave you alone for more than a few days I would have come with you right away," she laughs and I see more of the old Zara emerge.

"Are you feeling better?" I ask.

But the question has the opposite effect of what I was hoping as her face darkens again. "I don't know. It's hard sometimes."

"Sorry," I say. "I didn't mean—"

"No, it's not you," she says. "It's just…I feel this underlying fear all the time now. It wasn't there before Simon. And now it never goes away."

"Did you feel it last night?" I ask as gingerly as I can.

"That's when I felt it the most," she says. "You didn't see because they were stitching you up. But I spent half the night curled up in one of those hospital chairs trying not to lose it."

"Why didn't you say something?" I ask, feeling like maybe I should have told Wallace to pull both of us after all.

"Because as much as I hate to admit it, you've rubbed off on me. And I'm not about to let the person who almost killed you get away with it. But once we find them, I'm done. For real this time. I *have* to be." She looks at me, her eyes pleading.

"I get it," I say. "And I'm sorry if I've been putting any undue pressure on you. I think…maybe both of us have some healing to do."

She takes a deep breath, then shuts off the car. "Yes, we do. But for now, we just need to shove it into a little box in the corner of our brains and focus, right?"

I tilt my head toward her. "A completely healthy and normal plan."

Both of us laugh as we get out and make our way into the station. I lead Zara back to Detective Lowe's desk, which only seems messier since I last saw it. "You said the forensics team finished gathering all the evidence from your second victim's house?" she asks.

"I assume they did," I say. "We were all there late last night. Though I'm sure they haven't had time to process it. They probably had to head straight to the Ramada Inn. My bet is this town doesn't have more than one CSI team."

"Maybe it's better that way," she says. "At least we can get a look at all the evidence they collected without anyone's… biases leaking through."

I shoot her a finger gun. "Good point."

It takes me a few minutes to find an officer who can give

us the access we need for the forensics data from Dr. White-side's house. Some of it is in the computer, but the rest is still in a box for processing. Zara and I find the boxes in a secure area like someone just dropped them off without any ceremony whatsoever.

"You know we're going to have to do all the grunt work, right?" Zara asks.

I sigh. "Yeah. But I don't think waiting on anyone else to do it does us any good. It'll just delay us more." We both get to work categorizing everything the forensics team pulled from the site, including all the photographs, physical samples as well as any control samples they picked up. What we don't have are the biological samples, which are sent to the lab as soon as they come in as they have to be cooled in order to be preserved.

"God, you weren't kidding," Zara says as she looks through all the photographs that were on the memory cards included in the box. "This doesn't even look real."

"Tell me about it. It almost didn't *feel* real being there." I pray for the poor soul who has to come in and try to clean that house. I've seen difficult crime scenes before, but this is on a different level.

"You know, if I didn't know better, I'd say this entire scene was *staged* to look this way."

I glance up. "What makes you say that?"

"I don't know," she says, looking at the screen as she flips back and forth between two of the pictures. "It's just...it looks too clean."

I'm sure my eyes are as big as saucers because when she looks at me she stifles a giggle. "No, not clean like that. I mean it all just lines up too easily. He's right in the middle of the broken bed, the blood is everywhere. He's lying face up so that when you come into the room you're assaulted with this image..." She trails off.

"What are you thinking?"

"I'm not sure yet," she says. "But I want to see the blood samples."

"We'll take a look as soon as we're done here," I say, turning back to the evidence in the box. I've gotten most of it organized and entered into the station's record for the scene. But as I'm going through the personal information gathered on Dr. Whiteside I stop at his personal property list, doing a double take. "What the…?"

"What?"

I roll my chair over to hers, fast enough I feel that pull on my neck stitches again and I wince. "Is there a picture of Dr. Whiteside's garage?"

"Um, I think so," she says, scrolling back through the pictures. "Is this it?"

I nod, looking at an image of the detached garage I saw last night when I was walking around the property with Detective Lowe. "Is there a picture of what's inside?"

"Yeah, I just passed it," she says, and scrolls back a little more. Finally, she lands on the picture showing the garage door open and my heart just about jumps up in my throat. "Em, what is it?"

I find myself staring at the exact same van I saw on the security tape from *Daryl's Custom Car Care*. The one parked outside Lovely Hearts the night Cameron Bright disappeared.

"It's our missing link."

Chapter Twenty

"C'MON, we need to head over to investigate that van," I tell
Zara. The fact that Dr. Whiteside's vehicle could very well be
the same van we've been looking for all this time means we
finally have a solid connection between our first two victims.
Something that will allow me to establish a pattern and build a
profile on our unsub. Since the evidence hadn't been checked
into the system yet, I doubt Lowe or anyone else even made
the connection. The forensics team just photographed everything on site and left it up to the investigation team to put the
pieces together later.

"We will, just...trust me on this," she says, packing up the
rest of the evidence from the site and filing it in the system. "I
think it will be worth it."

As far as I know the van is still at Dr. Whiteside's house,
and I'm anxious to get eyes on it in person. But Zara has
insisted we finish looking through all the evidence collected
from the scene first, including the biological samples. I don't
know why she's so determined; we have a solid piece of
evidence out there and we need to go secure it before something happens to it.

It turns out the police don't have their own lab, so they

send everything to the Bellefleur medical center, where they treated me earlier today. I don't look forward to going back so soon, but if it will satisfy this need of Zara's so we can focus on what's really important, then I'm all game.

Because my arm is still sore, she insists on driving and we're back at the hospital in only a few minutes, having been directed to the lab where they process and analyze all biological samples from both the hospital and the police.

"C'mon, Z, is this really worth it?" I hate that I sound like I'm whining, but I'm also anxious to get back and take a look at that van. Something about it links to Cameron Bright's death, and I'm going to find out what.

"Oh, my dear, sweet, simple Emily," she chides. "You are going to be so glad we made this little side trip. Just wait."

"Wait for what? It's just blood, right? Are you thinking they might have pulled something from Whiteside's wounds? Because I'm not sure Agent Phillips had the time."

She turns, pressing one finger to my lips. "Shh, shh, shh. Just…trust me. K?"

I relent. "Fine."

We manage to find the lab with a few technicians working in different areas. Zara shows them her badge considering mine is MIA and explains that we're looking for the evidence submitted from the Whiteside case. It turns out no one has taken a look at any of it yet since things have been so chaotic overnight. But Zara manages to use her charm to convince one of the technicians to pull the samples and start examining them, looking for any irregularities.

I want to interrupt and say this is nothing but a waste of time, but if she's this insistent on taking a look, then she really must have something. So I keep my mouth shut and wait with her as the lab technician goes over the evidence that was submitted.

"Is there anything specific you're looking for?" the tech asks, a young man named Mihir.

"The blood samples," Zara says. "I want to know if there's anything inconsistent about them."

I furrow my brow. "Inconsistent? Like what? Some kind of mutation?"

She pulls me to the side. "I don't want to influence his analysis," she says. "But I'm looking to see if all the blood matches up."

"Why wouldn't it?" I ask. "Whiteside didn't have any defensive wounds. It's unlikely he took a chunk out of his attacker."

"I know," she says, shooting a glance over at Mihir as he analyzes the samples. "Just wait, though. This is gonna be good."

Whatever she's on about, she seems confident enough, so I stand back and watch as the tech goes through each of the sixteen samples that was provided from the forensics team. When he's done with his analysis, he turns to us. "Okay, looks like we have two separate samples here."

I incline my head forward. "Two? You're sure?"

"Absolutely," he says. "One is type-A and the other is type-O. A DNA analysis will provide more information, but right now I can confidently say these samples are from two different people."

"So then Whiteside did manage to harm his attacker after all?" I can't believe I'm going to ask this, but I need to put this insane theory to rest. "They are both human blood samples, correct?"

"Oh, definitely," he says. I breathe a sigh of relief, only to turn to find Zara staring at me and trying not to burst out laughing.

"Okay smartass, how did you know?"

She giggles but gets it under control and returns to Mihir. "Can you tell me which samples were from which person?"

"Samples one, seven, nine and thirteen all originated from subject A, and the rest of the samples from subject B," he says.

Zara takes the accompanying paperwork and reviews the notes from forensics. "Okay, samples one through six were taken from the body of Dr. Whiteside himself, according to the notes here. And samples seven through seventeen were all taken from surrounding areas, such as the walls, curtains, furniture, et cetera."

"Wait a second," I say. "That means that both blood types were found on Dr. Whiteside *and* the surrounding areas?" She nods. "So that means he must have really gotten a chunk out of his attacker."

"Not so fast," she says, turning to Mihir. "Can you pull up the data on the Bright case?" He types a few keys into the computer, bringing up Cameron Bright's file. "What was her blood type?"

"Type A," he says.

"And Dr. Whiteside's?"

"Type O."

"Hang on," I say, holding one hand to my temple as my head is beginning to pound. "Are you telling me that's Cameron Bright's blood in that room? Her *missing* blood?"

Zara nods, a large grin on her face. "I got suspicious when I saw the pictures of the scene. While the human body contains a lot of blood, about one and a half gallons in fact, I could tell just by looking that there was a *lot more* at the scene of the crime."

I have to admit I'm floored. I turn back to Mihir. "Can you match the Type A blood to Cameron Bright?"

He gives me a short of shrug. "Like I said, you'll need a DNA analysis for full confirmation. And we have to send those out; we don't have the equipment here. It will take a few days, at least."

"Em, think about it," Zara says. "Someone staged this crime scene to make it look like a massacre. Whoever drained Cameron of her blood was keeping it for something dramatic, and *this* is exactly what they wanted. A scene so gruesome no one would think twice about double-checking. You said it yourself, the people in this town are so wrapped up in their superstitions they wouldn't even think to look."

I'm taken aback. She's right. *I* didn't think to look either. I accepted it on face value, and I should have been more cautious. Scrutinized the situation more. "Damn."

She grins and slaps my good shoulder. "I told you it was worth it."

"You were right. Holy shit, Z, you just blew this whole thing wide open!"

She gives me a skeptical look. "I don't know about that—"

"No, really. This gives us our killer's M.O. They're trying to make each death look as dramatic as possible. First with Cameron, leaving her bloodless on the side of the road. Then with Whiteside, in a blood-soaked room. It's like you said, it's all for the *drama*." I think back to what Liam said about someone with experience in the movies. Someone who was an expert in this kind of thing. "Remember even you said it looked too 'clean'. That's what you meant, wasn't it?"

"I suppose," she says.

"Thank you for your help," I tell Mihir who seems anxious to get back to his work. "If you could put a rush on the samples it would help us out a lot."

"I'll see what I can do," he says, separating the samples by blood type. "But don't expect a miracle."

We thank him again and head back to the car, thankfully without running into any of the personnel who saw me earlier this morning.

"Bet you're glad I showed up now," Zara says as we climb back into the car.

"Are you kidding? If you hadn't you wouldn't have had anyone to wow with that revelation. I was just glad when you stopped my head from being cut off."

She pulls out, headed for Dr. Whiteside's house. "I'm sure

you would have found a way to disarm them," she says. "You always do."

"Not this time," I say. "I wanted to, but it's like I was stuck in molasses or something. I couldn't move as fast as I normally do."

"That was probably just because you were waking up. I've seen you disarm people with a lot more."

"No, I'm serious, Z. I think…I think I might have frozen."

She looks over and a dark shadow comes over her face before she pulls the car to the side of the road, putting it in park. "But you never freeze."

"I know. That's what's so scary about it."

She reaches over and gives my sore arm a gentle rub. "Did you talk to Dr. Frost?"

"Yeah, about how worried I was about you," I say truthfully. Frost knows I often deflect my own pain so I can focus on the problems of others and he's had to remind me on numerous occasions I have to also consider my own trauma. "I think maybe I didn't want to admit just how much what happened up in New York affected me."

Zara takes hold of my hand, giving it a squeeze.

"And I think focusing on you allowed me to bury it all. Last night, in the motel, that was the first time I was really under pressure since everything happened. And I just… couldn't make my body do what I needed it to."

She nods. "I know. I feel it too."

"What are we supposed to do?" I ask, feeling the first modicum of fear about my ability to remain an agent with the FBI. If I can't fight back, if I can't protect myself, how in the hell am I supposed to do this job?

"I'm not sure," she says. "Which is why I tried transferring to intelligence again before *someone* needed me to come save her." She says the last part in jest, but I can hear the very real pain behind her words too.

We sit in silence for a few moments, listening the rumble

of the engine and stare out at the flat landscape before us, dotted with small, one-building businesses. My mind feels like that sometimes, like an empty gray landscape. And for the first time in my career, I don't know what to do about the future.

"One thing's for sure," I finally say. "Not a word to Wallace. He'll pull us both from duty so fast that we'll never operate in the field ever again."

"But Em, we can't keep going like this," she says.

"I know." I take a deep breath in through my nose and out through my mouth. "Let's just…finish this up. We have something tangible to hold on to now, a way forward. And once this case is wrapped up, we'll figure it out. Together. Deal?"

She nods. "Deal." Zara takes a deep breath of her own and puts the car in drive again. I have to admit I feel anxious about what awaits us, but at least I don't feel alone anymore. Whatever future we're about to face, we're going to do it as a team.

Chapter Twenty-One

ON THE WAY to Dr. Whiteside's I call Lowe to get an update. According to him they've managed to secure the scene and have already transferred Agent Phillips's body back to the morgue and Dr. Hansen is already working on the autopsy. I silently curse, hoping we could have kept Agent Phillips' body away from Hansen until after our backup arrived, but if she was going to tamper with evidence then she's already had the chance to do it. I don't mention Zara's revelation about the blood, however, because I want to keep as much of a lid on this as possible. Whoever our killer is, they want their kills to look like something out of a bad monster movie. I don't want to show our hand just yet. Lowe is the only other person who knows we're on the lookout for the van that's sitting in Whiteside's garage. And right now, I want to keep it that way.

"Why didn't you mention it?" Zara asks once I hang up.

"Because I honestly don't know who to trust," I tell her. "This van could be the key to telling us who our unsub is. And right now, you're the only person in this town who is thinking with a clear head. We can't take any chances until we're sure of our killer."

"What, you don't have a clear head?" she asks.

"I didn't even think about the blood angle. You caught that because you haven't been subjected to all this…" I wave my hand dismissively.

"Em, you gotta relax," she says. "You're putting too much pressure on yourself. Per usual."

She's right. I made a promise to stop doing that. It's just when you've almost been killed it tends to ramp up your emotions and I'm still riding that wave of anxiousness.

When we pull up to Dr. Whiteside's house, the police tape is still in place and there's a patrol car sitting nearby, keeping anyone out of the scene. The house is dark; hopefully Mrs. Whiteside has somewhere else she can stay for a while. I know how she feels. Staying in that house after something like this is going to be difficult, if not impossible.

Zara shows the officer her badge as we pull up, informing him we need to take another look at the scene. He waves us on without even getting out of his car and Zara pulls into the driveway, so her car blocks the view of the garage from the road. The garage door is back down and as far as I can tell the scene is quiet.

"I wanna see the scene first," Zara says. I motion for her to go ahead while I head for the garage. There's a regular-sized door on the side of the building which is unlocked and provides access. Once inside I flip on the light and find myself staring at the white van, which has been backed into the space so that the nose is facing toward the door. The rest of the garage is spacious, there's an old tool bench along the side complete with tools laying about, and the back has rows of shelves filled with what look like paint cans and old house supplies. The floor is concrete, though it's cracked in a few places. There's also an old musty smell that I always associate with old houses. The smell that tells me this place probably hasn't changed much in the past thirty years.

I pull out a couple of gloves and slip them on before approaching the driver's side door, which is unlocked, thankfully. It saves me from having to search around for the man's keys. I can't help but wonder if this was Dr. Whiteside's primary mode of transportation, or if he was keeping it for whatever he was doing at Lovely Hearts that night.

I fully expect to find the van packed with boxes of drugs that Dr. Whiteside has been selling on the black market, but once I get inside, I find it's empty. There's a row of seats behind the driver and passenger's seats, but I don't see any boxes full of oxy, fentanyl or Adderall. I search under the driver's seat before making my way around to the side of the van and rolling open the side door.

"Hey," Zara says, coming into the garage. "Find anything yet?"

"Still looking," I say, climbing into the back of the van. "Did you see it?"

"Yeah, and I'm not surprised you didn't catch the blood thing. It's meant to be shocking, so much that your normal problem-solving skills short-circuit. It's like suspension of disbelief, right? Whoever did this was counting on the drama of it all to keep you from thinking logically."

"That's no excuse," I say rummaging around in the back. There are a couple of compartments back here, and I start going through each of them in turn. It looks like they've been added to the van at some point after it was manufactured.

"Whoever this is, they are showing the town exactly what it wants to see," Zara says.

"I suppose." I reach into one of the compartments and remove a black satchel. "Finally, jackpot."

"What'd you find?" she asks, sticking her head in the van.

I make my way back to the side door, setting the satchel down beside the seats. The overhead light in the van and the light from the garage are more than enough to see. It's an expensive looking bag, all black leather with brass buckles and straps. It takes me a minute to figure out how the bag opens, but when I get it, I'm still surprised not to see any bags of pills.

Instead, I'm looking at vials of different liquids, all of them with official labels on them. "Pentobarbital, diazepam, digoxin, morphine, amitriptyline," I say. The bag also has a supply of needles and syringes, along with some additional drugs. "What the hell?"

"Where did he even get pentobarbital?" Zara asks. "That stuff has been scarce for a decade now."

I shrug. "He was older, maybe he's just had it for a while? But what is the rest of this stuff?"

"Hang on a second," she says, pulling out her phone. After a quick search her face falls. "Em, a lot of these drugs, especially in this combination are used for assisted suicides."

I carefully place the vials back into the bag, where they have specific holders keeping them from clanking together. "Are you sure?"

"It's known as DDMA, and it's common in states where assisted suicide is practiced."

I sit back on one of the seats, looking at the bag. "But it's still illegal in Louisiana. And most of the rest of the country. Do you think that's what Dr. Whiteside was doing? Lowe said he just made house calls to the sick and elderly who couldn't make it to the medical center."

"Maybe his house calls weren't just checkups," Zara replies, her face grim.

"We need to get a look at his records," I say, closing the bag back up. At the very least, it's coming with us. I don't know if this has anything to do with his death, but I'm not willing to leave it here for someone else to find. There are some very dangerous drugs in here and I'll feel better once we have them under lock and key.

"I spotted an old desktop in the house," Zara says. "Wanna take a look?"

I shrug. "Can't hurt." We head back into the house and

through the halls until we reach a room that I missed on my first visit last night. It's opposite the room where Dr. Whiteside was found and is decorated in what I'd have to describe as "grandma" décor. There's a bed with a small side table, complete with a doily and a small lamp. The chest is full of pictures of younger people, some of them probably the Whitesides themselves. I take particular notice of one picture featuring a young couple and I can see the younger face of Mrs. Whiteside as she hugs the man in the picture, both of them standing in front of the ocean with a lighthouse far in the background. I get a good look at who I presume is the younger version of Dr. Whiteside. He has a kind face; I can see why people trusted him.

"Here we go," Zara says, sitting in the chair in front of the computer in the room. It's situated on a small rollaway table and looks like it hasn't moved in a decade. Zara stretches her hands out in front of her, interlocking her fingers and cracking every one of them before she powers on the computer and waits for it to boot up.

"Remember when you used to turn the computer off after using it?" she asks.

"Not really," I say.

"Give me a minute, this thing is ancient and may take—" The screen flickers to life and the desktop appears, with about a hundred icons scattered all over it. "Whoa." Zara scans the field until she finds a word document marked "appointments". "There's something to be said for people who aren't proficient with technology. But at least they were trying.

When Zara opens up the document it populates a list of appointments, names and dates of what look like all of Dr. Whiteside's patients.

But as Zara scans through the list there's no mention of anyone at Loving Hearts or anything listed for the night Cameron Bright died. "Sorry Em, looks like a dead end."

"Maybe he was just smart enough not to make a record of

it," I say. "Still, it was worth investigating. We still need to find out—" All of a sudden the room begins to spin and I feel like I'm about to collapse. Zara is up and holding on to me, guiding me to the nearby bed where we both take a seat.

"Okay, yeah. First thing you need to rest. Let's not forget you just had surgery this morning."

"It wasn't surgery," I tell her. "Just a couple of stitches."

"And you lost a lot of blood. Even with a refill I think you might need to take it easy for just a few hours."

"I'm fine," I say and attempt to stand, only for the room to spin again and I end up back on the bed. "Okay, maybe not."

"Give me just a second," she says. "I'll get things wrapped up here and then we need to get you horizontal. You probably also need some food. Have you even had anything since that coffee this morning?"

I give her a sheepish look and she blows out a long breath, ruffling the few pieces of platinum hair that have fallen into her face. "What would you do without me?"

"Fall asleep here?" I suggest.

"Sit tight," she says. "I'll be right back." She takes Dr. Whiteside's bag, and turns off the computer, leaving me in the guest room for a minute. I've never been great about sitting around, and even though my head is spinning I can't help but get up and walk to the door, keeping one arm on the wall as I go. When I reach the doorway where we found Dr. Whiteside, I find I'm looking at it differently now. The bed hasn't been moved and as far as I can tell nothing has been disturbed, but I make my way into the room anyway. I pull back the blood-soaked sheets away from the base of the bed, exposing the frame. Instead of being splintered and cracked, like one would think if it had been broken under the pressure of someone being thrown on it, there are a few saw marks halfway up, suggesting someone compromised the frame of the bed *before* it was broken.

Just another sleight of hand to help set the scene and make it look as dramatic as possible.

"Jeez, I leave you alone for two minutes and you can't even sit still," Zara says, coming into the room and taking my arm, even as I wobble a little.

"Look," I say, pointing to the bed frame. "Someone primed it."

Zara pulls out her phone and snaps a few pictures. "There wasn't a mention of this in the evidence boxes. I'll get these into the file later. Right now, we need to get you some food and rest." She gets up under one of my arms and helps guide me back out of the room and through the back door to where she already has the car running and waiting.

As much as I want to keep going, I have to accept my own limits. But we're close.

I can feel it.

Chapter Twenty-Two

AFTER FEEDING me and heading back to the police station to retrieve anything that wasn't taken for evidence from the crime scene that was my room, Zara checked us in to the local Hilton, which seemed like a much nicer option than the Gator Motel. I'm sure Wallace will balk at the expense, but seeing as I was almost murdered in that place he won't have much ground to stand on.

Zara takes it upon herself to make sure I'm in bed at a reasonable hour and that I'm taking all the medication that came with me from the hospital. I haven't felt so taken care of since I was a teenager, and part of me actively resists it. But she's as stubborn as I am and practically forces me to stay in bed so I can get at least ten hours of good rest.

Somehow, I actually manage to sleep. Maybe because I know Zara is there with me and there is no window accessible to the room without someone climbing two stories and breaking through solid plate-glass. Whatever the reason, I don't wake up until early the next morning, both my arm and neck feeling like they've been run over by a van. The thought immediately makes me sit up and I look around only to see Dr. Whiteside's satchel on the floor close to the dresser. I was afraid Zara might have forgotten it as the rest of yesterday is kind of fuzzy.

"Morning," Zara says, already sitting up and in her work clothes. It seems I slept straight through her shower and getting ready. "Sleep okay?"

"Yeah," I say, rubbing my neck where the bandage covers my stitches. "Pretty hard, actually." I don't recall any strange dreams about Dr. Frost or anyone else for that matter. It was one of those nights when I think I was just so tired that my brain didn't want to work to conjure anything. "You?"

"Bed's lumpy. But other than that, yeah." I try to get up, but I'm sore all over, which is frustrating. My body still feels like I'm moving in slow motion, but as I walk around the room I begin to feel a little better. At least I'm not dizzy anymore.

Zara monitors me in and out of the shower, but thankfully doesn't have to come in or give me a sponge bath. I don't know if I could manage the humiliation of needing someone to help me bathe or go to the bathroom. But it does bring my thoughts back to Loving Hearts, seeing as most of their patients are at that stage in life.

"We need to get over to the nursing home and speak with the manager again," I say as I'm carefully drying myself off. "I want to know if he knows anything about Dr. Whiteside."

"You think he might be involved?" she calls back through the cracked door.

"If anyone would be, it's him. I also want to talk to the residents, see if anyone saw Dr. Whiteside or anything suspicious." I recall that Gallagher, the manager at Loving Hearts said one of their residents died the night Cameron Bright went missing. At the time I hadn't thought much about it other than wanting to see her room, but now I'm wondering if it's connected.

Once I get my clothes on and my hair in out of the way, I head back out, looking for my shoes. "There was a resident that night…I forget the name. Gallagher said she'd passed overnight."

"And you're thinking Dr. Whiteside had something to do with it," Zara says, offering me my boots.

I take a careful seat and slip them on one at a time. "Gallagher said they'd all been hoping the patient would go for some time. And we know Whiteside was there that night; we have his van on security footage. Which means Cameron Bright *had* to know something."

"You think that's where her extra money was coming from?" Zara asks.

"Makes sense, doesn't it?"

Just as we're finishing getting ready, there's a knock at the door. Zara furrows her brow, then pulls out her service weapon and checks the peephole. "Oh. That was fast." She opens the door to reveal Special Agents Nadia Kane and Elliott Sandel. I admit seeing them here comes as a surprise. We've been working with both of them on some recent cases, including the Magus case that almost ended up killing both of us in New York a few weeks ago.

"Agents," Sandel says in that maddeningly stoic voice of his. "You look surprised to see us."

"It's just…when I asked Wallace for help, I figured he'd just coordinate with the local New Orleans office to send more agents."

"Apparently the SAC in New Orleans wasn't too happy about their agent," Kane says, taking a step into the room. "Wallace is doing damage control. In the meantime, he sent us." Her eyes drop to my neck where my bandage covers my wound. "Oh, Emily. Are you okay?"

"Oh, yeah, I'm fine. Nothing that a few stitches couldn't fix."

"A-*hem*," Zara fake coughs into her hand.

"And a good night's rest."

"Agent," Sandel says. "I must ask to see your firearm."

It takes me a second to realize he means Zara, not me. "Wait, what?" she asks.

"According to my information, Agent Foley discharged her firearm at a suspect. There needs to be a record and third-party investigation of the incident."

"I didn't even hit anyone," Zara says. "The bullets are buried in the wall of the Gator Motel!" Unfazed, Sandel holds out his hand. "Man. And to think I invited you to Emily's birthday party." She removes her gun from its holster, ejects the clip, then unchambers the last round.

"It's just a precaution for your own protection," he says, taking her weapon and the clip. He examines it for a moment, then the weapon itself. "Did you warn the suspect to put down their weapon?"

"Yes," Zara says, exasperated.

"Is this really necessary?" I ask.

"Did the suspect comply?" Sandel asks, continuing to inspect the weapon as if he hasn't heard me.

"At first. Then they turned and ran for the open window."

"So the suspect was fleeing, and you fired anyway," he says.

"I knew at least one shot was going wide, so I fired a few more to try and scare them into stopping," Zara says. "But I'd be lying if I said I wasn't trying to hit them at least to slow them down."

Sandel looks at her under hooded eyes. "You'll need to put that in your report."

"Oh, trust me, I will," Zara says.

Sandel loads the last round back into the clip, then inserts it back into the weapon before handing it back to Zara. "The Bureau is under a lot of scrutiny. A dead agent is going to bring a lot of questions. Just make sure you include all the details of the encounter when all this is over. I expect you'll have a visit from IA."

"I can't wait," Zara says, taking the weapon back and

holstering it again. "Doesn't matter anyway. I'm not going to be in the field for much longer." I think back to our conversation yesterday. There's a good chance I might not be back in the field after this either, depending on how my next psych eval goes.

"What's the latest on the situation?" Kane asks, taking a seat at the small table in the room.

We give her the rundown of what we discovered about the blood and Dr. Whiteside's van yesterday, as well as my hesitations about the local police and their willingness to properly investigate what's really happening here. I haven't had a chance to catch back up with Lowe this morning but seeing as no one attempted to murder either Zara or me overnight, I'm hoping we can at least take a breath and get a handle on this thing.

"If you two wouldn't mind investigating Agent Phillips' death, I think it could be a real help."

"But you think the body may have been compromised?" Kane asks.

"I can't say that with any certainty, but I will say that you should take whatever Dr. Hansen says with a grain of salt. As soon as Zara pretended to buy into her conspiracies yesterday, she was practically rabid to get a look at Phillips. We were too occupied to get to her before she had the chance."

"That's unfortunate," Sandel says. "Because if she is involved with this in some way as you suspect, then she's had ample time to plant evidence."

"Exactly," I say.

"What evidence do you think she might have planted?" Kane asks.

"I don't know yet, but I have a feeling deep in my gut she's involved. The way these two bodies were staged...it would take someone with some medical training to be able to pull that off. And we still don't know exactly what or how either of them was killed. But we have found evidence not everything was as it seemed on the surface." I inform them about the compromised bed we discovered yesterday.

"But you believe it was meant to look like a monster attacked them?"

"From what we've been able to gather, yes," I say. "Add the fact that Cameron Bright's blood was used to make the scene appear even more gruesome tells me we're working with someone who has zero human empathy. They just see people as tools to be used in whatever game they're playing."

"Does Dr. Hansen fit that profile?" Sandel asks.

"It's hard to say. Not traditionally, or if she does, she hides it well. Still, she's at the center of all this. And I don't think it's too much of a reach to keep an eye on her."

Kane nods, standing. "We'll take over the investigation on the Phillips case. I want to get a look at those bodies. What are you two going to do?"

"We need to speak with Mr. Gallagher again to try and find out if Zara's suspicions about Whiteside are true. If he really was helping people commit suicide, then someone had to have seen something. And Cameron Bright had to have been involved. I think if we can find the money trail it will lead us in the right direction."

"One last thing," I say as we all make our way out. "Be careful who you identify yourself as FBI agents to. Someone in this town is gunning for us, and the less people that know more agents are here the better. At least until we can flush this person out."

"Agreed," Sandel says. "We'll keep a low profile."

The four of us head out of the hotel, and as we do I can't help but glance around, looking for someone who might be watching. But the sun is already up and the land around the hotel is relatively flat, leaving few places for someone to hide. I guess I'm just jumpy, though I have good reason to be.

"Bad memories?" Zara asks as we get back into her car. As

I slide in, I accidentally brush my arm on the seat and a fire burns through my wound.

I give it a gentle rub to calm it down. "Just keeping a look out."

"I'll tell you one thing, whoever is out there doing this, they picked the wrong agents to mess with," she says.

"Damn right." I give her a reassuring nod. "Okay, let's go solve this thing."

Chapter Twenty-Three

WHEN WE PULL up to Loving Hearts Nursing Home, I notice Cameron Bright's car is no longer in the parking lot. It looks like Lowe finally had someone come and move it. I want to check for any prints on the car, though there is no evidence to suggest Cameron even got that far when she left work that morning. By all accounts her attacker grabbed her before she managed to reach it. Still, knowing what we know now, it might not be a bad idea to cover our asses. Our killer may have inadvertently touched the vehicles while waiting.

As we get out of the car I have to admit I do feel a little better now that I've had a good night's rest. I'm not sure I realized just how much the thought of someone being in my room was weighing on me. Then again, it's not like I would have admitted it to myself even if I had realized it. Still, I'm grateful that I can proceed with a clearer mind.

"This place looks cozy," Zara says as we enter through the sliding front doors. "In a mausoleum sort of way."

I stifle a laugh as I spot the nurse from the other morning: Tricia, working in the back office. "Over here," I say, heading in that direction. Tricia looks up, a smile on her face that falls upon seeing me.

"Agent Slate! What happened?"

I rub the bandage on my neck. "Hazard of the job, I'm afraid. This is my colleague, Agent Foley. Is Mr. Gallagher in? We need to speak with him."

"Pleasure," she replies, nodding to Zara. "Unfortunately, he's not in yet this morning. Would you like to wait?"

I exchange glances with Zara. We don't have time to sit around for this guy to decide to waltz in around ten a.m. Some of us are on a tight clock. The way this killer or killers are operating suggests we could have another victim already and not even know it. They aren't being shy about dropping bodies, and their M.O. seems to suggest they will not hesitate to kill again. Which is part of the reason I keep looking over my shoulder.

"Could we get a look at your patient records, instead?" I ask. "We're not looking for personal information," I add before she can object, which I can already see she's about to do. "We just need to know when they became residents and when they...left."

She screws up her face for a second. "I...guess that would be all right. Obviously I can't give you any sensitive informa-tion as all records are protected under HIPAA and I'd—"

I hold up a hand. "I understand completely. We're just looking for the basics. Occupancy only."

"All right, just give me a minute. How far back do you need?"

"A year would be great," Zara says.

Tricia indicates the main gathering area near the front doors. "Feel free to take a seat, I'll bring you the records as soon as I have them."

"Thanks," I say as we retreat back to the sitting area. It's quiet, at least, and it doesn't seem like any of the residents are up and about yet.

"I know it's probably not very *p.c.*," Zara whispers once we've sat down. "But places like this give me the heebies."

"I know how you feel," I say.

"It's just...so much death in one place. It's like living in a crime scene."

"That may be what these people have been doing and haven't even been aware of it." I glance down the hallway where an older man emerges from his room. He's dressed in slacks and a polo shirt, and is using a cane to make his way down the hall as he's slightly hunched over. As soon as he sees us his eyes brighten and I swear he picks up the pace a little.

"Uh oh," I whisper. "Get ready to put on your signature charm. This one is all yours."

"Don't I always?" she whispers back.

"Ladies, good morning," the older man says, tipping an imaginary hat at us. "I know it's too much to ask that two beautiful young women are here to see me, but I hope you wouldn't mind some company for a minute."

"Of course not," Zara says.

He smiles and makes his way around the couch until he's backed up to a chair, which he lowers himself into gingerly, keeping his weight on his cane. Even after he's sitting, he still keeps both hands on it. Though as soon as his eyes fall on my neck they go wide.

"We're FBI agents," I explain. "I was injured on the job."

"Oh, my," he says. "I hope you're okay." Then he sits up a little straighter. "You're here about Rebecca."

"Rebecca?" Zara asks.

He nods. "Rebecca Berger. You suspect something happened to her. That she didn't just...pass."

Now he has my attention. Mrs. Berger was the patient that died the night Cameron disappeared. "Why do you say that?"

"Rebecca was one of the strongest-willed people I know. Where most people come into this place have lost most of their willpower either from a disease or age, Rebecca had done neither. But she was in a great deal of pain. It had been going on for months. She confided to me that she was going to be done with all of it. That she wasn't sitting around any longer waiting for death to come." He leans forward. "She was going to go seek him out."

"That's...quite a statement. When did she tell you this?" I ask.

"A couple of weeks ago," he replies. "I asked her what she meant, but she wouldn't say any more. But it seems like she managed to pull it off, whatever it was."

I want to ask him more details, but Tricia comes out of the office with a bundle of papers in her hand. "Oh, good morning, Charlie," Tricia says. "What brings you this way so early?"

"Morning, Trish. Just having a nice chat with these two lovely ladies before breakfast." He doesn't meet my eyeline again, which tells me he may not want to say anything else in front of Tricia. Did he know what was going on here?

Tricia hesitates a moment then walks over and hands me the bundle of papers. "Here's everything you asked for. One year."

Zara and I stand. "Thank you. Do you know what time Mr. Gallagher normally comes in?"

She holds her gaze on Charlie for a minute before looking at her watch. "He actually should be in by now. Usually, he's here by nine. Let me try him at home, sometimes he accidentally sleeps in." She retreats back to the office for a minute.

I lean close to Charlie. "Is there something going on here? Something you think we should know about?"

"Not if you're going to ruin it for everyone," he says. "People get left in places like this to die. Is it too much to ask that some of them keep a little autonomy? At least a say in how and when they should go?"

While not a straight-out admission, that confirms there is some kind of *program* here that residents can opt into. But it's obviously kept on the hush-hush since it's still illegal in the state. But I get the feeling Trish knows nothing about it.

"One more question. Say someone was interested in this… option. Would they go to Nurse Bright?"

He doesn't flat-out refuse the possibility, which tells me everything I need to know. "We're not looking to get anyone in trouble here," I say. "We just want to understand what happened."

"Cammy was the most helpful person in this place," he whispers. "She was always willing to help."

"I can't get him at home," Tricia says, returning. "He must be on his way here."

While I can believe that Tricia might not know anything about the "special program" the nursing home offered, I can't believe Gallagher wouldn't. And yet he stood there and never said a thing when I first interviewed him.

I hold up the papers. "Thank you," I say. "We'll be in touch if we need anything else."

"Sure, just let us know if we can help." I take one last look at Charlie before we leave, his gaze is hard and intense. I'm sure he thinks he's already told us too much.

"That all but confirms it," Zara says once we're back in the car.

I split the papers in half and hand her a couple, while going over the others myself. "Do you have Cameron Bright's bank records from the case file?"

"I have access to it," she says. "Give me a minute." She goes to work on her phone and a minute later has the bank records pulled up. We go through and compare them to the dates patients have died in Loving Hearts.

"All her cash deposits line up with deaths at the nursing home," I say. "Deposits made two to three days later in each instance."

"Still, it's coincidental," she says. "No hard connection."

"No, but I'd be willing to bet anything Gallagher was the money man. Cameron might have given Dr. Whiteside access to perform the procedures, but Gallagher had to keep it all under wraps, and he had to make sure everyone got paid. Otherwise, someone could just whistle-blow the whole situation and get Loving Hearts shut down."

"But where did the money come from?" Zara asks.

"Probably funds from patient reserves, or he might have even found a way to finagle it through insurance. Only he can answer that for us."

"Convenient he isn't at work this morning," she says, putting the car into drive.

Yeah. Convenient. "I think it's time we gave Mr. Gallagher a house call of our own."

Chapter Twenty-Four

"IS THIS IT?" I ask, staring through the window at the house.

"According to the DMV, yeah," Zara says. We're parked outside Gallagher's home, which is a modest one-story white brick house with a large, flat lawn that sits at the corner of two residential roads. Two stone benches sit in the middle of one side of the lawn, serving no purpose other than lawn decoration while a giant tree dominates the other side of the property, covering a good portion of the house's roof. I motion for Zara to pull around to the side where the garage is just to get a better look and I realize the house goes back a lot farther than it seemed from the front. It almost seems like the side is the "front" as there's another entrance over here with a porch which sits right beside the garage.

"Let's try this one," I say.

I let Zara take the lead, since my arm is still sore and she can move faster if she needs to. Even though the house has a closed garage, there's a car in the driveway, though I'm not sure if it's the one belonging to Gallagher or not.

Zara rings the doorbell and knocks a few times before stepping back. The door has thin windows on either side and I catch some movement inside. But the door opens to reveal an older woman wearing an apron. "Yes?"

"Are you Mrs. Gallagher?" I ask.

"No, I'm Marie, the housekeeper," she says. "There is no Mrs. Gallagher."

Zara and I exchange a look. "We're looking for Mr. Gallagher," she says. "Is he home?"

"He left a few hours ago on his morning run," she says. I automatically begin looking around the neighborhood. "No, I mean, he always drives somewhere else to go run. He says he's run around this neighborhood too much; it's gotten too boring."

"Do you know where he might have gone?" I ask.

"I'm sorry, I don't. But he's usually not gone this long. I just figured he was having a good run and didn't want to interrupt it."

"What kind of car was he driving?" Zara asks.

"It's his gray Mazda MX-5," she replies. "Two-seater. He keeps the Explorer for his work."

"Thanks for your help," I say as we both head back to our car. I call Lowe before I've even reached the door. "It's Slate. I need an APB on a gray Mazda MX-5," I tell him. I look to Zara who already has the DMV info pulled up on the car. "License plate LMW-1113."

"What's going on?" Lowe asks.

"We have another missing person, someone who might be in the crosshairs of our killer," I say. If Gallagher was involved in the assisted suicides, then he would be the next logical target for the killer, after Cameron and Dr. Whiteside.

Zara puts the car into drive and peels out of the road.

"The potential target's name is Louis Gallagher. He left his home this morning for a run and hasn't been back since." I may have been too complacent thinking the killer hadn't struck again.

"On it," Lowe says. "By the way, there are two more

people here looking at Phillips's case, they say they're with you but they won't give me any formal ID."

"I know, I called in some specialists," I say. "Just give them whatever they need."

"Okay," he says, though there's some hesitation in his voice. "I'll get the APB out right now."

"What do you think happened?" Zara asks as soon as I'm off the phone with him.

"Someone figured out what was going on and is looking to put a stop to it," I say. "The motive could be nothing more than they believe assisted suicide is wrong. Then again, killing people to stop them from helping others die suggests a pretty fucked up moral system."

"No argument there," she says. "So where to?"

"I dunno, how well do you know the area? Where would someone want to run around here?"

"Beats me. Why drive somewhere just to run?"

I rub my sore arm, feeling the row of stitches underneath. "People are weird."

My phone buzzes before either of us can say anything else. "Slate."

"It's Lowe. Got a hit on your car."

"Already?" I ask, shooting Zara a look.

"Patrol noticed it earlier; it's been parked down near downtown along the canal for a few hours."

I mouth *downtown* to Zara. "Is there a running trail down there?"

"Yep. Runs right next to the canal."

"We're headed there now. Tell your patrols to keep a lookout for a middle-aged man, dark brown hair, may or may not be wearing glasses. Probably dressed in running gear."

"Already on it," he says.

"Any idea of when it showed up?" I ask.

"I'll check with patrol again. They run that area a couple of times per night, so they should have a window at least."

"I'm going to need a team to meet us at the car. I want to go over it with a fine-tooth comb."

He lets out a long breath. "I'll inform them. We may need to pull in resources from New Orleans, our people are being run ragged by all this."

"Whatever you have to do," I tell him before hanging up. "He's starting to resist."

Zara makes a hard left turn which points us back in the direction of downtown. "Didn't you say he was originally excited about the prospect?"

"I wouldn't say excited, at least not in the way Hansen was. But he seemed eager to prove some of his 'theories'."

"Does this mean he's off the suspect list?"

"No one's off the suspect list except for you, me, Kane and Sandel. Though I still want to take a close look at Hansen. Every time I see her she looks like she's just been run through the wringer."

"And her body type did match your attacker," Zara reminds me.

"It did, but I can't see Hansen vaulting herself through a window like that. Then again, I don't know anything about the woman, other than she has an affinity for the occult."

When we reach the parking area next to the canal a patrol car is already there, parked beside what I assume is Gallagher's Mazda. The first thing I do is check the license plate and sure enough, it's his.

"Anything suspicious around?" I ask the officer standing by the car.

"Just arrived a minute ago. Haven't seen anyone though."

"Em," Zara says, nudging me as she points at the canal itself. The murky brown water obscures anything that could be underneath. To be honest, for the city's source of drinking water, it doesn't look the best. Not to mention there are no guard rails or anything else to keep someone from falling or being pushed in.

"How deep is that canal?" I ask the officer.

"You mean the Lafourche?" Though it sounds like *le-foosh* when he says it. "I'm not sure. Maybe ten, fifteen feet in a 'coupla places?"

There's no way we can dredge the whole thing. This canal has to run for miles in both directions and it's at least fifty feet wide at its smallest point. "If he's down there, we'll never find him."

"C'mon," Zara says. "We can at least check out the car while we wait on forensics."

I motion to the officer. "Has anyone touched this car since you've been here?" He shakes his head as Zara and I pull on a couple pairs of gloves. The car is locked, which isn't a surprise, but fortunately the cop has a lockset in his vehicle. It takes Zara a few times, but she manages to get the driver's side door open.

The inside is small with not much room to move around. Technically it's classified as a sports car, so there are only the two bucket seats and no backseat at all. A power cord is still plugged into one of the vehicle's USB jacks, probably from where Gallagher kept his phone charged while he drove. The glove box only has the car's registration and service manual, while the center console contains a few tissues and some change. The registration proves it's Gallagher's car, but there's nothing else inside. No wallet, no phone and definitely no indication of where he went.

"Smell that?" Zara asks, sniffing.

"What?"

"Smells like…I dunno. Sewage."

I sniff a few times but don't detect anything. "Are you sure it's not just the canal? It is muggy out this morning."

"No, I only…" She pulls her head out of the car, sniffing again. "I only smell it in the car." We both look at each other, our eyes going wide. "*Trunk!*"

She pulls the trunk handle, and we rush around to the

back, only to find ourselves looking at the soaked and bloated body of Louis Gallagher. His eyes are open but it's obvious from the color of his skin and the fact he's not breathing that we're too late. I gingerly touch him in an attempt to roll him on his side and a mass of black water leaks from his lips, soaking into the vehicle's upholstery. I step back, not wanting to contaminate the scene any further.

"Well," Zara says, putting her hands on her hips. "At least we don't have to go diving."

Chapter Twenty-Five

BY THE TIME the body removal team and forensics shows up it's already past ten in the morning. They go to work on pulling Gallagher's body out of the back of the car and taking evidence samples. They focus on the trunk, though I doubt there will be any fingerprints left behind. Our killer hasn't been sloppy yet and I don't expect this death to be any different.

As we're heading back to the morgue behind the white minivan carrying Gallagher's body, I can't help but wonder about the nature of these deaths. The fact that this was another "staged" scene, while not as dramatic as the other two, still suggests to me we're looking at two killers. Or one killer with a seriously messed up M.O. Why would someone come at me and Phillips with only a knife, when they have the capability to drain the blood from someone, or slash them to pieces? Or drown them?

We have to be dealing with two different people here, but the only question is what connects them? Why come after FBI agents and how do we fit into the whole scheme? Due to the proximity of Phillips' death to the others, I have to assume it's all connected; I just don't know how. The odds of two killers working completely independent of each other within the same small town are roughly zero. Thankfully the news hasn't picked up on the savage nature of the deaths yet; they've only been reporting on the occurrences. Though I expect word to spread fast in a town like this. And once it gets out, we could even start dealing with some copycats.

But for now, these two killers are exhibiting separate patterns. One killer is going after people that may have been involved in an assisted suicide, while the other is targeting the FBI agents investigating it. Why not target the local police too? Could it be that because the local police harbor the same superstitions they're not a threat? Or could all of this be coming from *inside* the department itself?

I'm so lost in my thoughts that Zara has to nudge me to let me know we've arrived back at the morgue. She followed the white van around to the back and we accompany the men as they wheel Gallagher in on a gurney through the double doors. The morgue itself is empty when we arrive and I'm struck that not very long ago, Agent Phillips and I were in this exact spot, discussing Dr. Whiteside's situation. I look over and see her name written on a small card attached to the cooling drawers.

Life sure can be cruel sometimes.

"Where do you want him?" one of the medical techs asks us.

I don't spot Agents Kane or Sandel anywhere, so I just indicate for them to put Gallagher where Phillips was examining Dr. Whiteside. "Where do you think they went?" I ask.

Zara shrugs. "Maybe they finished up already." As soon as they finish wheeling him over, Hansen appears in the door, still frazzled as ever.

"Agents," she says, like she's surprised to see us. As she comes into the morgue, she tries flattening her frizzy hair, but it seems to be going in all directions today.

I had hoped with Agents Kane and Sandel we could have

distracted Hansen, but apparently they're already finished here. Which means we're going to have to let Hansen do an autopsy on Gallagher if we want any answers. But I'm going to be here to watch the entire thing, just to ensure she doesn't tamper with any evidence. The woman is walking on thin ice and I'm really not comfortable with her in this position. According to Lowe she's the only coroner for an hour in each direction and I'm not about to suggest the New Orleans field office send *another* agent. "Do you know this man?" I ask.

She approaches, then squints at his face as she takes him in. He's still just as we found him, soaked and in his running clothes, except now he's covered in a white sheet that has been pulled down to reveal his face.

"I don't think so. Should I?"

I can't tell if she's lying or not, but Hansen does seem jittery about *something*. "His name is Louis Gallagher. He was the director at Loving Hearts."

"Oh," she says, going still for a moment. "I assume you want the autopsy now."

"I want to make sure he died by drowning and nothing else. The other two deaths were more intricate, more involved. Whereas this one seems very simple. I'm just making sure we know what we're dealing with here."

"But…there have been three other deaths," she says, like I've somehow managed to forget Agent Phillips.

"I'm aware, but the attack on her and the one in my room don't line up. I believe Gallagher was killed by our original perpetrator."

"I see," she says, rubbing her hands together. "Of course, I'll get started right away. Just give me a moment to prepare."

I nod and she heads off. Once she's out of earshot I turn back to Zara. "Thoughts?"

"She's distracted with something," she offers.

"Maybe the fact she's about to autopsy the man she killed?"

"You think she knows something. Maybe even something that can tie our killers together."

"Bingo." I step forward, getting a better look at Gallagher. Discolored water is still leaking out of his mouth, which I guess shouldn't come as a surprise. Whoever is doing this, they have the uncanny ability to catch their victims unaware. Though in Gallagher's case it probably wasn't hard. Considering we found him with his headphones still stuck in his ears it's probably not a stretch to assume he never even heard his attacker. But Cameron Bright? *And* getting into Dr. Whiteside's house? We're dealing with someone who has serious skill; someone who isn't going to reveal themselves to us easily. It has to be someone strong enough to hold Gallagher underwater, and stealthy enough to get into Whiteside's house to stage it like that. *After* they'd already killed him. I'm still not willing to accept those cuts across his body were made by some monster. I'm not even sure they came from an actual animal. I think we're dealing with someone much more talented here.

Hansen rushes back in the room, tying a rubber smock around her before slipping on a pair of gloves and her mask and goggles. She prepares her documentation, moving back and forth between one of the computer stations and the body as she goes about the pre-work of an autopsy.

If our presence here bothers her, she doesn't show it. Instead she remains focused on her job; something I have to respect. But she does still seem anxious about something from the way she jerks back and forth from one station to another, almost like she's in a frenzy. When I listen close I can almost hear her mumbling something, but I can't make out what it is.

"What was that?" I ask.

She looks up. "Hm?"

"You sounded like you were saying something."

"Was I?" She holds my gaze for a beat too long then goes back to what she was doing, except this time she definitely isn't saying anything. I exchange a worried look with Zara. Given

Hansen's penchant for the *unusual*, I'm not quite sure how this is going to go.

"Friday, February twenty-sixth," she says, the computer near her catching everything she says and dictating it on screen. "It is one-oh-two in the afternoon and the subject in question is one Louis Gallagher, white male, age forty-six. Apparent cause of death is asphyxiation due to water in the lungs and we will proceed on that assumption until we learn more." She looks up. "I am joined by Agents Slate and Foley with the FBI." She stares at us almost like she's waiting for our permission before she proceeds.

There is *definitely* something off about this lady. I give her the nod to go ahead, and she nods back.

"First we'll begin by removing the victim's clothing, which will give us easy access for the autopsy." She takes a few minutes cutting away the loose fabric from Gallagher, exposing him completely. I notice that more liquid continues to seep from his mouth, pooling right beside his head.

"Bloating and the transparent nature of the skin does seem to indicate the victim was drowned," she says. "His condition and color are consistent with someone who was in submerged in water for an extended period of time."

"Wait," I say. "How long was he down there?"

"At least a few hours," she replies. "Why?"

"Because it means someone drowned him, then pulled him back out and stuffed him in the back of his car," Zara says. "Why leave him down there for that long?"

"That I can't answer," Hansen says. "Are you sure he was drowned on purpose? Perhaps it was an accident."

"Then what happened? He fell in and died, and some good Samaritan pulled him out, and conveniently stuck him in his own trunk?" Zara asks, not hiding her sarcasm. What little goodwill she seemed to have developed with Hansen has disappeared.

"That's not for me to determine," Hansen says, taking a

sharp scalpel from her tray of instruments. She makes a Y-incision along Gallagher's chest all the way down past his sternum. When she pulls the skin back I have to force myself not to turn away, though Zara does. Part of me wishes I had, because all I can see are a bunch of dark red blobs in the body, as well as some blood that transfers to Hansen's gloves and smock. But she goes to work examining the body cavity just like she was looking in a mailbox for a lost piece of mail.

"Maceration around the tips of the fingers and toes indicates the body was fully submerged and exposed to cold water temperatures," she says. "Initial estimates put the victim under the water at two or more hours."

Jesus. Someone must have gone after him right as he started his run. I can't believe no one saw anything. Or maybe they did and they're too terrified to come forward. Then again, it was early in the morning.

I can't help but inch forward to look at Gallagher's fingers to see if I can tell what Hansen is talking about. Sure enough, the tips of them are white, wrinkled and thick.

"It's possible only some liquid entered into the lungs, depending on if the larynx was spasming at the time," Hansen says, placing the tip of the scalpel against Gallagher's left lung underneath the ribs. As she cuts, it's like it happens in slow motion.

A black mass of liquid comes pouring out of the lung, breaking through the barrier and spilling over the body, as it splashes out over and onto my and Zara's pants and shoes. The liquid is thicker than water, and for a brief moment my gag reflex kicks in and I almost want to throw up.

"Whoops, sorry about that," Hansen says. "I should have warned you." I notice she managed to back up in time. Almost like she suspected it. Like she *knew* the lung would be full of this stuff.

Zara and I remain frozen as I assess the damage. My pants and shoes are soaked, as are Zara's.

"We need a minute to get cleaned up," I tell Hansen. She nods, and though her eyes are downturned and sympathetic, I can't help but feel like that was all a setup. "What is that stuff that came out of his lung?"

"Not sure," she replies. "But I'd be happy to take a look. It's almost like…tar, but with the viscosity of water."

"Work on that while we go get cleaned up, would you?" I ask, turning and heading for the bathrooms. My shoes make a sickening *squelch* sound with each step I take.

"Of course. I'll be right here when you get back."

Zara and I spend fifteen minutes in the bathroom trying to get the material from Gallagher's lungs off us with little success. Finally, I just have to admit we'll need to go back to the hotel to change, which means we'll have to leave Hansen with Gallagher. The smell alone is enough to make me want to retch.

"Think she did that on purpose?" Zara asks, trying to rub her pants with some paper towels.

"Sure seems like it," I say. "Maybe she wanted us out of her hair so she could come up with whatever bullshit finding she's got on this one."

"Black lagoon."

"What?" I ask.

"The Creature from the Black Lagoon," she repeats. "It fits. Dracula, Wolfman, Creature. We have ourselves a classic horror movie lover."

That reminds me. "Here, come with me. We need to make a short detour before heading back to the hotel to change." I pull Zara out of the bathroom and down the hallway until we reach Hansen's office. Thankfully she hasn't returned; she's probably still too occupied with the body.

"What?" Zara whispers.

"Look," I say, pointing to all her trinkets on her shelves, as well as the strange symbols I saw last time I was in here.

"They're runes," Zara says, turning to me. "You know, ancient letters or symbols from another alphabet."

"Do you know which one?" I ask.

"They look druidic," she says, taking a step inside and looking around. "In fact, all of this stuff seems to fit in with Wicca." She turns to me with one of those smarmy smiles on her lips. "I think Dr. Hansen is a witch."

Chapter Twenty-Six

SPECIAL AGENT LIAM COLL sits in his not-so-new-anymore Jeep Wrangler, waiting. Half this job seems to be waiting around and the other half seems to be going so hard your heart feels like it will explode any minute. While he prefers the former, it seems he keeps being thrust into the latter, no matter what situation he's in.

But this time will be different. He's been in Millridge, Emily's mother's hometown for almost two full days now, taking his time, not making any waves, and trying to be virtually invisible to the people here. So far, everyone has greeted him with a friendly wave, and the moment he starts speaking, he can almost *sense* them visibly relax. They think he's one of them, just a man passing through town who happened to find a quaint little place off the map which seems like the perfect place to get back to one's roots.

At least, that's the impression he gets from the people around here. There hasn't been a soul yet who hasn't seemed weathered in some way, be it their rough hands, the wrinkles around their eyes, or the permanent tans they wear from years of working outside. People here work hard to make a living, and they're proud of it.

And he's been nothing more than a shadow moving among them, a passing face, nothing special about him and nothing worth noticing. He thinks maybe that's the hardest part of this job, attempting to remain invisible, when so much of his life was about standing out from the crowd. Excelling in school to get his choice of careers, putting his best face forward to get the job at the Fairview Police Department, working under Chief Burke in hopes to make lead detective one day. Attempting to become the model officer, all while ignoring what was swept under the rug. Because that's what you did when you were young and just learning the ropes, right? Everyone else seems okay with it, so why shouldn't you? You don't want to hurt your chances of ruining your career, especially not in a small town like Fairview.

And then you meet someone who changes your perspective on everything. Someone who makes you want to be a better detective—a better person, no matter what it ends up costing you.

He wouldn't be here right now if it weren't for Emily. She may not realize it, but he owes her a debt that he's not sure can be repaid. It also doesn't hurt that he's deeply, madly in love with the woman. Ever since first seeing her, he'd felt that spark between them and until he was sure of her feelings, it was something he had to keep buried. He didn't want to accidentally make her uncomfortable or ruin their friendship.

And yet, he couldn't help how he felt. It had always been there. It was as if as soon as he met her, he'd found a missing part of himself. He had been willing to bury that as deep as possible, to never show his hand, but fortunately she had felt the same way. And the past six months had been amazing. It took a relationship with Emily for Liam to finally realize that every other relationship he'd ever had hadn't really been a relationship at all. Not in the truest sense of the word. They had been infatuations, partnerships, or nothing more than flings. But it had all changed when Emily Slate came into his life.

And so he finds himself, sitting here on the side of the road, watching a dirt driveway from a hundred and ten yards away, casing the location to see if anyone is keeping watch.

Because their boss seems intent on keeping Emily occupied, Liam volunteered to travel to her hometown and find out what he could about her mother's family, in hopes that they could put a stop to these letters. She hasn't said so, but they have to be weighing on her, especially after the whole *Organization* debacle. Emily has had more than enough to deal with in the past year, and she doesn't need some *buck eejit* as his father would say, attempting to intimidate her.

It's Liam's hope that once they find whoever is sending these letters, they will be able to put a stop to it and Emily can —for the first time in over a year—take a well-deserved rest. But he also has to admit it's self-serving as well. She has had to face so much trauma in her life that she has difficulty connecting with people. He doesn't want to pressure her, but he does want to help remove any obstacles in her way—not that she'd ever let him. She's one of the most bull-headed and stubborn people he's ever met, almost to her own detriment.

Regardless, Liam has spent the past two days in the Highland County Records Office, making friends with the ninety-year-old man running the desk and using the days to comb through property and birth records. He managed to find Emily's mom's record of birth in nineteen-sixty-two. He also found information on her parents and the location of their family home. What he can't seem to find, however, are any death records. As far as he can tell, both of Emily's grandparents are still alive, and living in the house that sits at the end of the dirt road he's been staring at for the better part of six hours. He arrived here early this morning, before five a.m. and has been sitting in the same spot ever since. But there's been no traffic in or out, no indication anyone has come or gone from the home.

Something tugs at him to investigate. He's always had a natural curiosity, something that's served him well as both a detective and a special agent with the FBI.

It's also almost gotten him killed.

But right now, that's secondary. His primary focus is finding out who is sending these letters and why. If both Emily's grandparents are still alive, it's possible they could be the ones sending them, though he can't figure out why. And why would they send letters to Dr. Archer as well? None of it makes sense, but that's exactly what Liam is here to uncover. And if he can find an answer to this mystery and uncover the culprit, then maybe everyone can go back to living their lives without this madness hanging over them.

He thinks back to his own grandparents, back in Ireland. They were kind, but also the type of people that had been weathered by life, much like this community. But he can't see them writing cryptic letters and then delivering them to him in some elaborate scheme to get him to come home. Liam isn't even sure that's the writer's goal. In fact, the letters—to him anyway—come across almost like some kind of penance. Like whoever is writing them needs for Emily to know something, though what that is remains a mystery to everyone.

Why do people have to be so complicated, he thinks. Why not just come out and say what you mean, instead of going to all this trouble? That will be the first question he asks when he gets up ʾ to the house to speak to someone. Well, no, his *first* question will be to determine if they are the ones sending the letters. According to Emily, she isn't aware of any living family on her mother's side. At the very least maybe he can open a door for her to connect back with her grandparents.

Liam puts the Jeep in gear and turns down the driveway, taking it slow. He spots the house in the distance, sitting at the end of the road and in the middle of a field that hasn't been tended in a while. The home is old, plank wood for siding and looks like it's falling apart. A single electrical line runs along poles parallel to the dirt road until it reaches the home. The field beyond looks like it's full of overgrown wheat, but he can't be sure. Farming was never his strong suit.

Liam pulls up to the house, parking directly in front of it, since there is no garage or dedicated parking area. What little grass that looks like it grows on the property is dead from winter. When he steps out of the vehicle, it crunches under his boot. Liam gazes at the home a minute, looking for any signs of life, but there are none. No movement at the windows, no voices on the air. The place has the distinct feel of having been abandoned for some time. A small barn sits off to the side of the property, about a hundred yards from the house. But the doors are open and part of the roof has caved in. He's not sure it's even safe to enter.

Clearly, he's made a mistake somewhere. Even if this was the home of Emily's grandparents, they obviously don't live here anymore. It doesn't look like anyone has lived here in at least thirty years or more. But Liam is nothing if not a little bull-headed himself, so he closes the door to his Jeep and heads up the porch steps. The wood bends under his weight, but not enough that he believes he's in any danger.

Just as he's about to knock on the door, he realizes it's already cracked, the latch either deteriorated or broken over time. He gives the door a gentle push, and it squeals on its rusty hinges, revealing the dark inside of the home.

"Hello?" Liam calls out. "Is anyone home?"

Silence. *This is a fool's errand*, he thinks. But maybe there is a clue here that will point him in the right direction. Something he can show Emily that could help—though he doesn't know how.

The home is completely furnished, though a thick layer of dust covers everything. A grandfather clock sits in the main hallway, its glass face so dirty Liam can't read the time on it anymore. It's a wonder no one has come in here to steal this stuff, or vandalize the house. But as far as he can tell, it's been untouched.

He strolls through the main floor, looking in each room and finding it much like the last: complete with furniture and decorations, abandoned at some time in the past and never touched since. He enters the living room and inspects the shelves at the far side of the wall by the fireplace. A couple of the frames have fallen over, while the rest remain standing. He wipes the dust from one to find a young couple, probably in their late twenties, with their hands on the shoulder of a little girl, no more than seven or eight. The woman is smiling, and he can just see the roundness of a baby bump beginning to take form. He assumes the girl in the photo is Emily's mother, Margaret. And the parents must be Bill and Janet Brooks. The photo is dated nineteen-sixty-nine. So Margaret would have been seven at the time. And apparently, she had a sibling on the way. Which is strange, because Liam hasn't found any records on another child being born in the family, he assumed Margaret was an only child.

Furrowing his brow, Liam removes the photograph from the frame, and puts it in his pocket. He'll need to do some more research.

It's then when he hears it, a skittering sound, like that of someone running quickly across the floor. And it has come from right underneath him.

His heart leaps into his chest and Liam pulls his service weapon, heading back for the door. There is definitely someone else in this house. But before doing anything else, he needs to call Emily and let her know what's going on.

He's not about to be ambushed again.

Chapter Twenty-Seven

"Okay, but there's a difference between being a practicing Wiccan and a broom-carrying, pointed-hat-wearing, soul-cursing witch," I say as we're driving back from the hotel after getting a fresh pair of clothes and quick showers. I was not about to go back into that room smelling like a rotting lung. I know Zara was just trying to get a rise out of me back at Hansen's office and I have to admit that my eye may have twitched once or twice when she said the word "witch". But I also know it is a very real religion that has nothing to do with anything nefarious.

Generally.

"Broom-carrying and pointed-hat-wearing, no," Zara says. "But soul-cursing?" She thinks about it a minute. "Maybe."

"Maybe?" I ask, arching an eyebrow.

"It's like anything else, there are going to be fanatics, right? People who take things too far, who believe themselves to be capable of performing…miracles. And people who believe everything they're doing is right, no matter what."

"Yeah, they're called assholes," I say.

She laughs. "I'm just saying that no matter what religion you look into, there will always be someone who thinks they're *special*, that they alone have been given the power or chosen to change the world for the better."

"And you think that's Hansen?" I ask.

"I don't know. It certainly seems like she has some strong beliefs. But would she go as far to kill people for those beliefs? I can't say."

"How much of Wiccan culture intersects with what we're dealing with? Victims that appear like they've been hunted by supernatural creatures?"

"I'm no expert," Zara says. "But I've never heard of anything like it. As far as I know those aren't typical aspects to Wiccan religion. And I'm pretty sure the Black Lagoon angle isn't in any ancient texts either."

"Still, to be sure I want to sit Hansen down and have a talk." Zara turns back toward the police station. Already the sun is getting low in the sky, and I don't want to think about what another night will bring. If we keep finding bodies with no answers, then we're going to have a serious problem on our hands.

"A talk, or a *talk*," Zara asks. She means do I want a friendly chat in Hansen's office, or do I want to pull her into an interrogation room and grill her for a few hours.

While I would love the latter, I don't think it would be very conducive. For starters, we still don't have any evidence that could directly link her to any of the murders. In fact, we still don't have anything, other than the supposition that Dr. Whiteside was performing assisted suicides and was coordinating with Cameron Bright and Louis Gallagher.

So it will have to be a "nice" chat. At least until we can find some evidence that links her to our killer or killers. I wish Zara had left me in the room and gone after the unsub who tried to cut my throat; at least then we'd have a suspect we could charge. But there's also the chance they could have gotten the drop on her out in those woods. Neither of us is at the top of our game lately, something that has been on my mind a lot over the past few days.

When we finally get back to the morgue Gallagher's body is no longer on display and the scene has been cleaned up from earlier. I check the coolers and his name is listed on the one right beside Phillips, which must mean Hansen has already finished her autopsy. All the computers are off as well, so Zara and I make our way back to Dr. Hansen's office, where we find her typing on her computer, her face only inches from the screen.

I clear my throat as she obviously hasn't noticed us yet and she looks up, furrowing her brow. But the look is gone almost as fast as it arrived and she adopts a more neutral face before raising her hand in a small wave. "Good afternoon. I'm afraid I'm not quite finished with the autopsy results yet."

"Were you able to determine what the liquid in his lungs was?" I ask.

"I sent it off to the lab for analysis. It looked like tar to me, but it was obviously much too fluid for that." She turns back and continues typing on her computer.

I turn, taking in the wall scroll hung on the wall to my left depicting the phases of the moon. It looks old, like it's been handed down for a few generations. "That's an impressive scroll."

"Thanks," she replies without looking up.

"Is that a pentacle?" Zara asks, pointing to the five-sided star with a circle around it in the center of the scroll.

Hansen takes a deep breath and stops typing, like she's gearing herself up for a battle. "Listen, I know you don't share my beliefs." She shoots Zara a quick look that hints at nasty but it's so brief I barely catch it. "You don't need to make small talk about my décor. I'll have the report to you in another hour, at the most."

I take a seat across from her without invitation, causing her brows to furrow again and this time I catch that flash of anger. If I were a betting woman, I'd be willing to say she doesn't like FBI agents very much. And she has done a good job at hiding it. What I don't know is if that's because I haven't believed any of her wild theories or if there's another reason. But if her anger at me is the reason someone is targeting FBI agents in this city, then I'm going to have a difficult time squaring that later. But for right now, I just need the truth.

Zara takes the seat beside me, a pleasant smile on her lips, which only seems to frustrate Hansen more.

"Let's be clear," I say. "I don't believe any of your theories. Not for a minute. But that doesn't mean I think you're completely incompetent. You obviously know what you're doing, or you wouldn't still be Bellefleur's medical examiner. What I want to ask is don't you think it's a little convenient that you just happen to be the one person who can identify these attacks as...supernatural?"

"No," she says instantly. "It's the opposite. You're lucky I'm here. Any other examiner, like your poor colleague, would probably misdiagnose the cause of death. I'm assuming that's what your killer wanted." She almost has an air of superiority about her.

"You're kidding, right?" Zara asks. "These deaths were professionally staged to look as though some monster appeared out of nowhere and murdered these people. If anything, the killer is looking to further cover their tracks by having *you* proclaim the victims couldn't have possibly been killed by another human."

Hansen sits back in her chair, glaring at us. "You're saying the killer is specifically preparing the bodies, so I'll mischaracterize them?"

My phone buzzes in my pocket and I see its Liam. But I'll have to call him back. I pocket it and lean forward, focusing all my energy on Hansen. "I think the killer is preying on the superstitions of this town in order to induce panic. We've been lucky it hasn't been leaked to the news yet. Imagine what happens when it does. How many of the local population has some sort of belief about *something*, whether that be spirits, voodoo, the power of nature, or creatures of the night? Can you tell me without a doubt that some people won't try to take the law into their own hands?"

She glares at us for a moment. "To what end? What is the killer hoping to accomplish?"

"Chaos? Pandemonium? Or maybe they're just doing everything they can to cover their tracks, either so they don't get caught or so they can keep killing. Whatever they're doing, they're using your own superstitions against you." I hadn't meant to go this hard on her, but for the first time since I've met her Hansen is coming across as combative, and when I get pushed I tend to push back, no matter who it is.

"Do you believe in vampires? Werewolves?" I ask.

"I do," she says, her voice unwavering. Her beliefs aren't just on the surface. They are deeply held.

"But that's not typical for Wiccans, is it?" Zara asks.

She swallows. "Not usually. There aren't any hard and fast rules to Wicca. This isn't Catholicism. People tend to believe what they want to believe. I've always known there were things out there that couldn't be explained by science. That dark creatures walked our world, hiding in plain sight. I just never had the evidence to prove it. Now, I finally do." She sighs, closes her eyes and winces before leveling her gaze at us again. "I'll admit, maybe I want it to be true too much. You know when you're a kid and the world seems infinite and magical? And then as you grow up more and more of that is stripped away until you're left with nothing but harsh reality? I don't want to live in that world."

"Rani," I say, leaning even farther forward. "You can't just pretend the real world doesn't exist."

"I know," she replies, like I'm a fool for even suggesting that. "But I'm also not so arrogant to assume we already know everything there is to know about every living creature on this planet. No one took Galileo seriously either, at first. And now the man is heralded as one of the great scientific minds in all of humanity. Imagine what will happen to the first person who discovers that vampires are in fact, real. The first person who opens up that door for everyone else to walk through. I'm willing to take that risk."

"And you're willing to let that door slam in your face when you're proven wrong?" I ask.

"*If* I'm proven wrong, yes."

I take a deep breath and sit back. It seems like there is no getting through to her. Though I'm not sure what I expected, coming in here. People's beliefs are held close to their hearts. Changing them is more difficult than almost anything imaginable, because often people build their entire identities around those beliefs. That, at least, unites all of us. It's just the specifics that get in the way.

Zara looks over and gives me a subtle shake of her head. We're not going to get anything going at her directly. We need another angle. And I'm not sure how long we can keep this up before she tells us to get out.

"Dr. Hansen, do you believe in suicide?" I ask. I'm hoping that by coming out of the blue like this I can hopefully shock an answer out of her.

Her eyes go wide. "No. Not at all," she says, emphatic.

"Why not?"

"Because it's an exercise in futility," she says. "Whatever demons you're battling in this life you're sure to face in the next. It's only by calming your spirit and allowing yourself to live in peace will you transition to a life free of regret, pain and misery. Suicide just…extends the pain. Makes it harder for people."

"So then you'd be against anyone practicing or assisting with the practice?" I ask.

"Yes, of course," she replies. "Beyond the spiritual, I don't approve of anyone taking their own life willingly. Life is such a precious, rare gift. It shouldn't be squandered."

"What about in instances of say extreme pain…or suffering?"

She hesitates a moment and I can't tell if I see a flicker of recognition in her eyes or not. If Hansen is our killer, I may have just played our hand. We know someone is going after people who are assisting in suicide for the infirm. But Hansen is particularly skilled at hiding her micro expressions, not something many people are able to do. I have to assume she's doing it consciously, which means she probably has something to hide. Then again, given her position in the community, maybe she's used to hiding her true self. "There are medications that can help alleviate pain and suffering," she finally says. "It's no excuse."

I lean forward again. "Then you would have a problem if you found out someone was planning on committing suicide. No matter the reason."

She sucks her lips between her teeth, hesitating again. I don't like how shifty she's being. She certainly isn't doing herself any favors as far as our suspicion goes. "I would."

I push a little more. "Are you currently aware of anyone in such a position?"

"Agent, I don't think I like this line of questioning," she says. "I'd like to know what this is all about."

"It's about whether you can do your job without your bias sneaking in," I say.

She puffs herself up, like I've just slapped her. "I think you should leave. I have a lot of work to get to and frankly you are keeping me from it."

We both stand. Even though she didn't come right out and admit it, she gave away a little too much. It's not enough for an arrest or even a search, but at least it's a start. "We'll let you finish, then. I look forward to your final report."

As Zara and I leave I swear I hear the doctor muttering

something else under her breath but it's much too soft for me to make out any of the words.

"Think that was smart?" Zara asks as we make our way down the hall back to the station side of the building. "If she's our suspect then she knows we're on to her."

"Good," I say. "Maybe the added pressure will force her to make a mistake. We need a break here, and so far we don't have much. If we want the truth, we'll have to take a few risks." My phone buzzes again and I remember I need to call Liam back. This is probably him, trying again.

"Slate," I say, answering.

"Emily, it's Kane. I think we have something on Agent Phillips' killer."

Chapter Twenty-Eight

"GLAD TO SEE you haven't accrued any more injuries since this morning," Sandel says after opening the door to their room. Despite normally being a very stoic individual, I've been trying to encourage him to lighten up lately. I guess this is his poor attempt at doing so.

"Very funny," I say, and he steps out of the way. Inside the hotel room he and Agent Kane have set up what looks like a mobile lab. One of the beds is covered in equipment while the desk has four different white blocks on it, all of them which look like they're made of plaster or something similar. A large microscope sits next to the floor and Agent Kane is sitting on the other bed, with one laptop on her lap and another by her side.

"Wow," Zara says. "Great setup."

"We came prepared," Sandel says. "Given the nature of the case."

"Is that...a blood centrifuge?" I ask, pointing to the circular device that's on top of an errant suitcase.

"You never know what you might need in a case like this. Plus, all of this is from my own storage unit. None of it is FBI property, so Wallace can't balk."

"I didn't know you collected medical equipment," Zara says, sitting down beside Agent Kane.

"It's mostly just stuff I've accumulated over the years. Some of it from back in med school."

I manage to contain my surprise; I had no idea she'd been to med school. She looks up from the monitor and smiles when she sees my face. "I dropped out in my third year. It was ' too much. Thought it would be much more exciting to work the criminal element instead."

I turn to Sandel. "Any helpful background skills you'd like to provide?"

"My skill is experience," he says, clasping his hands behind his back. So much for getting him to relax.

"Anyway, we've been taking a close look into the attacks on you and Agent Phillips. And we think we might have found something helpful." Kane sets the laptop to the side and gets up around Zara, heading for the desk. She moves one of the plaster blocks, turning it over to reveal what looks like a shoe cast, though there's no detail.

"Is this from outside Phillips' window?" I ask. She nods. "Lowe told me the ground was too soft to get a solid cast."

"He was only partially right. While we might not have been able to pull any specific details from the site like shoe type or depth, I was able to get a general size off the prints. I took a few just to be sure." She turns over a second one. "Both of these came from outside Phillips' window. And these two came from outside yours." She takes the next two and turns them both over to reveal the soft impression underneath.

"They all look identical," I say.

She nods. "More or less. I managed to get an approximate size, which was a women's size six. There's about a ten percent margin for error, but I'm pretty confident. We went back and checked all the prints that were left and they all conformed to the same parameters."

I turn to Zara. "What size shoe does Hansen wear?"

"I—"

"Already checked," Kane says. "We pulled a print off the linoleum in the morgue. The doctor wears a seven and a half."

"How can you be sure it was her print?" I ask.

"Because we happened to see what shoes she was wearing," Sandel replies. "And Agent Kane found they were a match."

"Don't worry," Kane says, leaning in. "We were inconspicuous. We did our best not to make waves or make ourselves targets."

"So then this pretty much eliminates the possibility of Hansen being the one who attacked Emily."

"Correct," Kane says. "According to your description, we're looking for someone who is probably very athletic. These impressions weren't very deep either, despite softness of the mud. Odds are they were running very fast to get away, but still that leaves evidence behind. I'd guess your attacker was no more than a hundred and twenty pounds. At most."

I shake my head. "Impossible. There's no way a hundred-and-twenty-pound person was able to get that knife—"

Zara clears her throat, reminding me that I may not be in top fighting shape. Normally I could take someone like that down with little to no problem. Even if they had some kind of combat or martial arts training. Usually, it's the bigger guys I have to worry about, and it's all about using their own weight and size against them. But it isn't often someone of this size gets the drop on me...and almost succeeds.

I scowl. "Okay, fine. So we know we're looking for a Caucasian female, five-four, hundred and twenty pounds, with crimson eyes—most likely contacts—and size six shoes. Does that about cover it?"

"Sounds like a good start to me," Kane says.

"And you're sure the same person that attacked me went after Phillips?"

"The shoe prints seem to indicate as much," she replies.

"Elliott and I went over that site with a fine-tooth comb. The killer didn't leave so much as a hair behind, which makes tracking them down nearly impossible."

"She also probably didn't expect me to see her face. Well, what little I managed to make out. Is there any way to track manufacturers of colored contacts?"

"Not anymore," Zara says. "Maybe twenty years ago before the start of online shopping. But nowadays you can order those things from almost anywhere. I got a pair of purple ones one time to complement my hair, but they just ended up irritating my eyes after a day or two. Are you sure they were contacts? Because people also do permanent eye pigmentation. That would be a lot easier to narrow down."

"Wait," Kane says. "How do they change their eye pigmentation?"

"Oh, it's really cool," Zara says. "First they cut a little hole right in your cornea and then they shoot a laser down in there and fill the space in front of the iris with a new color, so it's like painting a wall, except, you know, it's your *eye*."

Kane shudders, hunching up her shoulders. "Nope. No way, not for me, thank you." I have to agree. Messing with your eyes is asking for nothing but trouble.

"Sandel? Maybe want to change those dark browns to a sky blue? Or even a forest green?" Zara teases.

"I'll never understand the desire for people to undergo cosmetic surgeries," he says. "It seems like the risk is never equal to the reward."

"Says someone who is completely comfortable with who they are," I say. "But not everyone is lucky enough to be in your position. Some people know they won't feel like their true selves unless they go through some changes. Though, I'm not sure anyone could make that argument for red eyes."

"Maybe instead of looking for the source, look for groups of people who might be into that kind of thing," Kane suggests. "There have to be a few pockets of people, even here in Bellefleur, who are into body modification."

Zara jumps up. "That's a very good point. You are just full of good info today, Nadia."

Her cheeks flush and she turns back to her computer. "Just thinking the problem out."

"It may be worth a look, too bad you don't still have your blue hair," I tell Zara.

"I know! How many times did I have to argue with Janice that it could be a benefit? But no, it was all, *blend in* this and *don't make a scene* that." She crosses her arms. "I tell you one thing though, as soon as I'm back on intelligence permanently, I'm going hot pink."

"Maybe I'll join you," I laugh. "Good work guys, thanks for getting on this so quickly. I think we can say without a doubt now that our killers are not one and the same. But just because she couldn't have come after me, doesn't mean Dr. Hansen isn't still involved with the other three deaths." I quickly fill Kane and Sandel in on our conversation with Hansen earlier. Sandel takes care to point out that while she didn't do herself any favors, she didn't incriminate herself either.

"While we investigate this other angle, would you mind looking into Hansen's schedule for us?" I ask Agent Kane. "Every time we see her now she seems like she's just rushing back from somewhere and I want to know what has her so frazzled. But primarily I'm looking to see if she had the opportunity to go after each of the three victims."

"Sure, we can do that," Kane replies, nodding to Sandel. "Still keep a low profile?"

"Until we can be sure of who came after me and Phillips, definitely," I say. I'm still not convinced that someone in the department didn't leak something, intentionally or not. Either way, someone knew we were here and where we were staying before they struck. That information shouldn't have been easy to come by.

As we split off again and Zara and I head out, I can't help but feel a sense of foreboding about all of this. Someone is going to a lot of trouble to make their point, and they've already proven they're not shy about coming after federal agents in order to do it.

I just hope we're quick enough to see them coming next time, before it's too late.

Chapter Twenty-Nine

LIAM HAS WALKED the property three times already. The sun has begun to set in the sky and despite his attempts to call Emily, she has yet to pick up. He's not even sure they've gone through because his texts certainly haven't. Service out here is virtually non-existent. Part of him wants to leave, to round up some backup and come back, but he knows the moment he pulls away, whoever is in that house is bound to run out and possibly disappear forever. It may just be some kids who are messing around, or some homeless person who has decided to make the house their personal sanctuary now that the original owners are no longer around. The footsteps he heard were quick, light. Not the slow, plodding steps of someone of advanced age.

Then again, this was what the writer of the letters wanted, wasn't it? For Emily to come back to where it all started? So there is a good possibility the person he's looking for is running around in that basement. Liam just has to go in there and find out what's going on.

The problem with blending into a town where no one is supposed to know who you are or what you're doing there is you can't call for backup when you need it. He'd have to go back into town, explain himself to the local Sheriff, and return to the house with some additional units. But that just leaves him with the same problem. Whoever is in the basement could be long gone by then. And they obviously aren't supposed to be there, otherwise they would have answered when he called out.

Liam makes sure the safety on his service weapon is engaged and heads back to the house, this time approaching from the back. An old screen door sits at the top of three steps, but Liam has also noticed a pair of doors set at an angle to the back of the house. They're cellar doors, and he would proceed down into them directly from here, were it not for a large chain and lock holding the doors tight.

He approaches the door and takes a deep breath, centering himself. Emily would probably kill him if she knew what he was doing right now. But they can't lose this opportunity, not if they want to put an end to all this. He opens the back door, which makes a different kind of squeal from the front door and finds himself in the home's small kitchen. Linoleum floors that are peeling at the corners stretch out under his feet, but the home is dead silent. The difference with the front of the house is the kitchen isn't covered in dust. In fact, it feels like it's been used recently, though he can't say exactly why. He knows he's announced his presence, so there's no point in attempting to be stealthy.

"Whoever is in this house, identify yourself, this is the FBI!" he calls out. But there's no response. No sound whatsoever except for the occasional creak from the house settling. He spots the living room where he removed the picture. It's possible he imagined the sound in the basement, which, if it turns out to be the case, he'll feel pretty stupid. A door sits closed in the hallway off to his right. He approaches and opens it, finding a flight of old stairs that leads down into the dark basement. The smell of mold hits his nose, telling him there's a good chance the basement has taken on water at some point in the recent past. But it's completely black down there; if someone was there, how could they see anything?

Liam reaches over and flips the switch next to the door, but nothing happens. Unsurprisingly, no one is paying the electric bill. Which makes the possibility that someone is still down there even more remote. He pulls out his phone and turns on the flashlight, using it to see down the old stairs. They look more brittle than the ones out at the porch, little more than planks nailed atop wooden slats that lead down. At the base of the stairs he can at least see the floor is concrete.

"Hello?" he calls out again. "Anyone there?"

Silence.

Steeling himself and cursing at the same time, Liam slowly descends into the basement, taking each step carefully. There's no telling if any of them could have deteriorated enough to break under his weight, but they hold him until he reaches the floor. He sweeps the light back and forth in both directions, but can only see so far. His weapon remains in his other hand, though he keeps it at his side. He's not usually one who panics, but usually he's also not one to enter into a dark basement alone. The last time he was in a place like this, his life had been on the line...or at least that's what the assassin had wanted him to think. He still doesn't know if her threats on his life were ever serious, all he knew was he was tied to a chair in a cinder block room with no way out. Part of him thought he'd die in that room, and being down in this basement isn't doing much to assuage his PTSD from that experience.

Liam turns to the left first, following the wall with the light until he comes to an old, rusted water heater beside an old air conditioning unit. Both have seen better days and he doubts either works. Red rust stains the concrete around both units and the smell of old water and mold is stronger over here.

He turns back and heads in the other direction, passing the stairs again until he comes to what looks like a partition wall, with a door. He's not sure if the wall was part of the original house, it looks slightly newer, but is still old. Along the base of the wall, water stains creep up to about five inches, though everything seems dry now. He almost feels like he should knock, but as far as he can tell, this part of the house is as abandoned as the rest.

Hesitating a half-second, Liam opens the door with the hand still holding the phone, to find himself in a room that's been partially finished. Another linoleum floor covers the concrete, and the walls have all been covered in wood paneling. And an old, red recliner chair sits in the corner, across from a TV. On a hunch he flips the light switch next to the door and the overhead florescent lights come on. Huh. The bulb at the stairs must have just been burned out.

Then he sees it.

All along the wall are photographs on top of photographs of Emily. Most that look like screenshots from various news interviews she's either given, or has been a part of over the past few months. Liam immediately spots some of the largest ones are when she was standing behind Janice during the press conference after they had found and dismantled the Organization. Because they're zoomed in on her, the photos are a little fuzzy. And most are haphazardly taped to the wall.

Below them is a desk, covered with articles of cases Emily has been working on; including the one from Liam's own hometown: Stillwater. The headline reads *Killer off the streets thanks to FBI working with local police*. The case where he first met Emily. The case that made him want to become an FBI agent. Off to the side of the desk are a stack of blank papers. Normally, he wouldn't think anything of them. But he recognizes the cream color: they're the exact same shape and size of the letters Emily has been receiving. Whoever has been contacting her, has been doing it from here.

Liam doesn't touch anything; he knows better than to contaminate the scene. But he's going to need a full unit out here to begin gathering this evidence. He begins taking pictures of the desk, as well as all the images that have been hung up. Someone is definitely keeping track of her cases, though he doesn't get the sense that this is anything friendly. These images haven't been framed in a loving manner, like the pictures upstairs. Instead, all of them are haphazardly placed, like the person who captured them was in a hurry to get up as many as they could. A frenzy, even.

Just as he's about to pull out a pair of gloves and begin going through the papers on the desk, an acrid smell catches in his nose. It's not the smell of mold that permeates everything down here, no, it's something much more…volatile.

Liam rushes out of the room where the smell is even stronger. *Kerosene*, he thinks, his heart dropping. But where could it be coming from?

As if to answer his unspoken question, there is a flicker of light at the top of the stairs, and suddenly the entire staircase is engulfed in flames, causing Liam to stagger back. The fire lights up the entire basement and he can see clearly now this place is little more than a repository for junk and old furniture. But what's more distressing is there don't seem to be any windows, or any way he can see to get out. The staircase is out of the question; he'd die before he could reach the top and the fire at the bottom is only spreading. Someone must have poured the kerosene down the stairs, allowing it to pool while he was in the other room.

The fire is spreading quickly, and Liam is already having trouble breathing; the fire sucking all the oxygen out of the room. He looks around, knowing if he doesn't get out of here quick, he'll cook to death at the same time he asphyxiates from smoke inhalation. Then he remembers the cellar doors. It takes him a second to orient himself before he heads for the low stairs that lead to the doors themselves. He hesitates for a brief second, thinking he should go back for the evidence in the room, before the fire spreads too fast and cuts him off from that part of the basement.

He curses again, coughing this time and runs to the concrete stairs that lead to old wooden doors. He pushes up as hard as he can, knowing full well they're chained from the other side, but trying anyway. The air is already getting thin and every breath he takes produces nothing but coughs. Liam struggles with the door, his phone still in his hand as he hits the doors over and over with his shoulder.

The fire threatens closer, advancing on him like a roman legion, cutting off any possible exit as it searches out a source of fresh oxygen. Liam continues to focus his efforts on breaking the old, rusted lock and chain. It's his only hope. But the fire is coming too fast.

Gritting his teeth, Liam shoves one more time, hoping it's enough, but the doors barely move. He looks into the fire, fear taking over, but he doesn't stop. And yet, he knows this is the end. He hopes wherever Emily is, she can feel him reaching out to her. Because he knows he'll never hold her hand again.

As the fire licks the edge of his boots, the door finally begins to budge. Liam pushes with everything he has left.

The fire advances, unrelenting.

Chapter Thirty

ZARA and I spend a good portion of the rest of the evening driving around. It's Friday night, a perfect time to go out looking for people who are obsessed with "the darkness" as Zara says. She's coming back into herself a little more, and I'm not sure if she realizes it or not, but I'm not about to say anything again. The last thing I want to do is remind her of her trauma. But I hope she's at least regaining some of her former confidence.

"If you were a goth, where would you go to hang out?" Zara asks as we drive. We've cracked the windows to let some of the air blow in as everything tends to cool down at night.

"I dunno, the *mall?*" I say, somewhat sarcastically. I haven't encountered anyone who embraces goth culture since high school, though I know it's an entire subculture in some cities, and especially in Europe. But it's not something I encounter in my day-to-day life, so it never really crosses my mind.

"I'm not sure this town has a mall," she replies. "But I bet they have a couple of clubs." She shoots me a wicked smile.

"No way, I am not getting dressed up in one of your crazy outfits just to get into some EDM nightmare," I say, laughing.

"Cool your jets," she says. "I'm not gonna make you dress up. But you do have to pretend to be my sub."

"Your *what*?"

"Don't worry about it, I just need to find a pet store. You need a collar and a leash."

I grab hold of her arm. "You wouldn't dare."

"Hmm, I wouldn't dare? Or would I?" she teases. "Plus we need something to cover up that bandage on your neck. I think a spiked collar would work perfectly."

"Zara—"

She bursts out laughing before I can say anything else. "You are too easy sometimes."

"That's because I know you'd do it if I let you!" I say.

Her laughter dies off. "Well, maybe once upon a time. But don't worry, I think we can probably get in with our badges… or, I guess *my* badge. Have you told Wallace yet?"

"No, and I'm not about to," I say. Losing my badge was bad enough, but my service weapon as well? "When we get back I'm going straight to Janice. Maybe she can help before Wallace finds out."

"It's not like you could have stopped them," she says, pulling the car to the side of the road. "But he'll probably pitch a fit anyway."

"I'm sure you're right," I say. "What are you doing?"

"Gonna find a club. Maybe someone there knows someone who likes to wear crimson-colored eyes."

"But no leashes," I say, my voice stern.

"That's right, no leashes," she replies, tapping away on her phone. "Here, this looks promising. As far as I can tell it's the only club of its kind in town. *Shadowscape*."

"That does sound promising."

It only takes us fifteen minutes to get to the club's address, but the alley where it's supposedly located is empty when we drive by. Because the alley isn't wide enough for more than one car, Zara finds a place to park on one of the side streets and we make our way back to the address, looking for anything that might clue us into where the club is located.

"This is a real place, right? It's not just an online club or something?"

"No, real place. Real reviews, real photos," she says, looking at her phone. "I just don't…" She trails off as we both search the area. As far as I can tell, we're standing in an empty alleyway, with brick buildings on both sides. There is a small sidewalk barely wide enough for one person, and the alley itself is made of old cobblestones.

"Wait a second," I say, something catching my eye. I bend down and notice a symbol very much like what we saw in Dr. Hansen's office etched into one of the bricks. "Isn't that a pentacle?"

"Yeah," Zara says, bending down to look. She reaches out to touch the image only for the brick to move. Beside us there's a thump, and part of the brick wall swings in, revealing a hidden hallway.

"That's not creepy," I say.

"No, it's *cool*," she replies. "A hidden entrance. C'mon, we gotta see what's inside."

"Z, maybe we should…" I begin to protest but she's too excited and takes my hand, pulling me along with her. The hallway inside is dark, but there are purple strip lights along the floor which tell us which way to go. Behind us I hear the false brick door close, effectively trapping us in. Normally I wouldn't be too apprehensive, but I'm a little more on edge since the attack, especially considering I'm not armed.

Somewhere in the distance I hear the thumping of a bass, though I feel like the hallway is pitched down, like we're being led underground. But Zara isn't being shy about heading in, she turns a corner and we find ourselves looking at another door. This one is similar to the metal door that separates the morgue from the police section back at the Bellefleur Station.

It has a simple lever which Zara pushes down, and the door opens.

We're hit by a wall of sound, blasting heavy metal music from an artist I don't recognize. But it's so loud I try calling out to Zara and can't even hear myself yell. A woman with spiked blonde hair stands just inside the door, next to a room that seems to be made up of entire of wire cage. Inside sit two more people on computers, and it looks like they might be controlling the volume and sound.

The woman pushes her open hand to us but Zara and I only stare at each other, unsure what she wants. She points to the sign above her head which states it is thirty dollars per cover. Zara rolls her eyes and shows the woman her badge. She glares at us a minute before finally letting us pass. Beyond her is a staircase which leads down to the main floor below, which is packed *full* of people, most of them sweaty and jumping to the music. It looks as though a makeshift mosh pit of people have formed close to the front of the room where a small stage supports a DJ in front of a couple of turntables and mixing equipment.

There's also a bar opposite the stage, which is also packed, with two bartenders doing their best to keep up. All along the stairway that leads down to the pit people are leaning up against the rails or sitting on them, watching the action. More than a few are too engaged with each other to even notice us or anything else going on around them. And absolutely *everyone* is dressed head to toe in black, though some are showing a fair amount more skin than the others.

"How are we supposed to find anyone in here?" I yell at the top of my lungs.

"Show them a picture?" she shouts back.

I roll my eyes and pull up a picture of someone with crimson eyes and begin showing it to people we pass. At first they seem confused, until Zara flashes her badge, but then they all begin shaking their heads "no". I don't feel like we're going to make a lot of progress in here, but Zara seems determined, so we make our way down into the main glut of people.

There's barely enough room to move without being crushed by everyone so I have to be careful as we push our way through until we get to the bar at the back. On the way I continue to show people the image but most just ignore me. I am *way* out of my element here. What I do notice is the high number of people with some kind of body modification, whether it be as simple as a couple of extra piercings, nose rings, or even elongated ear lobes. But a couple have even more extreme modifications, including one guy with a split tongue, which he seems to enjoy showing off, while another girl's face is practically *covered* in dark tattoos.

"Yo!" Zara yells, banging on the bar with one hand while waving her badge with the other, trying to catch the bartender's attention. Thankfully there are less speakers back here which means I can actually hear something, though it's still like trying to scream over a jet engine.

"Whaddaya want?" A woman at the bar yells back. Her red hair is tied back in thick dreadlocks and she sports tattoos down both of her exposed arms. She's wearing what looks like a black leather vest designed to accentuate her chest, probably an attempt to encourage tipping.

"We're looking for anyone here who wears red contacts or even permanently changed their eye color," she says. I show her the picture, even though it's not of our actual suspect.

"That could be half the people in here," she yells back. "Red is a popular color."

"She'll be on the smaller side, athletic," I say. "About my height."

"White girl?" the bartender yells. We nod. "Sounds like one of the Ravens."

"Who are the Ravens?" I ask.

"Just this group that likes to think their shit don't stink.

They show up in here every now and again, but usually keep to themselves. Don't like interacting with anyone else."

"Then why come?" Zara asks.

The bartender shrugs. "Don't know, don't care. They order drinks, they pay for them. That's as far as I go."

"Are they here now?" I ask, looking around.

"Haven't seen them tonight. They don't show up every weekend. Only sometimes."

"Do you know their names? How many are in this group?" I ask.

"Usually see four of 'em, but I dunno who they are. We don't check IDs at the door, not that kind of place."

"Isn't that required for you to keep your liquor license?" Zara asks.

"Hey, you want to bring that up to Midnite, be my guest," she says. "Look, I got people waitin'." We nod and she goes back to serving the rest of the customers. Speaking of which, the patrons here seem to have given us a wide berth. I no longer feel like I'm about to be crushed. Instead, there's a circle around us of about two feet where people have moved away.

"Looks like we're not going to get much else," I say.

Zara gives the place a longing look, then relents. I can tell a place like this really energizes her; it's the kind of atmosphere she's used to thriving in. At least, it was before everything with Magus. I bet this is the first time she's been to a club since everything went down.

"Do you want to stay for a drink?" I ask.

She shakes her head. "Nah, we should probably go." We find an exit near the back right which leads us to another set of stairs up, taking us to a different door clearly stating it is an exit only and there is no re-entry from this point. Zara gives the dance floor one final look, then pushes through the exit as the sounds of Rob Zombie's *Living Dead Girl* reverberate through the air.

Chapter Thirty-One

WITH NOTHING else to go on, Zara and I head back to the hotel for the night. But as soon as we pull into the parking lot my phone buzzes, notifying me of a new email. It's from Agent Kane, showing a detailed list of Hansen's schedule for the entire week.

"Damn," I say, reading over the list.

"What is it?"

"Looks like Hansen was on duty at the police station when Dr. Whiteside was killed."

"Is there visual confirmation of that?" Zara asks.

"No, just a clock-in on her work computer and the system scanning her badge. But that's pretty conclusive, wouldn't you say?"

"Probably," she relents, getting out of the car. "I'm getting real tired of not making any progress here, Em."

"Me too," I say. "*Ravens*. Could they have a more generic name?"

"I'm going to grab a couple of winks and then I'll get started on social media in the morning," she says as we head in through the lobby. "Odds are if they're young-ish girls they're on at least one of the platforms."

"Yeah, but I'm not sure it fits. Traditionally young women aren't a good fit for a serial killer profile."

"Then again," Zara says, pushing the elevator button. "We are in the land of the strange down here."

I concede the point as we make our way back to our room. Once inside, both of us are in our pajamas and our respective beds in less than ten minutes. It has been one long-ass day and I'm exhausted. But as I'm trying to sleep I can't seem to turn my mind off and end up turning over half a dozen times only to find myself more awake than when I laid down. Across from me, Zara is sound asleep and I can't help but wonder if she has some Melatonin stashed in her bag somewhere.

I think about checking, then abandon the idea and decide that if I can't sleep, I can at least be useful. I can already hear Dr. Frost in the back of my head telling me I need more *balance* in my life but balance has never been my strong suit.

As soon as I sit down and open my computer I almost curse at the screen remembering Liam called earlier and I never called him back. He didn't leave a message, which is strange, but it might have been something that was too sensitive to leave over voicemail. He also didn't email or text, which means it really probably is pretty important. I take a second and slip out into the hallway so I won't wake Zara. Unsurprisingly, my call goes straight to voicemail. He's probably asleep by now.

"Hey," I say. "Sorry I missed your call. It's been a little crazy here. Give me a call tomorrow when you wake up, I should be around. Kay, sleep good. Love you." I end the call and hold the phone to my chest for a moment. I don't know why, but I have a strange feeling in the pit of my stomach. It's probably just frustration about this case.

I slip back inside and return to the list we got from Loving Hearts. There are forty-six names on the list, and I start at the beginning, doing a background search on each one. Whatever this is, it all points back to the nursing home and Dr. Whiteside's operation there. I'm not ready to narrow the list down to just the names that coincide with payments in Cameron Bright's bank account just yet, because I can't afford to cut corners, not right now. I need to do this right.

As I'm working I hear Zara turn over a couple of times, but she doesn't completely wake up. She does mumble a couple of times in her sleep though, and I'm sure I hear the name *Theo*. I have to bite my lip to keep from giggling, and instead try to focus on the work in front of me.

It's slow going at first, and the first eight names aren't anything special. I can find nothing on any of them that connects them back to anything to do with the case. As far as I can tell, they were just old and died at the nursing home. Number nine, however, is the first name on the list which happens to coincide with one of the payments to Cameron Bright. A Mr. Willard Chess, originally a resident of England who moved to the United States in the fifties and spent most of his life as a public school teacher. He was diagnosed with pancreatic cancer eight months before his death and only given four to live. So I guess it's no surprise he died when he did, but the paperwork would suggest that Dr. Whiteside paid him a visit on the night of his death as there was a deposit in Cameron's account two days later, with no other deaths occurring for another week prior or after.

I wish there was someone I could ask about it. I'm sure his patient records list his primary care doctor who could probably tell me exactly what was going on with Mr. Chess, but I'm unlikely to get access to those. Not unless I can prove a connection and right now I'm still working with nothing but circumstantial evidence.

I move on, going through the next five names without incident. It continues like this for a good two hours. I'll get through a few names, then come to one we suspect is an assisted suicide, only for the details to be shrouded in the patient's file and inaccessible. I feel like I'm spinning my wheels, until I come to another one of Dr. Whiteside's "patients". Mrs. Willow Fletcher. What little information I can find on her puts her age at around ninety-two, and a lifetime resident of Bellefleur. She passed on February second, much in the same pattern the other people we suspect Dr. Whiteside was involved with. Death came during the night with no witnesses, nurses found her the following morning.

Fletcher wasn't the last patient Cameron Bright saw, but she was one of the most recent. There were only two more deaths until Cameron herself was abducted and killed. I'm about to move on, but something is sticking in my craw about this one, and I do a general search for Willow Fletcher.

What comes up are a bunch of local articles about community involvement in the sixties and seventies. Featured in the middle of the old black and white photos is Willow Fletcher herself, a woman with long, graying hair and a deep-lined face. In what few pictures I find, she's always wearing a long, oversized dress that covers her feet and arms all the way to her hands. She's also sporting what look like necklaces made of beads or some other material, and a headband of some sort. But when I look closer, I see that one of the necklaces a very familiar sigil.

"Wait a second," I say, pulling up the county records and searching through them. "Son of a—Z! Wake up!"

"Hmm?" she barely stirs.

"Wake up, I found something."

"Can't it wait? I was having a good dream."

I practically pull her from the bed. "No, it can't. I need you to look at this."

"Em, I'm really tired," she says as I sit her down in front of the computer. "What time is it anyway?"

"About one-thirty," I say. "Look, this is one of Whiteside's 'patients'."

She squints at the screen. "Willow Fletcher. Okay?"

"Now look here. According to the county records, Willow

Fletcher had a daughter in 1976. Look at the birth record."

"Rani Fletcher," she says, then her eyes widen. "Wait, Dr. Hansen?"

I nod. "Turns out Rani Fletcher married Ty Hansen in 1999. He passed in 2005, but she kept the name."

"So Dr. Hansen's mother was in Loving Hearts," Zara says.

"*And* it looks like she was one of the people who benefitted from Dr. Whiteside's…services."

She turns to me. "Motive."

"Exactly," I say.

"But she was working at the time Dr. Whiteside was killed."

I hold up a single finger. "She was *clocked in*. But unless we have video evidence of her sitting at her desk from six p.m. until eight-thirty on Wednesday night, then there's nothing to say she couldn't have slipped out, committed the murder, and come back in time to 'receive' the news and head back out there. I bet there's at least one entrance or exit on that station that doesn't have a camera watching it. And if that's the case, then I think we might have just re-identified our primary suspect."

Zara goes over to her suitcase, pulling out a fresh set of clothes. "Is it enough for an arrest warrant?"

"I don't know," I reply. "It depends on the judge and who we can find that's awake at this hour. We'll see what we can get. At the very least, it finally gives us a direct connection to Hansen." I shake my head. "I should have seen this all along. *She's* been the one setting these things up, in order to 'prove' her own theories."

"You think she's that fanatical?" Zara asks.

"I think she found out about what Dr. Whiteside, Cameron and Gallagher were up to, and decided to use it as an opportunity to 'open the door' as she called it."

"And the attack on Agent Phillips? On you?"

"Phillips was the only other person that could refute her claims," I say. "And I was the one who ordered her down here. Maybe Hansen got worried we'd find out the truth. Hired someone for the hit."

"Someone from *the Ravens*," Zara says.

I nod. "It sounds like maybe they run in similar circles. She might have already had a contact in that group. Someone she knew could do the job." I head over to my own suitcase and begin digging around for some fresh clothes.

"Should we wait until morning?" Zara asks.

"I'm afraid if we do, someone else is going to get killed. I don't know how deep this operation went, or how many people knew about it. But our killer sure seems to. Who knows how many other names are on her list. We'll wake a judge up if we have to." I pull out my phone and call Lowe.

"Detective Lowe," he says, his voice groggy.

"It's Slate. We've made a breakthrough in the case. Do you know of any federal judges in town?"

"I don't think so," he says, yawning. "I think the closest is on the other side of Lefourche County, in Greenbow."

"How far is that?" I ask.

"'bout an hour and a half at this time of night," he says.

"I might as well go back to New Orleans," I say, frustration leaking into my words.

"Whatever's easiest. What's going on? What's the breakthrough?"

"I'll tell you when we get back. Thanks." I hang up before he can ask another question. It's not that I don't trust Lowe, it's that we're dealing with an internal leak here, and I don't know where it's coming from. Right now I suspect Rani Hansen, but until I'm sure I'm not about to put us or anyone else at risk. We'll need to hit her hard and fast, especially after our illuminating conversation earlier this afternoon.

"What's the plan?" Zara asks.

"Pack a coffee. We've got a long drive ahead of us."

Chapter Thirty-Two

BY THE TIME we get the sign-off from the judge—who wasn't very happy about being woken up in the middle of the night—and get back to Bellefleur, daylight is threatening the sky. We gather Agents Kane and Sandel and the four of us make our way over to Rani Hansen's home, pulling up to the house just before six. I'd prefer to have more backup, but right now these are the only three people I trust, so it's just going to be us.

The home is isolated, at the end of a long, private road that leads deep into some overgrown trees. The driveway itself is unpaved, and mostly just dirt and mud all the way from the main road. The house itself looks old, though it seems to be maintained well. A pitched tin roof peeks out above some of the trees and a large front porch encompasses the front of the home, with stairs leading up. As best I can tell, the house sits on sets of brick or blocks of some kind, probably to keep it dry when the water rises, and the wooden beams which make up the home's siding are covered in algae and moss. The house has green shutters on each of the four windows flanking the door directly in the middle and a red brick chimney on one side. It looks at least a hundred years old if not more.

Certainly not where I would have pictured a local doctor living.

A Subaru is parked off to the side of the house and the property is surrounded by trees and marshland. I'd be willing to bet this house has been passed down through a few generations, and I'm almost certain Willow was a prior resident.

I motion for Kane and Sandel to cover the back of the house while Zara and I head for the front door. There are a few lights on inside, but curtains prevent us from spotting Rani herself. She's probably looking forward to a day off after the glut of bodies that have been through the morgue in the past week.

We climb the steps, and I don't bother worrying about if she hears us coming or not. We have a federal warrant to search the home and confiscate anything inside that might be useful to our case. I couldn't convince the judge to sign off on an arrest warrant yet, but he said to come back with solid evidence connecting Rani to the murders and he'd be willing.

I just hope she's arrogant enough to think we'd never come to her home and there's evidence for us to find.

I give the door a hard knock and step back. Zara stands ready, though her weapon is still in its holster. I'm sure by now Kane and Sandel have the back covered.

"Rani Hansen, open up. This is the FBI. We have a search warrant for your home."

After a minute without answer I bang again. I'm giving it one more minute before I start kicking this door down.

But I finally hear footsteps on the other side and a bolt slides before the door opens to reveal Rani, mug in hand and robe wrapped around her. Her hair is still disheveled, and she has her glasses on. "Agents? What's going on?"

I show her the warrant. "We need to search your property," I say. Zara rounds the woman and heads through the house until she reaches the back, where she opens the door allowing Kane and Sandel to enter. All four of us put on our gloves and go about the business of searching the home.

"Wait a second, you can't do this," she says, following me into her living room. "I haven't done anything wrong."

"Please," I say. "Stay out of our way or we will have to restrain you." She takes a few steps back and I begin looking around for anything that might connect her to the deaths of Cameron, Dr. Whiteside, or Louis Gallagher. I thought her office was full of Wicca-related materials, but it's nothing compared to her house. At the end of the living room, in front of the fireplace is a large altar-like structure, covered in candles. It doesn't look like it's been used in some time and almost functions as a piece of furniture, but it's hard to miss the symbols and runes carved into it. Next to it sits a normal-looking couch across from a TV on a stand, which is in front of some of the windows we saw from outside. The rug in the room is more like an old tapestry and shows the giant image of a crescent moon. I can hear one of the other agents rummaging around in the kitchen, but I keep my focus on anything in the living room that might be useful. But other than a large number of crystals displayed on the windowsill, I don't see much. I turn to find Hansen watching me closely, and I gingerly walk around her to continue with the rest of the house.

Sandel is in one of the back rooms, what looks like a den or library of some kind, so I leave him to it. Kane is the one in the kitchen. Zara must be upstairs rummaging around. It looks to me like Kane and Sandel have this level covered, so I head up the narrow stairs to the landing above, which splits off in two directions. One heads for a large bedroom at one end of the house, and the other leads to a closed door. Zara is in the primary bedroom rooting around, so I head to the closed door, which sports a small black cross right below the handle.

Finally. I open it, fully expecting to find a room full of equipment tying Hansen to the scene. But instead, I find myself looking at another bedroom. Except, this isn't just *any* bedroom. All the walls have been painted black and have been decorated with silver runes, though they're in an intricate pattern, almost like wallpaper. A desk sits to one side, with a laptop, along with a few knick-knacks, including a skull pencil holder. The bed is a queen and sports a purple comforter, though it appears unmade, but the headboard is opulent and is hand-carved wood. Black and gray clothes are strewn all over the floor and the closet door is open, revealing even more clothes inside. The furniture is old, but well taken care of. Beside the bed is a bookcase filled with dozens of books. Strings of lights line the walls in places, and when I flip one of the switches at the door, two candelabras attached to opposite walls come on, giving the room an ethereal glow.

I recall Dr. Hansen saying she had a daughter, though I was thinking she was younger. This room seems to belong to a teen or maybe even young adult.

My first target is the laptop, but of course its password protected. I leave it for Zara and instead begin going through the desk drawers, finding a lot of pamphlets and old books inside. These are different from the books on the bookcase. They are much older and seem like they are hand-bound. In fact, the leather on one of them feels particularly strange, and I find myself feeling the inside cover, noting that it must have been bound in a different kind of material than I've ever felt before. All I find inside are pages and pages of runes, almost like they've been written in code. But I have no way of deciphering what's inside. There are a few images, but nothing I can make any sense of, just more symbols I don't recognize. Though I do see the pentacle appear many times.

"Hey, Z," I call out.

"Yeah, what's—whoa," she says, appearing at the door. "Who gets points for the awesome room?"

"Her daughter, I presume."

"I didn't know she had a daughter." It had slipped my mind too until I opened this door, though I do recall her saying something about needing to drop her kid off one morning. I dig a little further in the desk until I get to the very bottom where I find a long, sharp knife. I gingerly pull it out. The blade itself is about eight inches long and it has a cross guard, like a sword would. The handle is made of leather just like the book, and is cross wrapped to provide extra grip. In the base of the hilt is what looks like some kind of precious gem embedded in the metal. It's red, though I don't know if it's a ruby or not.

I didn't get a great look before, but this very well could be the knife that was held to my throat.

"Get Hansen up here," I tell Zara, holding up the knife so that it catches the light. I can't see any blood anywhere on it, but that means very little. Obviously, its owner didn't want it found.

She returns a moment later with Hansen in tow, though she's no longer carrying her coffee mug. "What are you doing in Saffi's room?" she asks. When she sees the knife her eyes go wide.

"Do you recognize this?" I ask.

"No," she says. "Where did you find that? In *here*?" I point to the drawer where it came from. "I've never seen that before." Her micro expressions seem to indicate she's telling the truth, but at the moment I'm not sure I trust her. She's proven herself to be a master of her emotions.

"I'll go ahead and assume Saffi is your daughter." I hold up the strange book for her. "What about this?"

She furrows her brow. "It looks like one of my mom's old books. A lot of the stuff in this house was hers. The house has been in the family for a hundred and fifty years."

"The knife too?"

"Like I said, I've never seen that before. I don't know

where it came from." Kane and Sandel have appeared behind Zara.

I hold the knife for Agent Kane. "Can you bag this up for me?"

"Sure," she says, taking it and pulling out an evidence bag.

"Do you know what this book says?" I hold out the book for Dr. Hansen, but don't allow her to touch it.

"I never learned more than a few phrases," she admits. "But my mother was fluent."

"Did she write the book?"

"I don't think so," she says. "It's a family heirloom."

I hold it out for Sandel. "We'll need to get it translated. I'm curious as to what's in that book."

"Why?" Hansen asks. "It's just a book."

"Are you sure about that?" I ask. It seems like Hansen's daughter might be into more than her mother is aware. I point to the laptop. "Do you have the password for that?"

"No," she says, somewhat defiant. "I don't violate my daughter's privacy."

"Z," I say and she nods.

"On it." She sits down at the desk and begins working on the computer, doing what she does best. While she's working I turn back to Dr. Hansen.

"How old is your daughter, Dr. Hansen?" I ask.

"She turned twenty-three about a month ago, why?"

"Is she a practicing Wiccan too?"

"Of course," she says. "My entire family has been Wiccan. For over two-hundred years."

"I'm in," Zara says, bypassing the login screen. "What am I looking for?"

"Check her search history and all her files. I want to know what she's been working on recently." Zara works silently for a moment while we watch. She's moving through files and systems almost faster than I can keep up with. I slip a view to Hansen, though she seems more worried than distressed. Whatever her daughter is into, I'm not sure she's a part of it.

"Whoa, okay. I…uh…there's some rough stuff here, Em," Zara says. "She's been spending a lot of time on the dark web, and not doing a very good job of covering her tracks."

"The dark web, what's that?" Hansen asks.

"It's where people go to find everything illegal," Agent Sandel answers. "It's usually a haven for criminals and the mentally disturbed."

"My daughter is not mentally disturbed!" Hansen says. She's clearly frustrated now, but there is also an undercurrent of fear in her words.

"Whatcha got?" I ask Zara.

"A lot of sites about human disembowelment. Graphic sites too, with instructional pictures. There's some messed up stuff here. And it seems she was on a few chat sites, none of them good."

"What was she talking about?"

Zara turns to me. "She was looking for advice about the repercussions of killing figures of authority or the law. In other words, us."

I'd say that's enough for an arrest warrant. "Anything else?"

"Lots of discussions about how to make bodies look unnatural after death." She scans row after row of text. "And there are some suggestions here about making kills look supernatural. People are even chiming in with advice on how to pull it off."

"Son of a bitch," I say. "So we are looking at one killer. It's been her this entire time." I turn to Hansen. "Where is your daughter now?"

"I can't believe this," Dr. Hansen says, spite leaking into her words. "This can't be true. Not Saffi."

"Dr. Hansen," I say, getting right in front of her. "I need you to focus. Where is your daughter right now?"

"I—I don't know," she admits. "Half the time she barely comes home anymore. She's an adult now; she comes and goes as she pleases."

"But you said the other day you had to drop her off."

"That was only because her car broke down that day. She needed a ride for work."

"We need to get an APB out on Saffi Hansen," I tell Sandel. "Rani, I need you to give us a full description of your daughter and tell us what kind of car she drives."

"It's...it's a gray Elantra. Two-thousand-and-fifteen."

"And Saffi. What does she look like?" I ask, looking around the room, though there isn't one single picture frame anywhere. Now that I think about it, I haven't seen a picture anywhere in this house.

"Um...she has black hair, is about...about your size," she says, though I can tell we're beginning to lose Dr. Hansen. She's starting to slip into the realization that her own daughter might be a cold-blooded killer and isn't going to be useful to us much longer. We need to make sure someone keeps an eye on Dr. Hansen; I don't want her doing anything rash.

"Call Lowe," I tell Sandel. "Get him over here to watch her." I turn back to Rani, trying to keep her attention, but her eyes have gone glassy. I take her by the shoulders. "Where does your daughter work?"

"I gotcha, Em." Zara says. "*Morbid Masterpieces Taxidermy*. It's right here on her LinkedIn Profile."

"Does she normally work Saturdays?" I ask, realizing that Liam was right. He originally suggested someone who might work in taxidermy and I didn't even pay very much attention to it. Somewhere deep in my subconscious I realize he never called back, but it only tugs on my mind for a brief second before I'm wrapped up in finding Saffi Hansen. I can't believe we're looking for someone who is only twenty-three years old. To demonstrate that amount of viciousness and callousness toward another human at such a young age…All I know is we need to find her and we need to do it *fast*.

"*Doctor Hansen*," I shout. "Saturdays!"

"S-sometimes," she stutters.

I shoot Zara a look. "Stay here, preserve the chain of evidence," I tell Kane and Sandel. "We'll get on the horn as soon as we have eyes on the daughter." I motion for Zara to follow me as we rush out of the house.

"Let's get that APB out but tell anyone who spots her to keep their distance," I tell her as we reach the car. "Whoever this girl is, she's obviously not afraid to go after cops."

"Great," Zara says. "Out of the frying pan and into the pit of boiling acid."

Chapter Thirty-Three

"Em, I just need to tell you right now that if things get hairy, I'm going to be okay," Zara says as I speed down the one-lane road, headed back into town. She's already called in the APB and units are keeping a look out for Saffi Hansen. I had Lowe hold off on sending someone to Morbid Masterpieces as I don't want to spook her with an officer showing up to their door. But if she is the person who attacked me, she'll know what Zara and I look like, so we need to be careful.

As I consider what she's said, I take a second to assess her condition. She's holding the "oh shit" handle so tight her knuckles are white. Even though I'm driving fast, she's normally not one to do that. I think it's more out of stress than anything else. Despite her assurances, I'm not sure Zara is in any condition to go into a situation like this. Maybe it's best I go in there alone, or we at least have some additional backup. We may need to wait until Kane and Sandel can give us some backup. Then again, something inside me says that we need to get this girl in custody sooner rather than later. She obviously has no compunction for taking lives, no matter who they are. And there's no telling who could be next on her list. I wouldn't be surprised if all four of us were her next targets, since I'm the only one to escape her wrath so far.

"I appreciate that, but I'm not going to do that to you," I say. "You've already had to pull your weapon once; I don't want to put you in that situation again. You're here as a favor to me; I can't imagine how hard this is for you."

"That's just the thing, though," Zara says. "Back there, in the house, felt like the most normal thing I've done since the undercover assignment. Searching for clues, working on the tech, I *like* those things. I'm good at those things. I want to keep doing them. Which means I need to face the other side of it too. I can't be an investigator if I'm not willing to put myself in the crosshairs every now and again."

"But what about working in intelligence? Where you don't even have to leave the building if you don't want. You can color your hair back to electric blue." I glance over to see if maybe I've been successful in getting a smile out of her, but her face is dead serious.

"That's just it, though. Do I want to be that person?" she asks, though I don't think she's really asking me. "Do I only want to do what's comfortable? Or do I need to push myself to grow through the pain and struggle? And even if it's the hardest thing, do what I don't want to, so that I don't get… stuck." She turns to me. "Does that make sense?"

"Yeah, I think it does," I say. Zara is an extremely resilient person. She always has been, which is why I knew she would always make a great field agent. I think, maybe my fear about losing her as a working partner might have pushed me to try too hard to keep her around. Even though I thought I was giving her the space she needed. Maybe I wasn't really doing that at all. "Somehow, you never cease to amaze me."

She scoffs. "Tell me that when my shots go wide again. I can't *believe* I did that. I need to get back on the range, brush up."

"You don't have to go whole hog all at once," I tell her. "Give yourself time to get acclimated to the idea again."

"We don't have time for me to get used to the idea," she says, pulling out her weapon and checking the chamber to make sure there is a round loaded. I have to admit she looks kind of badass as she does it. "But like I said, I'm solid. You don't need to worry about me."

This time I actually believe her. "Okay. But if you need me to—"

"Em, stop babying me," she says. "I've got this."

She's right. I need to stop trying to control everything around me. "Okay. What's your assessment of our suspect?"

"Extremely dangerous," she says. "Someone without the ability for compassion or empathy. I think we're probably dealing with a true sociopath here, given the breadth of her killing style. That she was even able to make it look like two different killers is enough to give me pause."

"That is disturbing," I say. "But I don't understand how she was able to accomplish such a feat in such a short amount of time. Staging each of the bodies would have had to have taken hours, at least. Not to mention she was able to catch them unawares and overpower them without any other obvious signs of struggle is concerning." *That* is the real trick that Saffi seems to have pulled off. Not that any of these people were killed by any supernatural means, but that she was so expertly able to perform these kills with little to no resistance. It's not something we often see in our victims. Then again, nothing about this case has been routine from the beginning.

"She is obviously disturbed," Zara says. "Which means if we get her into a corner, she's going to be very dangerous."

"Then we need to make sure when we do find her, she's alone," I say.

It turns out Morbid Masterpieces Taxidermy isn't a business that's easy to find. We end up scouring the streets of

Bellefleur, looking for anything that might point to the business. Zara has it pulled up on her maps, but without a storefront and the address being an entire block of buildings, it's difficult to locate. Finally, she manages to spot what looks like a door at the top of a row of stairs that lead up to the second floor of a brick building in the back. We park in the small lot behind the building even though there isn't anything to indicate we're in the right place.

"How do they even get mail?" Zara asks.

I shrug and climb the stairs. At the top is a metal door with no signage or windows indicating we're in the right spot. I try the door and find that it's open. "Be on your guard," I whisper.

Inside the room is bright with all white walls. On said walls are what I would have to describe as an excessive amount of heads, belonging to all manner of animals. Many of them deer heads, but there are also moose, elk, a yak I believe, and various other long-legged herbivores.

In front of us is a partition about four feet high, like you'd normally see in any other kind of office with a reception. Except this one is covered in with different animals, all lined up next to each other. The frozen eyes of squirrels, badgers, otters, ducks, and a few others are all staring at us, like they're daring us to take one more step. I happen to look down and just about jump half a foot when I see a full-sized alligator on the ground, its mouth stuck open and its eyes staring up at us.

"Dammit," I say, once I get my heart rate under control. I don't like being scared, even if it is by nothing more than a stuffed alligator.

"Watch out, he almost got you," Zara jokes.

"Funny," I say, walking up to the desk, looking for a bell of some kind. "At least we're in the right place." There's no bell, but I look up to the corner to see a camera which can see the entire reception area. What are the odds Saffi Hansen is watching us on that camera right now?

Before I can decide if we should power forward or not, the door behind the reception desk opens to reveal a young woman who can't be more than twenty-one or twenty-two. She's dressed all in black, with black lipstick and black nail polish. Though her shoulder-length hair isn't black, it's a dark chestnut. Her eyeliner is as heavy as I've seen it on a person, and she regards us with a bored look that's meant to indicate she could care less that we're here.

"Help you?" she asks.

"You're not Saffi Hansen, are you?" I ask.

"No," she says, like I've insulted her. "I'm Cora."

"Is Saffi here?" Zara asks.

The girl shrugs. "Haven't seen her this morning. Why? You got an order in or something?"

"Just need to ask her a few questions," I say. I can't help but notice Cora's body language and posture—while she's trying to project nonchalance, the way she's holding herself is like she's silently screaming that she's nervous. She's not as aloof and unbothered as she'd like us to think. And the one hand she's holding to her side keeps flexing, enough that her black fingernails are digging into her palms.

"Do you know where Saffi might be? Is she supposed to be in to work today?"

She narrows her eyes. "No. Not today."

"Tomorrow?" I suggest.

"Yeah, maybe. I don't make the schedules. Kenny does that."

"Who's Kenny?" Zara asks.

"Runs the place. Takes all the orders. We—I just work here."

A little slip. I let it pass by to hopefully make her think I didn't notice. "Okay. Well, if you happen to talk to Saffi, let her know we'll be back in a few days." I catch an errant glance from Zara, but its brief.

"Sure," the girl says, leaning on the counter. She's still

doing her best not to show any emotion at all, but her body gives everything away. She can't wait for us to get out of here. If Saffi really isn't here, then Cora is going to be making a phone call in about twenty seconds.

We thank the girl and leave, heading back down to the car. "Notice anything odd about that?" I ask Zara as we reach the vehicle.

"Yeah, she never asked for ID. She never even asked who we were. How is she supposed to tell Saffi who came looking for her?"

"She already knows," I reply. "I'd be willing to bet Saffi told her friend who we are. Which means there still might be more than one person involved in this whole scheme."

"You think she's in on it?"

"Maybe. If not, she knows something's up, at least. I'd be willing to bet she knows exactly where Saffi Hansen is, and is probably talking to her right now."

"Too bad we can't see in there," Zara says.

"No, but we can keep an eye out." I back out of the space, then pull the car around the block where we can watch the exit without being easily seen.

"What are you looking for?"

"I just want to watch for a minute. And let's hope if that place has any other exits, they're fire exits."

From our vantage point we have a line of sight on the door at the top of the stairs, but we can't see the area behind the building where we parked. I have to go out on a limb and assume at least one of those cars belonged to Cora.

But the longer we wait the less confident I feel. I had hoped Cora might play her hand quickly and leave to warn Saffi, or Saffi herself might come barreling out of that place, looking to run. But neither is happening and I'm beginning to get nervous we might have just tipped off our suspect who is about to disappear forever.

As we're waiting and watching, my phone trills. "Slate."

"It's Agent Kane. Lowe and his people have arrived. We're bagging up the evidence and we have Hansen on watch."

"Good," I say. "Stay there in case the daughter comes back. We're at her work now, but there's been no sign of her yet. And no sign of her car either." Not that it means much. I would assume someone smart enough to elude us this far and set everything up probably isn't using her own car much these days. Even her mother had to drive her around the other day.

"Ten-four," Kane says. "And Emily, as soon as we get the all clear, I'm heading back over to take a look at those bodies. I need to figure out what's going on there."

"Be my guest," I tell her. "We'll be in touch as soon as we know something."

The minutes turn into an hour and with every passing second, I feel like we're wasting time. But what else can we do? Cops all over the city are looking for her and right now, her co-worker is the best lead we've got.

"You didn't pull anything from socials on her, did you?"

Zara shakes her head. "Nothing that I can find. Unlike ninety-nine percent of the population out there, the girl doesn't seem interested in having a social media presence."

"Maybe we could all take a page from that book," I say, keeping an eye on the door. Though, given what I know about Saffi Hansen, it doesn't surprise me. She may consider social media something that's "beneath" her, or that she doesn't have time for.

I find I can't help my leg from being restless as we wait for something—anything to happen. If my phone would just ring, letting us know someone had spotted her, or if someone would come out of that door, or even if we'd get call from Lowe saying she showed up at her house and is now in custody. *Anything* would be better than just sitting here, watching the clock tick by with nothing to show for it. This is why I've avoided stakeouts until now. Too much time to allow my thoughts to marinate, though it's always something Dr. Frost advises.

I reach into my phone, preparing to call Liam to check back in, only for Zara to shake my arm. "Em, look."

I lock my gaze on the metal door, which has opened to reveal Cora. She stands at the door a moment, fiddling with keys in her hand, then locks it behind her and quickly descends the stairs, not even bothering to look around. We could have been parked next door and she wouldn't have known. I inch the car closer to the curb and we watch as a black Toyota Matrix pulls out of the lot.

"*Finally*," I say, putting the car into gear.

Now all she has to do is lead us to Saffi Hansen.

Chapter Thirty-Four

I'M KEEPING a safe distance behind Cora's Matrix, and from what I can tell, she's not paying much attention to anyone behind her. Maybe she thinks she stayed at work long enough we wouldn't still be around when she left.

"Do you really think she's heading to see Saffi?" Zara asks.

"I don't know. For all we know, Saffi could be halfway to Dallas by now." Though we still haven't gotten any hits on her car, wherever it is. That makes me think she's either using someone else's vehicle to get around, or she's already long gone. She's obviously not stupid; she had to know we'd come looking for her eventually. But why leave her laptop at home, unless she thought maybe we wouldn't be able to crack it?

"I still don't understand the motive," Zara says. "People die in nursing homes all the time. Do we really think this…girl went after all these people just because they may have helped her grandmother ease her suffering?"

I admit, it's hard to believe. "My first priority is finding her. We can sort out all the details later. Though, you're right. It doesn't make a lot of sense." But we'll have to worry about that once we have her in custody. Right now, I don't see any way that Saffi isn't our killer. Specific mentions to killing law enforcement officers, detailed notes on preparing bodies, her background...not to mention that freaky book in her desk. And the knife? I can't prove it because it was so dark, but I'd be willing to bet that was the blade that almost ended my life.

Cora leads us further and further from the center of town, where it becomes more and more difficult to keep up the appearance that we're not following her. Soon enough, we're the only two cars on the road headed west out of Bellefleur. We've been following her for at least forty minutes now, where on earth could she be going? But as we get closer, a pit forms in my stomach.

"Run her plate," I tell Zara.

"What? Why?"

"Just indulge me."

Zara shrugs and calls it in. I glance over and see her face pale slightly when she gets the information from the phone. "Right, thanks." She hangs up and turns to me. "It's registered to a Kenny Boloway."

"Dammit," I say, pressing my foot to the gas and moving into the other lane, despite there being a double yellow. I pull up beside the white Matrix and look in the driver's side only to see an older man, probably in his mid-forties, with shoulder-length, chestnut brown hair. He turns to look at us like we're crazy.

"Em!"

I hit the brakes and yank the car back into the right lane just as a huge truck comes barreling down the other side, barely missing us. His horn blares and I'm sure the driver has more than a few choice words for me.

Checking to make sure the lane is clear this time, I pull up beside him again and motion for him to pull over, Zara holding up her badge. It's times like these when I really wish some of these cars had sirens and lights on them. It really makes getting people to pull over or get out of the way a big pain in the ass.

Thankfully he seems to get the picture and pulls on to the soft grass beside the road, putting his flashers on. I pull up behind him and am out of the car before Zara can stop me. "Are you Kenny Boloway?"

"Yeah? Who are you?" he asks, his accent heavy.

"You own and run Morbid Masterpieces Taxidermy?"

"Been doin' it since I was twelve," he says as Zara comes up to the other side of the car. "What's goin' on?" He squints. "Wait, were you two the ones who were in my shop earlier?"

"Yes, were you there?" I ask.

"Sure. I'm always there. 'cept when I need to head home to get some supplies. Ran out of Styrofoam sheets. Need 'em for the bodies. I was runnin' home to get some more."

"Where do you live?" I ask.

"About two miles down the road," he says.

"Why didn't we see you come out of your main exit?"

"Why were you watchin'?" he asks, his voice accusatory. But then he looks over and sees Zara has her badge out and pressed up against his passenger window. He clears his throat. "I mean…we have a service elevator that lets out on the ground floor. Cora asked me to leave out that way as she'd forgotten to lock the door down there and she didn't like it unlocked when she worked alone." He shrugs. "Girls. You know how they are."

Damn. I underestimated her. "What's Cora's last name?"

"Lockwood."

"And what kind of car does she drive?"

"Oh, I'm not sure. It's some kind of old minivan. Chrysler maybe?"

My impatience is getting the best of me. "What color?"

"Um, gray? But it's got a lot of rust."

I reach into my pocket for one of my cards, then remember they're with my missing badge. I motion for him to roll down his passenger window and Zara passes him one of her cards. "If you hear from either Cora Lockwood or Saffi

Hansen, you give Agent Foley a call immediately, do you understand?"

"Sure," he says, taking the card. "What's all this about?"

"Just call us," I say and head back to the car.

"She played us," Zara says.

I nod, getting back behind the wheel. "She sure did. I'm wondering if they aren't in on it together." I picture Cora Lockwood in my mind, and as far as I can remember, her size matches up with the woman who attacked me. And while the eyes weren't a match, I can see Cora as the exact kind of person who would wear crimson contacts. "She must have been watching us somehow, or she knew we wouldn't leave until she did. That's why she made such a big show about locking up. She must have stayed behind until she was sure we were gone, using Boloway as a decoy."

"Which means she could also be on her way out of town by now," Zara says.

I hate to admit she's right, but we just got schooled by a twenty-two-year-old. I should have known better than that. Now she's got at least a thirty-minute lead on us. I pull out and do a U-turn, headed back for town.

"Now what?" Zara asks.

"Now we go back to Hansen," I say. "She's the next best lead we have."

WE GET ON THE HORN TO SANDEL WHO TELLS US THEY'VE taken Rani Hansen into protective custody for her own good, and have transferred all the evidence back to the police station. A patrol unit is standing by at the Hansen property to keep an eye out for Saffi. I also have Lowe assign a unit to Cora Lockwood's home, though I don't expect her to turn up there. Wherever these girls are, they're not stupid enough to go to the first places someone would look for them.

"Agents," Detective Lowe says as Zara and I head into the office. "If you'd told me what you were working on we could have provided immediate backup."

"Would it have mattered?" I ask. "Saffi Hansen is still in the wind."

"We could have coordinated around the friend, at least," he suggests, walking with us as we head through to the office. He's right, we could have. But the problem is I don't trust Lowe, even though maybe I should have. I know he's a competent detective, and so far hasn't put his own beliefs over the good of the case. Not like Dr. Hansen has, anyway.

"You're right," I say. "I'm sorry. From here on out, we'll be more transparent."

"Good," he says. "Are there any other FBI agents here that I should know about, other than Agents Kane and Sandel?"

I grin. "I'll be sure to let you know when we call in the whole department."

"At the rate this is going…" Zara mutters and I can't blame her. We're both burned out and not to mention the fact we just got checked by someone who's barely a few years out of high school worries me.

"Where's Hansen?"

"We've got her in one of the offices, lying down on the couch. She's been mostly quiet since she's arrived. Hasn't been talking much."

"We need to change that," I say.

"Agent Kane wanted to see you first," Lowe says. "She's down in the morgue with the bodies."

Right. I recall her saying something about wanting to take a look when she had a chance. I thank him and ask him to please try and get Dr. Hansen talking. Right now she's our only hope for finding her daughter. She might think she doesn't know where she is, but I've found family members often know more than they think they do.

When we get down to the morgue, I find Agent Sandel

standing off to the side, his arms clasped behind his back as he studies the intricacies of Dr. Hansen's office. "Not in a mood to look at bodies?" I ask as we pass.

"Just seeing what I can learn from the doctor's personal effects," he replies. "Perhaps there is a clue in here that will help lead us to her daughter."

"Knock yourself out," I tell him and we continue on to the main room where Agent Kane is dressed in full gear, examining the body of Cameron Bright. In her getup, she reminds me of Agent Phillips, though she's not nearly as tall.

"Oh, good, you're here," she says, pulling off her gloves and lifting her visor. "I decided to get started once we were done at Hansen's home. Originally I'd planned to do this after we found the footprints outside the motels, but things have just been so hectic..." She trails off, making a motion with her hand.

"Made any progress?" Zara asks, taking a closer look at Cameron's almost transparent quality. As far as I can tell, the body hasn't changed since I first arrived earlier in the week.

"Yes, thanks to Agent Phillips," Kane says.

"Really?" I ask. Agent Phillips never had a chance to tell me what she thought happened to Cameron, though she said she'd had a theory. But unfortunately, she died before she discussed her theories with anyone.

"I found some notes that had been discarded," Kane says, holding up a few pieces of paper with scribbling on them. "I assume Dr. Hansen threw these out."

"If it was anything close to coherent, you can bet she did," I say. I should arrest her just on that basis alone. Not to mention interfering with another medical professional's work? One thing is for sure, Rani Hansen will never practice any kind of medicine ever again by the time I'm done with her.

"She almost looks like a ghost," Zara says, peering at the body.

"I believe that's on purpose," Kane says. "I believe, and I

think Agent Phillips would agree with me here, that a dialysis machine was used on Cameron Bright, to drain her of all her blood."

"A *dialysis* machine?" I ask.

She nods. "Except in her case, the unit was never hooked back up to her so in effect it acted like a vacuum. And I believe this wound here," she points to one of the two identical holes in Cameron's neck, "was where the needle was placed to drain the body."

"Where would she have gotten access to a dialysis machine?" Zara asks.

"The local hospital has two, I checked," Kane says. "And one is still out for service. My guess is it ended up in the killer's hands."

"What about the other puncture wound?" I ask.

"I can only speculate, but I believe it would probably have been the sedative that was administered. Because that's the only way I can explain the lack of any kind of residual wound, lack of head trauma, or anything else that would indicate she was attacked. I think her attacker put her to sleep first, then slowly drained the blood from her body. They may have even suspended her so the blood wouldn't pool in any areas of the body."

Zara stands back and makes a face. "Gah."

"Wouldn't she have woken up?" I ask.

"Depends on how heavy the sedative was, but probably not, because the lack of blood flow would have caused her brain to stop functioning. If she wasn't already unconscious, she was close to it, and as the blood left her body, she probably just drifted off."

"I mean…I guess that's one way to go," Zara says.

Honestly it sounds horrifying to me. "And you think this was the conclusion Agent Phillips was coming to?"

"Most people in the medical field tend to think along the same lines. Eliminate the impossible first, then go about eliminating the possible, based on the evidence." She smiles. "Oh, and the office received the rushes you placed on the evidence found at Dr. Whiteside's. Turns out it was Cameron Bright's blood all over the room after all, mixed in with the doctor's of course."

"Maybe you should have stayed in the field," I say. "You're pretty good at this."

"Aww," she says, beaming. "Thanks. But I'm just following the evidence. Plus," She turns and heads back to the coolers, opening the drawer where Dr. Whiteside is stored. "I don't think you'll be so complementary when you hear I don't have any theories on his actual murder yet."

"Do me a favor," I say. "And see if you can match up any of these wounds to an animal claw of any kind. Ignore the shape of the hand, I just want to see if you get anything."

Zara walks up beside me. "Taxidermy?"

I nod. "Yep. I'm wondering if Kenny's young workers haven't been getting a little...*creative* with their materials."

"Sure," Kane says. "But it will take me a while. I'm not as well-versed in Zoology. But I have made some progress on Mr. Gallagher. We got the samples back from the lab. The liquid in his lungs? It was water mixed with corn flour and food coloring."

"Food coloring?" I ask.

"For the appearance. Best I can tell, he drowned all right, but then corn flour and color was added to the liquid in his lungs, to thicken the material a bit and give it that dramatic flair." She turns to another report, handing it to me. "I checked Hansen's notes. Even she indicated his throat was swollen and raw, though she didn't have an explanation. I believe it was from a tube or funnel of some sort being pushed down into the airways to deliver the additional materials to the lungs."

"Damn. This is good work, Nadia." She's just given us

plausible explanations for what had been very difficult circumstances.

"Thanks. And I'll get right on this taxidermy angle for Whiteside," she says. "But no promises on how soon I can deliver."

"Take your time," I say, nodding to Zara. "I just need to know if it's possible. In the meantime, we have some Wiccans to find."

"And here I didn't think you believed in witch hunts," Zara says with a smile.

Chapter Thirty-Five

"DOCTOR?" I say, walking into the room with two evidence bags in my hand. Zara is close behind and shuts the door behind us. Rani Hansen is on the couch in the office, curled up under a blanket, though her eyes are open and it seems like she's just staring at the wall. As soon as we enter, she shudders and sits up, keeping the blanket wrapped close to her.

"Did you find her?" she asks.

I set the two evidence bags down on the desk in the office. One contains the blade we found, the other holds the strange book with the leathery binding. "Not yet. We had a lead on one of her coworkers, Cora Lockheart?"

"Oh, yes, I know Cora. She's a sweet girl," Hansen says.

"Wasn't so sweet to us," Zara says. "She deliberately gave us the slip."

"How close are Cora and Saffi?" I ask.

"They've been friends for years," Hansen replies. "Ever since they were kids. They always just seemed to fit with each other."

"And you didn't think to tell us about her?" I ask. "That could have been pertinent information."

"Look, my daughter is missing, okay?" Hansen says. "I'm not exactly thinking straight."

I scowl and don't bother to hide it. I'm not entirely convinced at least some of this isn't an act. And I'm getting tired of being jerked around. "We need to know if there is anyone else your daughter might seek out, anyone she might be trying to stay with or who could be harboring her."

Hansen seems to sink back into the couch. "I don't know, she has other friends, Alicia, Elenor, they're always hanging out together."

"Full names," I say.

"Alicia Winters and Elenor Rosewood," she says. "They were all in the same grade at school."

I turn to Zara. "See if you can't find them, home, work, wherever. Check back with the school for their records. Might be quicker than the DMV."

"On it," Zara says, and leaves me and Hansen alone.

I pick up the book still wrapped in the bag. "What is this? I know you know, so don't play dumb."

Hansen regards me with what I'd describe as a modicum of disdain. "It's a book of spells, all right? But I know how you don't believe in that sort of thing, so I don't know why it matters."

"It matters because I think *your daughter* believes in these kinds of things. Currently we're looking at her for four murders and one attempted murder. And I think some of it has to do with this book."

"That's not—" She stops herself, her frustration seeping through. "They aren't *bad* spells. They're for protection, for communing with nature, for healing. Nothing nefarious."

"Are you sure about that?" I ask. "You said yourself you don't know how to read all of it."

"I'm sure," she says. "It's what my mother told me."

"Willow," I say. She nods. "How was your relationship with your mother?" I ask, though I can't help but feel like something of a hypocrite. Here I am dealing with my own complex situation with my mother and I'm interrogating someone else about their relationship. But as far as I know, my mother isn't the reason four people are dead.

"Fine, same as anyone else, why?"

"Because these murders didn't start until *after* your mother died at the nursing home."

She gives me a nonplussed look. "What are you saying? My mother has risen from the grave and is out for blood? Even *I* won't go there, Agent Slate."

"No, but I find the timing curious, don't you? Your mother passes at the nursing home, then not more than a month later, people begin mysteriously dying." I pause for dramatic effect. "Did you know Loving Hearts was practicing assisted suicide?"

Her eyes grow as wide as saucers. "That…can't be true."

"It's what we believe," I say. "Unfortunately, everyone who was involved with the program seems to have died recently."

"But…my mother didn't commit suicide," she says, her voice more urgent. "She died of natural causes. A heart-related condition."

"Who told you that?"

"Mr. Gallagher, the manager," she says. "He called me personally to offer his condolences."

"We believe Gallagher was in on the operation," I say. "And I think his killer knew it too."

She begins shaking her head back and forth, violently. "No, my mother would *never*. We don't believe in it. Never have. It's one of our most sacred…our most…they must have, they must have done it without consent," she finally says, hunching her shoulders and dropping the blanket. She's riling herself up.

"Dr. Hansen, calm down," I say.

"Those…*butchers*, they killed her," she says, though it comes out more like a scream. "They killed my mother!"

"*Rani*," I say, raising my voice above hers. "Calm. Down. We will investigate and if we find they did as you suggest, then you will be the first to know." Though, it's not like much more can be done to punish those responsible, *if* that's what ultimately happened.

"They deserve to rot in the ground," Hansen growls.

"Do you think your daughter would have a similar reaction? If she believed your grandmother was murdered?" I ask, jumping at my opportunity.

She knits her eyebrows, then releases her face as realization dawns on her. She knows something about her daughter she's not telling me. But by the way she's staring off into space, running the scenario through her mind, I can tell it isn't something minor.

"Rani, tell me what you're thinking."

She cocks her head but doesn't look directly at me. "There's something you have to understand about Saffi. She's a very…special girl, okay? She's very passionate, about everything. She and her grandmother were very close."

I hold up the bag with the knife. "Have you ever found her using this before?" The doctor hesitates before finally nodding. "Why did you lie to us?"

"Because you were held at knifepoint," she says. "And because of what happened to Agent Phillips. I…I didn't want you to suspect Saffi."

The lies we tell ourselves. I can't allow my emotions to get in the way right now. I need answers. "Was this your mother's knife as well?" She nods. "When did you last see Saffi use it?"

"I promised her it wouldn't be a big deal," she says, trying to explain it away. "It was nothing. Just girls being girls."

"Tell me," I say.

Her shoulders collapse. "I found her and the other girls carving runes into their forearms with it about two months ago. I took it and thought I hid it, but Saffi must have found it again. She's…tenacious."

"Why were they carving runes into their arms?" I ask, my heart beating faster.

She lets out a long, defeated breath. "They were attempting a blood rite…in order to form a coven. The one they were performing isn't done anymore, it requires the blood of all members. I don't know why they chose such an ancient ritual, but they weren't deep cuts, and I was able to stitch them back up without anyone knowing. I didn't want word to get around town. All they had to do was keep their sleeves down until they had a chance to heal."

"And that didn't concern you?" I ask. "Did you ever attempt something like that?"

She shakes her head. "Never. I was never—I never found a coven. And even if I had, forming a bond in that manner… it's…unnatural." She pauses, pinching her face. "But my mother did."

"Your mother carved runes into her arms?" I ask.

She nods. "When she was about Saffi's age. I remember as a young girl always running my fingers over the bumpy scars."

"Do you think that's why Saffi did it? To honor your mother?"

"I…I don't know," she admits. "I was more concerned with making sure she was okay, that they hadn't seriously hurt themselves…I didn't give it a lot of thought."

"Who else was in your mother's coven?" I ask, recalling that she had been from this area as well, living in the same house that Rani and her daughter currently occupy.

"Most of them are dead now," she says. "Roberta McGuire, Andrea Patsworth, along with a few others. Her best friend is a woman named Georgia Aucoin. Georgia is the only one still alive that I know of."

Zara comes back in, her face flushed. "Just checked on the other two girls. No sign of them since this morning."

I turn back to Hansen. "Does Saffi know who Georgia is to your mother? Have they ever had any contact?"

"Of course," Hansen says. "Georgia is Saffi's great godmother."

I grab both evidence bags and pull Zara to the door. "We need to find Georgia Aucoin. C'mon, I'll fill you in on the way."

～

"So all these girls, they formed some kind of pact?" Zara asks. In the distance the sun has already set and the last light is leaking away from the sky. Stars have already come out on what looks like a cloudless night, and the full moon is large above the horizon.

"That's what it sounds like to me," I say, pressing the accelerator to the floor, the car lurching forward. "And it explains how they were able to kill so quickly and leave the sites so clean. If there were three or four of them working together, that's a lot more manpower to help stage a scene."

"I still don't get the whole vampire-slash-werewolf thing," Zara says. "And how does this Georgia Aucoin fit in?"

"I can't be sure yet, but I think she might have started this whole thing, perhaps even unintentionally. She was Willow Hansen's best friend, according to Rani. I don't know, maybe somehow she said something to Saffi that set her off. I still don't understand their full relationship yet, or how Saffi knew about what happened to her grandmother. Whatever the connection is, we're going to find it by speaking with Mrs. Aucoin immediately."

"Should we call for backup?" Zara asks.

"To interview an old woman?"

Zara's hand is on her cell phone, but she slips it back into her pocket. "No, I guess you're right."

"My hope is that Mrs. Aucoin has some information that could lead us to Saffi's whereabouts. If she's involved with this in any way, maybe she can give us some additional information."

"And what if she's not?" Zara asks. "For all we know she could be a senile old woman who can't even answer a simple question. When I pulled her address, I checked out her birthdate. She's ninety-two years old."

Not ideal. Still, we need to at least try and see if she has any information that can help. If she's spoken to Saffi lately, she might know where she and the other girls would go. Even as the girl's great godmother, she might have some insight Rani didn't.

Much like the Hansen residence, Georgia Aucoin's home isn't close to town. It's off the state highway about ten miles outside of town, down a series of one-lane roads that the car's GPS only shows blurry images of because the service out here is so bad. The home itself is small, one-story and was probably at one time painted white. Now though, it's in a serious state of disrepair. A sloped overhang built on the side of the house covers what looks like old appliances, odds and ends, and a lot of trash. A filthy nineteen seventies truck sits off to the side of the home, its bed rusted and broken.

"How does anyone live out here like this?" I ask as we get out of the car. A single light is on beside the home's only door. Unlike the Hansen house, this home doesn't sit up on bricks or anything, though the ground around here is slightly higher, so I suppose flooding isn't as much of an issue. Dense woods surround the house in all directions. I feel like if we walk a hundred feet away from the home we wouldn't even be able to see it anymore.

"Maybe she has someone who comes in to help her?" Zara suggests.

"I wonder if that's one of Saffi's jobs," I say. The mailbox to the house was all the way back at the state road, a good mile away. Then again, I don't know anything about Mrs. Aucoin. She could be a very agile and capable woman.

We walk up to the door and just as I'm about to knock, something stops me. Something feels…off. I don't know why.

"Em, what is it?" Zara asks.

"I don't know," I say. "I'm sure it's nothing." I give the door a good knock. But there's no answer. I knock again, listening for anything inside, but the house is silent.

"Think she's in there?" Zara asks.

"Car is here, but I'm not sure," I say, trying the handle. It won't budge. I walk over to the side of the house where the old appliances and junk have been piled up under the sloped roof. Nothing about it seems odd, other than it's a breeding ground for rats and the like. Walking around to the back of the home there's a couple of old metal "T" structures that have been erected in the backyard, with lines strung between them. A place for the woman to dry her laundry. I haven't seen those in a while. The back door is as solid as the front. We're not getting in there unless I'm willing to break down the doors. And given that the old woman could very well be asleep and can't even hear us, I'm not ready to do that. At the same time, we can't just wait around until she wakes up tomorrow morning. We need to get her attention now.

I'm just about to knock again when a flicker of something in the corner of my eye grabs my attention. There's a bright, warm light, way out in the depth of the woods. "You see that?"

"Is that a fire?" Zara asks.

"Looks like it to me," I say. I turn back to the house. What are the odds the woman isn't in the home at all? "I think we need to investigate. As quietly as possible."

Zara pulls her weapon. "I knew we should have called for backup."

"Let's just see what we're dealing with first," I say and head into the woods, watching my foot falls so I don't make any noise. The fire is deep within, and it's about a ten-minute walk to reach the location since we have to watch where we're putting our feet.

But as we draw closer, I notice four figures surrounding the fire, which has been built atop a stone altar that looks like it has been part of the landscape for the better part of a century. All the figures are wearing black robes and chanting something, but I can't make it out. And in the center, standing right behind the blaze, is a fifth figure, though she's wearing what looks like a gray cloak with black wraps. The garment has no hood, and her white, flowing hair is clearly visible. I am sure without a doubt this is Georgia Aucoin. She's positioned herself in front of the fire with her arms out to the side and her eyes closed. I exchange a quick glance with Zara as we both come to a stop about ten feet from the clearing. The other four figures all have their hoods up, but I can venture a pretty good guess as to who is under each one.

Suddenly, the chanting stops.

"We call upon the power of mother earth," Aucoin says, clearly. "We call upon our sisters to touch our souls, for this night we have come to end our journey."

She's in charge of it, I think, not daring to share my words with Zara. I don't know exactly what's going on here, but it seems like they are performing some kind of closing ritual. Perhaps because they've completed their mission?

Aucoin raises her arms above her head and then lowers them again, almost as if she's about to embrace the fire itself. For a split second I think she might jump into the fire, until I recall what Hansen told me about Wicca and suicide. Instead of folding herself into it, she opens her hands and something falls out, but the flame itself momentarily flashes a bright shade of green, causing me to cover my eyes for a second.

When I look back, all four of the other figures are gone, and only Georgia Aucoin remains, though her eyes are closed.

I don't like this. We need to get out of here, and do like

Zara said, come back with backup. I didn't think a simple discussion with an old woman would turn into…this.

But as I turn to chart a path back to the house, I see all four figures have gathered behind us, almost surrounding us.

"Shit," I say.

The closest figure raises one arm, my service weapon in her hand. She pulls back her hood to reveal the young face of Saffi Hansen. "Welcome, sisters," she says. "So glad you could make it."

Chapter Thirty-Six

I CAN'T TAKE my eyes off Saffi Hansen, though I'm seething. They've gathered us into the center of the clearing, beside the fire, and have bound our hands with ropes so tight they almost cut off the circulation. They've also bound us in such a way that Zara and I are back-to-back, sitting on the ground next to the stone altar.

The entire time Georgia Aucoin hasn't said a word. The other figures have removed their hoods as well. I only recognize Cora Lockwood, but I'm reasonably sure the other two girls are Alicia and Elenor.

Cora disarmed Zara, and now has her weapon. Both our badges sit on the stone altar, right next to the fire, along with Agent Phillips' badge. Where her weapon is, I don't know. Whatever is about to happen here, I don't think we're supposed to make it out alive. But as I watch Saffi Hansen's face, I can't help but see the hint of a smirk.

"Which one of you was it?" I ask. "In my room that night? Was it you?" I make a nod at Saffi. "Or her?" I jerk my head to Cora.

"Now, now, there's no need to speak of the past," Georgia says, walking around the altar so she can see us better. "What matters is you're here now. You may not realize this, but you are our honored guests. All of this, has been for the two of you."

"*Us*," I say, incredulous. "I think if you wanted to talk you could have just called." I'll admit, for a ninety-two-year-old woman, Georgia Aucoin doesn't look it. Nor does she move like one. She carries herself like someone fifty years younger, and her eyes are bright and full of life. Perhaps she doesn't need as much assistance as I'd first assumed. She obviously has no trouble getting around.

Aucoin smiles, the wrinkles reaching her eyes. "Don't you understand? We *summoned* you here. For a purpose."

"Yeah, a deadly purpose," Saffi says, her grin breaking through.

"Now granddaughter," Georgia says. "We do not take pleasure in this act."

"But you said it yourself," Saffi says, not taking her gaze off us. "The eyes of their ancestors have vanished from their souls. Their lines are broken."

I almost lurch forward at the accusation. Does she mean my *mother*? How could they possibly know? "What about your ancestor? Your mother? Haven't you forgotten her?"

Saffi trills, and I admit it's not a pleasant sound. Like the scream of a banshee. "Rani is an idiot, always has been. My grandmother knew she wasn't truly one of us, with her odd beliefs. Which was why she made the perfect unwitting accomplice."

So the deaths *were* staged so Rani would rule them as supernatural. "Why?" I ask. "To what purpose?"

"The people of this town, they need something to believe," Aucoin says. "Humans are not designed to deal with so many changes. Do you know when I was born there were no highways? No fast-food restaurants? Life was simpler, closer to nature. All of that has been stripped away. It is our goal to bring people back to belief in the miraculous."

"Even if you don't believe it yourselves?" Zara asks.

"Wonder comes in all forms, young sister," Aucoin says. "And faith is built on the back of the miraculous."

"Grandmother," Saffi says, her voice impatient.

"Yes, let us be done with this deed. It is the necessary final stroke to complete our sworn oath."

I try to redirect, to get the focus off us. "What oath are you talking about? Vengeance?" I ask.

"*Balance*," Aucoin says, her voice stern. "We seek balance in all things. Our sister was murdered, taken from us unfairly and unjustly. We cannot leave matters in the hands of mortal men, as they do not know justice in their hearts."

I know she doesn't mean men as in the gender, but rather in those that built the entire system. The patriarchy. It's something I've clashed with myself on occasion. It's a system I work within, and it's one I've been fighting to change my entire career. "What you're doing is vigilante justice," I say. "We live in a system of laws and rules. And you can't just break them at your convenience."

"No, sister," Aucoin says. "*You* live in that world. We do not. We follow the guidelines of the natural world, the *essence* of life. The natural energy that flows through all things. It was how we attracted you here. It is how we have accomplished our goals."

"Whatever. You're just trying to make people panic." Zara says, incredulous. "To make them afraid. Well guess what? We're not afraid of you. You're nothing but frauds."

Aucoin smiles, folding her hands together. Though I see her motion toward Cora, who approaches. "You are a strong one. You *both* are. I detect a powerful energy between you. With the right training, you could have had a very resonant coven. But unfortunately, we must finish what we started."

"Which is what, eliminating anyone who comes to question your *evidence?*" I ask. "You can't just kill every FBI agent that comes into your town. If Agent Foley and I disappear, the

FBI will send a legion into this town to find out what happened."

Aucoin's mouth turns down. "Sister, that is not my concern. They will never find you. And by then, the attention will have been drawn away from our work. All will fade into memory, into legend. And we will be but leaves on the wind, finding new places to call home."

"No," I say. "You can't expect to hide behind the fear you tried to create. We've already convinced the local police you were behind all the murders." I nod to Saffi. "We have the evidence. No one is going to believe your lies. They will never stop looking for you. They will start a national man hunt if necessary. None of you can run forever." I see a few furtive looks between the girls before Aucoin holds out her hands.

"Granddaughters, be calm. This sister does not know of the power we possess. She speaks lies in which to frighten you."

"When I say that the FBI will never stop hunting you, I mean it," I say. "Better to turn yourselves in now and hope for leniency rather than let them catch you and throw you in a cell for fifty years."

"We are children of the moon," Aucoin says, lifting her hand to the sky, where the full white moon has appeared in the opening above us. "It does not matter where we end up."

"Easy for you to say," I spit back. "You're at the end of your life, they're only at the beginning of theirs. They'll be the ones who pay with the time you no longer have left."

For the first time I see the serene visage of Georgia Aucoin falter. "I was left with no choice. They murdered my sister. If you were faced with the same choice, would you have not taken the same action? If your sister here were taken from you, would you not seek vengeance on those responsible?"

"I would," I reply. "By following the law. By arresting them, charging them. Not by unleashing a psychopath to kill them in the most brutal ways possible." Saffi's smile turns into something of a snarl, but I can see she's still enjoying this. Her grip on my weapon tightens.

I turn to try and catch Zara's eye, but we're too close to each other and while I can feel her against my back, I can't see her. "I almost did lose her a few weeks ago. I can't imagine what that would have been like."

"And tell me, sister," Aucoin says. "In that moment, that brief second when you believed her to be gone. When you believed someone had taken her from you. Tell me your vengeance didn't burn just as bright as mine."

A cold shiver runs through me as I recall the words I said when I thought Magus had killed Zara. But what bothers me even more is this woman seems to know more about this situation than she should. I look up into her green eyes, and it's like I'm looking into the depths of the universe. Like she can see into my soul, into my past, and she already knows the answer before I'm going to give it.

"It is as I said," Aucoin says quietly. "The two of you would form a powerful coven on your own. But we cannot allow it to be. This is our final act, an act demanded by the brutal sacrifice of our sister, Willow."

Both Saffi and Cora raise their weapons at the same time, each one pointing a gun at our heads.

"What if Willow wasn't sacrificed," I say, trying to get the words out fast enough before they pull the triggers. "What if she chose to leave?"

"Impossible," Aucoin says. "We have a strict code against suicide. Whiteside, Gallagher, and the Bright girl, they were only interested in money. It led them down an unforgivable path."

"But what if it didn't?" I ask, turning to Saffi. "You visited your grandmother, right? How many pills was she on? How much pain was she in on a daily basis?"

"Shut. Up." Saffi says, her grip on my weapon tightening.

The girl is like granite, I'll never be able to break through to her. I turn back to Aucoin.

"What was she like when you visited her? Was she pain-free? Or was she in constant turmoil? Constant pain?"

"It doesn't matter," Aucoin says. "She never would have violated our most sacred beliefs."

"Are you a hundred percent sure about that?" I ask. "You can't tell me that when faced with possibly years of debilitating pain, someone might not change their minds. Unfortunately you've murdered the only people who could have ever told us the truth."

"I don't need the truth," Aucoin says. "I know it in my heart."

"And yet instead of doing something about it yourself, you conspired with these girls to do your work for you," I say. Knowing Saffi is a lost cause, I turn to Cora. "Trust me when I say you will never not be looking over your shoulder for the rest of your life."

"Enough of this," Aucoin shouts. "Sisters, I am sorry. But this must happen. We must eliminate any doubt regarding our power."

"Then you better be prepared to kill the other two FBI agents back at the station who are looking into the bodies right now," I say. "Dialysis machine for Cameron Bright. A makeshift claw made out of animal parts from the taxidermy office for Whiteside. And plain colored water mixed with corn starch poured into Gallagher's lungs after he died. All three , simple enough to detect with enough scrutiny."

"You said they wouldn't find out," Saffi says, turning her gaze to Aucoin.

"She is only bluffing, child," Aucoin says. "Once they are dead, it will be over."

"What if it's not," Cora replies. "What if there are other FBI agents on the case already? There weren't supposed to be any. And then *she* showed up." She points at me.

"Followed by the FBI doctor," one of the other girls says, her voice shaking.

"What if it's true?" the fourth one asks.

"And then that one nearly blew my head off," Cora says, indicating Zara this time. "I don't want to be running for the rest of my life." She turns her weapon on Aucoin.

"Now, granddaughter," Aucoin says, holding up her hands.

"You *bitch*," Saffi spits. "That's my *family*." She points her weapon at Cora. The other two girls remain frozen in place.

Cora shoots us a glance, then another at Saffi. "If I cooperate, what will happen to me?"

I open my mouth, but Saffi steps forward, striking me with the butt of the gun and I topple over. "Shut up! No one is talking to anyone." As I've fallen I've pulled Zara down with me and we're both lying on our sides.

"Em," she whispers as the other women are arguing. "Here." She passes a rock into my hands, and I can feel one edge is sharp. I begin working on cutting the rope, while trying to make it look like I'm not moving.

"I'm not going to their prisons!" Saffi yells.

"Granddaughters, calm yourselves," Aucoin is trying to say as all the girls begin talking at once. As best I can tell, at least two of them favor turning themselves in. But I don't think Saffi is going to let that happen. Nor is Aucoin.

"Don't point that at me, Saf!" Cora yells. "I just want this be over. I want to go home!"

"Then put it down," Saffi yells.

"You first!"

I feel the rope begin to give and I pull hard against it, Zara doing the same thing. But before we can get it apart I hear the first gunshot.

The ropes go loose, and I sit up to see Aucoin looking at her chest while Cora is frozen in place, a small wisp of smoke trailing from the barrel. "I—I'm sorry!" Cora yells. "I didn't—"

Her words are cut off by another gunshot. Cora staggers back and falls to the ground just as Aucoin collapses to her knees, both of them falling at the exact same time. The other two girls begin screaming but all I see is the rage on Saffi's face as she looks for any other targets. I'm up in seconds and barrel into the girl just as she swings her rage in our direction. I manage to knock her off her feet and the gun goes flying.

This time, I am focused and I can feel my body responding like it's supposed to. Saffi attempts to fight back, but I manage to block and dodge each of her hits, striking in strategic places quickly enough to incapacitate her. She's a fighter, but she's not trained and she's uncoordinated. I have her on her stomach with her hands behind her back in under a minute. "I need something," I yell.

Zara runs over and helps me bind Saffi's hands behind her back as she squirms and writhes, even though she's probably in a considerable amount of pain.

Once we're sure we have her secured, Zara and I check on Cora. The other two girls are still screaming and holding each other, tears falling down their faces. I place my fingers against Cora's neck, but I already know it's too late. Her eyes are open, but they no longer see a thing. We rush to check on Georgia, only to find the woman face down in the dirt. Saffi, meanwhile, continues to curse and spit at us, speaking almost in another tongue.

Zara and I stand, looking at the carnage around us.

All of this because someone made a choice. And someone else couldn't live with the consequences.

Chapter Thirty-Seven

I'M SITTING in the Bellefleur's break station, a small room with three circular tables and a kitchenette that is bordered by a refrigerator on one side. A single cup coffee maker sits in the middle of the counter, and despite the late hour, I decided I couldn't sleep. After we apprehended Saffi Hansen and the other two girls, we led them back to our car where Zara called for backup. Lowe's officers were on the scene for a good two hours gathering evidence, and because both of our weapons were fired, Agent Sandel suggested we keep them bagged and unloaded until IA could come down and clear things up. I agreed, but at least I have my badge back.

Given that we both became potential victims, I decided it was best to hand off the case to Agents Sandel and Agent Kane, who have now taken over the investigation, working directly with Detective Lowe. They told us to go back to the hotel, but Zara and I stuck around just in case Lowe needed us. The survivors are all in interrogation, though, neither Alicia nor Elenor look like they'll hold up in the same way Saffi did.

Zara walks into the break area and smiles when she sees

me. She grabs a cup of coffee herself and sits down across the table, though she doesn't take a sip. "Hell of a night."

"Yeah," I reply. I can't quit thinking about Georgia Aucoin's accusation. That had I been in her position and Zara had been murdered, wouldn't I have sought the same kind of vengeance? After all, I did tell Simon Magus I wouldn't hesitate to kill him if Zara had been hurt, and I meant it. I can sit here and espouse all the legal justification I want, about how we live in a society of laws and we have systems in place to enforce those rules, but the truth is, I know the system isn't perfect. I know people slip through the cracks all the time. And if I were seeking justice for someone I loved, I'm not sure I wouldn't bend or even break the law to see that justice was done.

"I can almost hear those wheels grinding in your head," Zara says.

I grin. "Sorry. Just…a lot to process, you know?"

"How about a little roleplay?" she asks. I arch an eyebrow. "You be you, and I'll be Dr. Frost. Go."

"Oh no, not this again," I say. "Plus, your impression of him is not at all flattering."

"And that's a bad thing?" She chuckles. "Okay, you be you. I'll be me. Gimmie what you got."

"It's nothing," I say.

"Bad liar," she replies, smiling again. "C'mon Em. I'm not going to sit here and guess all night. And didn't Dr. Frost say you needed to communicate more?"

I huff. "Fine. I'm worried about what Aucoin said. That I might do something similar for someone in my…coven."

She shrugs. "So?"

"So? I'm an officer of the law," I say, looking around to make sure no one else can hear me. "I can't go out and start playing vigilante when the law doesn't suit me." I shake my head. "You don't know how…*close* I came when I thought you might be dead."

"But you didn't, did you?" I look up as Zara reaches across the table and pats my hand. "The fact that you're even questioning yourself already means you're not the same as them. All those thoughts about what you would do, those didn't necessarily come from your own brain. They may *seem* like it, but really that's you just attempting to process outside information from somewhere else. They aren't your own thoughts, which is why you're struggling with them so much."

I sit up a little straighter. "That...actually makes a lot of sense."

"You sound surprised."

"No, it's just that...I'd never thought about it that way. And I'm supposed to be the psychological profiler."

"Well, maybe I picked up a few things," she says, winking. "One thing is for sure. I can't go back to desk duty now, not after realizing that without me you'd already be dead four times over."

"I don't know if—"

She slaps a closed fist on the table, extending one finger. "Knife to the neck in the hotel room." Another finger comes out. "Rock to cut your hands loose." A third finger. "Gun to your head at the altar." Another finger. "Truck barreling down the road at sixty miles per hour."

"Okay, yes, but two of those are the same thing," I say.

"Still. You, Ms. Slate, are your own worst enemy sometimes. I'm afraid if I'm not around to save your butt, *I'll* have to be the one swearing for vengeance and finding a psychopath to go kill all your murderers for me." We both laugh. It warms the deepest parts of my heart to see Zara back and feeling more like her old self. She'll never be exactly the same again, but then again, will any of us? Isn't that what experiences do? Change us in small, or sometimes big ways? Isn't that what living is?

"I'm glad to see you two so happy," Detective Lowe says, walking into the break room, a folder under one arm. He takes it out and slaps it down on the table between us. "You have good cause. Full confessions from both Winters and Rosewood. They gave us everything. All four of the girls were involved with each murder, though Hansen seems to have been the ringleader. And all of them under the direction of Aucoin."

"What'll happen to them?" Zara asks.

"Hansen isn't talking; she's lawyered up and will fight, I'm sure. But with the testimony of the other girls, the fact she killed Cora Lockwood and your statements, I don't see how she doesn't end up doing life. The other two may plead down, but they're all looking at serious time."

"It was a serious matter," I say.

He nods. "I hate that you both got caught up in things. I asked for the FBI's help because we weren't sure what we were dealing with down here. Not because I wanted you to become victims yourselves." He takes a breath. "And I have to admit I allowed my own biases to get in the way of this investigation. If I had just followed the evidence—"

"—you would have ended up in Aucoin's sights as well," Zara says. "They genuinely thought they could get away with it if they rid the town of non-believers."

"They certainly did give us a run for our money," he says. "I've spoken to Captain Decker, who is due to return tomorrow. As soon as he gets back, he's going to speak to the Mayor about a full overhaul of the department. Including specialized training and…" He bends down to whisper. "*Deprogramming.*" He stands back up straight. "A lot of us have some strong… beliefs. We may need to reexamine them."

"The fact that you're willing is a good first step," I say, shooting Zara a knowing look.

He nods, tapping the folder. "Well, I just wanted to let you know Agent Kane said you can head back to the hotel if you want. There will be plenty to wrap up tomorrow, but I think we're mostly done. Hopefully you folks can get back home. I know your families must be missing you."

"Thanks," I say as my stomach drops. I'm only now realizing I haven't heard back from Liam since I tried calling earlier. He's never taken this long to get back to me.

Lowe shoots us a little wave as he heads back out, and I retrieve my phone from my pocket. Zara's brows are knitted as I dial Liam's number. Despite it being late at night, I need to speak with him. Maybe I'll wake him up, but right now I don't care.

The phone rings three times before it picks up and my heart leaps. "Hello? Who is this?" An unfamiliar male voice says.

"This is Special Agent Emily Slate with the FBI," I say, my voice wavering. "Identify yourself. What are you doing with Agent Coll's phone?"

"This is Doctor Riley at Grey Ridge Medical Hospital," he says. "I'm sorry but your friend has been in an accident."

Chapter Thirty-Eight

"WHAT'S GOING ON, where is he?" I ask, storming into the hospital. After getting off the phone with Dr. Riley, I jumped in my car and drove straight to Louis Armstrong International and hopped on the last flight of the evening, taking me to Columbus, Ohio. There I rented a second vehicle and drove the hour and a half to Hickory county, the location of the hospital. My heart hasn't stopped pounding since. Zara insisted she come with me, but I told her to stay in Bellefleur in case they needed anything else on the case.

The truth was I didn't think I could keep myself together if she was there beside me. I think I'd be leaning too hard on her; I'd have been breaking down every five minutes. But alone, I can remain as stoic as I need to, as long as I focus.

"Where is who, ma'am?" the nurse at the duty station inside the door asks.

I hold up my badge. "I spoke with Dr. Riley on the phone. I'm looking for your John Doe that came in with smoke inhalation yesterday. Where is he?"

She points down the hallway. "He's in recovery, down there. But you'll need—"

I don't bother to wait around for her, instead I head down

to the recovery ward of this very small hospital. It's out in the middle of nowhere but is probably the closest hospital to my mother's hometown. I'm still fuzzy on all the details as I was running for the car, then driving as I was speaking with Dr. Riley on the phone.

Just as I enter the ward, an older man with a gray beard sees me and approaches. *Riley* is on his nametag. "I'm Agent Emily Slate," I tell him. "Where's Liam?"

"He's in recovery, right in there," Riley says, but holds his hand out, stopping me from entering. "I'm afraid he's had some severe burns to his lungs and is incapable of talking at the moment. So you can speak to him, but he's still recovering. Honestly, it's a miracle he's alive."

"What happened?" I ask. I can't see all the way into the room, but I can see a figure lying on the bed, motionless.

"As I said on the phone, he was found when emergency services arrived at the home. The house was engulfed in flames and Mr. Coll was found about a hundred feet away from the house, barely breathing."

"Why didn't you call sooner? Why didn't you notify the FBI?" I ask.

"We didn't know that's who he was with," Riley admits. "He didn't have any ID on him, just his cell phone, which we couldn't unlock. And to be honest, we were more concerned about the scorching in his lungs. We think he inhaled a lot of smoke and has singed the alveoli, which means he'll have to be on breathing assistance for a while until they heal. But of course, we can always transfer him to a larger hospital. It was just that when we didn't know who he was—"

"—you didn't know if he had insurance," I say, flatly.

Riley looks away for a moment. "We work with what we have, Agent Slate."

"Other than his lungs, is he okay?" I ask. "Will he recover?"

"As far as we can tell, yes. But he's been on some heavy

painkillers for the past day, so we haven't been able to get much out of him. We decided it was more important to save his life than figure out his identity."

"Is he awake? Can I see him?"

Riley nods. "Just try not to get him worked up. He needs as much rest as he can get."

I swallow hard, then head into the room. Liam is lying on the only bed, hooked up to a respirator that looks like it's breathing for him. Other than a few red spots on his arms and head, he looks fine. But his eyes are drooping, probably from the drugs.

"Hey," I say, sitting down on the bed and running my hand through his hair. "I'm here."

It takes him a second but his eyes brighten and he smiles. Then they travel down to my neck and they go even wider.

"I'm fine," I say before he gets worked up. "It's nothing, just a scratch." I remember thinking I didn't want him to find me in a hospital bed. And now here I am, in the same position. "Liam, I am so sorry," I say. I don't know what happened or why he was in a fire, but I do know it was because he was here and I wasn't. *I* should have been here instead. I should have been the one to deal with this.

He blinks slowly, then gives a small shake of his head, reaching out and cupping my cheek. I know he can't speak, but he says everything with that one gesture. "I guess it's my turn, huh? You scared the shit out of me."

He gives me a knowing nod, then reaches over to where they've folded his clothes on the chair next to the bed. "Doctor says you need to rest," I say, pulling his arm back. But he reaches out again.

"What is it? Your clothes?" I get up and take the pile, handing it to him. It's been bagged, and when he opens the bag, the smell of smoke permeates the room. He roots around in the bag for a second, before withdrawing a photograph, which he hands to me. "What's this?"

Liam drops the bag, so it hits the floor, but his eyes remain intense. I unfold the photograph and see it's the image of a smiling family. Mom, dad and daughter. But when I look closer, I see the young girl has more than a passing resemblance to my mother.

"Is this…did you find it?" I ask. He nods. "Then this is my Mom? And her parents?" I've never seen pictures of my grandparents before. Mom said she'd lost all the photos during a water leak after she moved. I take a minute to study their faces. I have my grandmother's strong chin. And my grandfather's soft gaze.

Liam reaches over and taps the photo, right at my grandmother's belly. It takes me a second, but I finally see it. A baby bump.

"Wait," I say. "Is this…do I…?" He nods, a smile on his lips as the machine breathes in for him.

I have an aunt or uncle. An aunt or uncle Mom never told me about. He's done it. He's found who has been sending these letters. But when I look at him, my heart drops when I realize the price he's paid for me. All its cost him is his voice, and almost his life.

Don't worry, he mouths under the transparent mask. *We'll find her.*

"Her?" I ask.

He nods. *Your mother. I saw her. Still alive.*

The End?

To be continued…

Want to read more about Emily?

. . .

IF A GUN GOES OFF AND NO ONE IS AROUND TO HEAR IT, DOES it make a sound?

When an innocent hiker is gunned down in the middle of the woods, Special Agent Emily Slate finds herself back in the . town where it all began, looking for answers.

After some harrowing cases and some narrow misses, Emily knows that an FBI Agent's job is never done as she returns to the small mountain town of Stillwater. What at first looks like an accident, is soon revealed to be part of something more sinister:

A hunter, using humans as his targets.

The only problem is, Emily can't prove it. But she's been in this job long enough to know a predator when she sees one.

As she fights to uncover the truth, she'll also have to face a personal choice, one that tests her loyalty not only to herself, but also to those she loves the most. Love, it seems, is always complicated, especially when your life is constantly on the line.

This time, though, she may have to make the ultimate choice.

JOIN EMILY IN THIS HARROWING NEW ADVENTURE WHERE THE hunter becomes the hunted, and no one knows what's around the next corner.

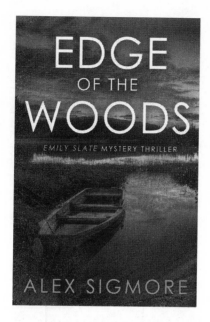

To get your copy of **EDGE OF THE WOODS, CLICK HERE** or scan the code below with your phone.

FREE book offer!

Where did it all go wrong for Emily?

I HOPE YOU ENJOYED *THE VANISHING EYES*. IF YOU'D LIKE TO learn more about Emily's backstory and what happened in the days following her husband's unfortunate death, including what almost got her kicked out of the FBI, then you're in luck! *Her Last Shot* introduces Emily and tells the story of the case that almost ended her career. Interested? CLICK HERE to get your free copy now!

Not Available Anywhere Else!

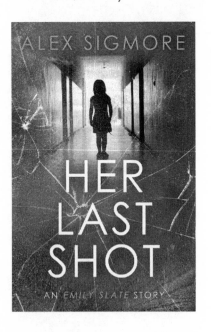

You'll also be the first to know when each book in the Emily Slate series is available!

CLICK HERE or scan the code below to download for FREE!

The Emily Slate FBI Mystery Series

Free Prequel - Her Last Shot (Emily Slate Bonus Story)

His Perfect Crime - (Emily Slate Series Book One)

The Collection Girls - (Emily Slate Series Book Two)

Smoke and Ashes - (Emily Slate Series Book Three)

Her Final Words - (Emily Slate Series Book Four)

Can't Miss Her - (Emily Slate Series Book Five)

The Lost Daughter - (Emily Slate Series Book Six)

The Secret Seven - (Emily Slate Series Book Seven)

A Liar's Grave - (Emily Slate Series Book Eight)

The Girl in the Wall - (Emily Slate Series Book Nine)

His Final Act - (Emily Slate Series Book Ten)

The Vanishing Eyes - (Emily Slate Series Book Eleven)

Coming Soon!

Edge of the Woods - (Emily Slate Series Book Twelve)

The Missing Bones - (Emily Slate Series Book Thirteen)

Standalone Psychological Thrillers

Forgotten

A Note from Alex

Hi there!

Thanks so much for reading *The Vanishing Eyes*! I knew when I first started writing Emily's story I'd want to venture into the world of the paranormal without actually having any real paranormal elements in it. I hope you enjoyed reading as much as I enjoyed writing it. The response to this series has been incredible, and as long as you, the reader, continue to ask for Emily Slate stories, you can be rest assured I will deliver them!

As I've always said, you are the reason I write!

If you haven't already, please take a moment to leave a review or recommend this series to a fellow book lover. It really helps me as a writer and is the best way to make sure there are plenty more *Emily Slate* books in the future.

As always, thank you for being a loyal reader,

Alex

Made in the USA
Columbia, SC
23 October 2023